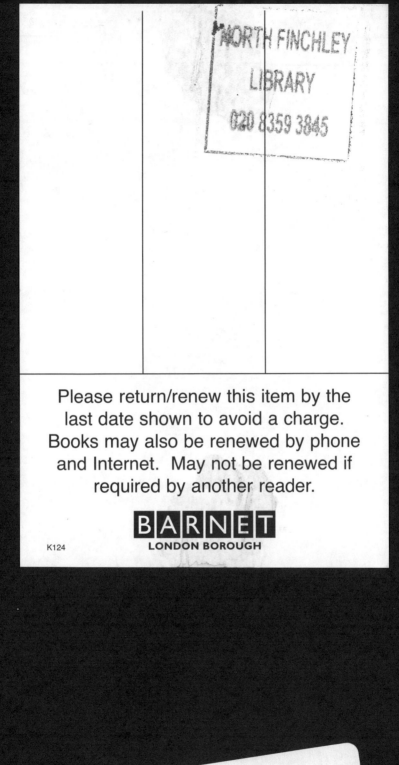

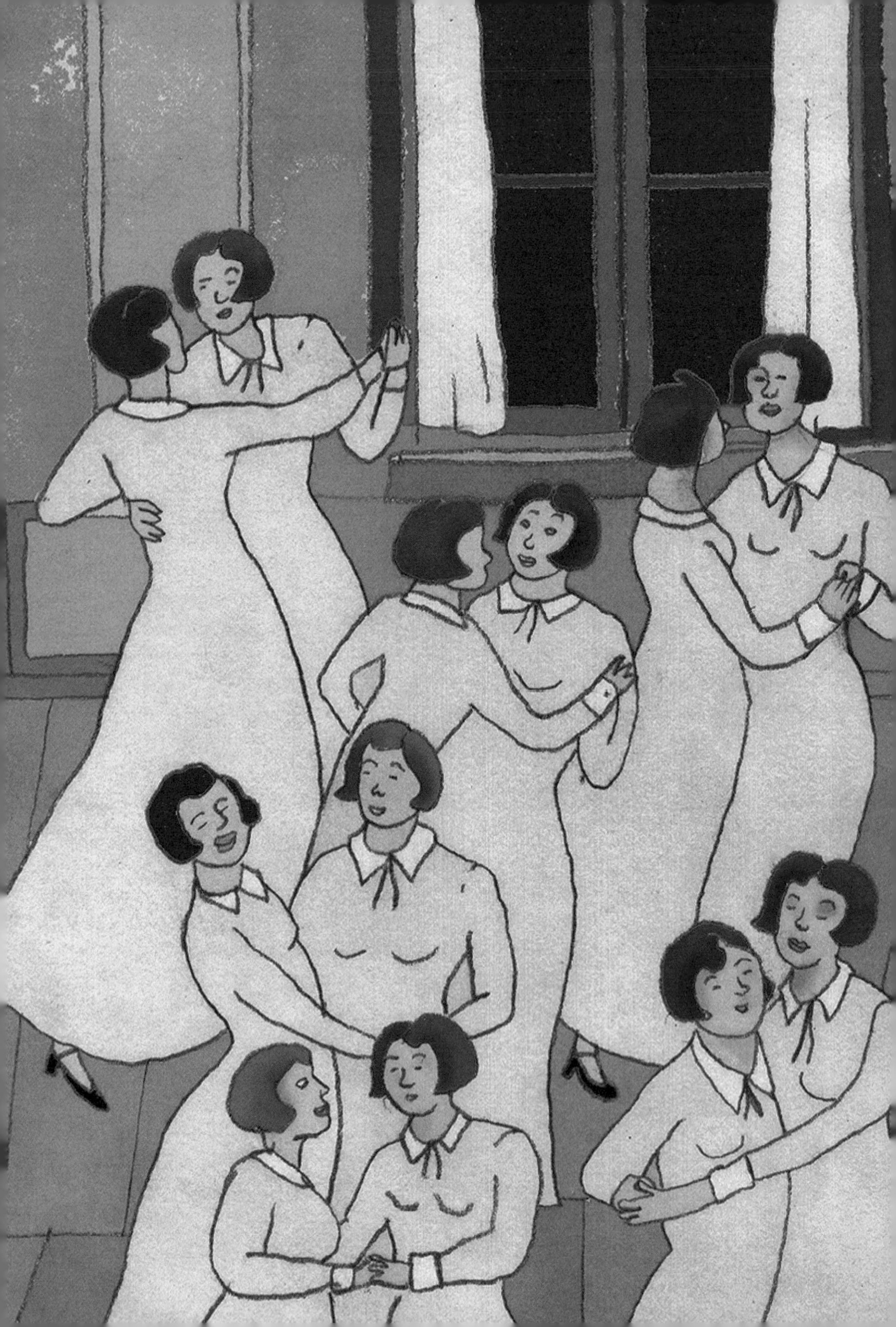

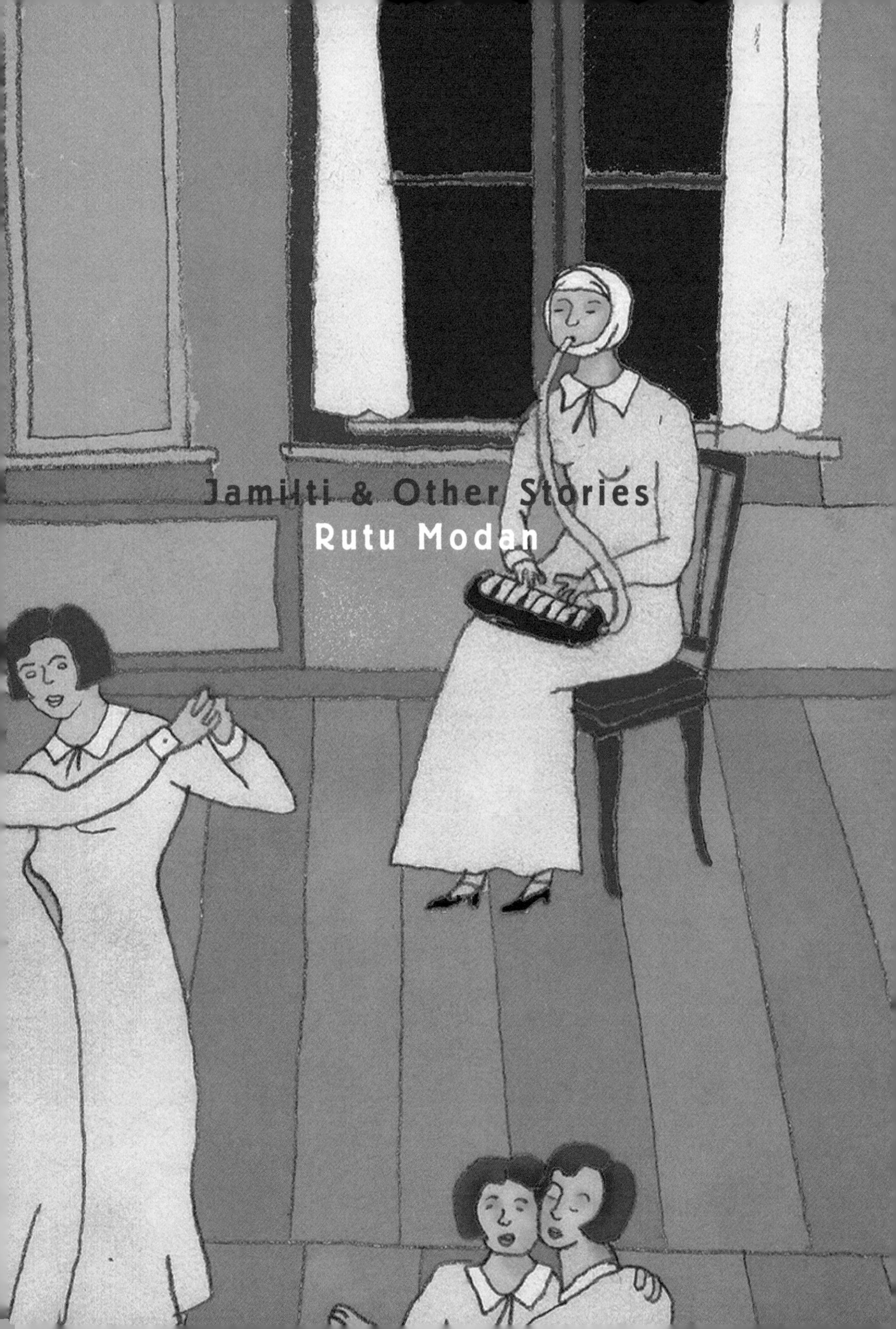
Jamilti & Other Stories
Rutu Modan

Published by Jonathan Cape 2009. Copyright © Rutu Modan 1998-2008. Rutu Modan has asserted her right under the Copyright, Designsand Patents Act 1988 to be identified as the author of this work. This book is sold subject to the condition that it shall not, by way of trade or otherwise, be lent, resold, hired out, or otherwise circulated without the publisher's prior consent in any form of binding or cover other than that in which it is published and without a similar condition, including this condition, being imposed on the subsequent purchaser. All the stories were originally published by Actus Independent Comics (actustragicus.com). Translation credits: 'Energy Blockage', 'The Panty Killer' and 'King of the Lillies' by Noah Stollman; 'Bygone', 'Homecoming', 'Fan', and 'Jamilti' by Jesse Mishori. First published in Great Britain in 2009 by Jonathan Cape, Random House, 20 Vauxhall Bridge Road, London SW1V 2SA. www.rbooks.co.uk. The Random House Group Limited Reg. No. 954009. A CIP catalogue record for this book is available from the British Library. ISBN 9780224087704. Printed and bound in China by C & C Offset Printing Co., Ltd.

Jamilti & Other Stories
Rutu Modan

Jonathan Cape
London

To Lilian

מביתי לביתך המרחק קילומטר
מליבי לליבך אף לא מילימטר

JAMILTI

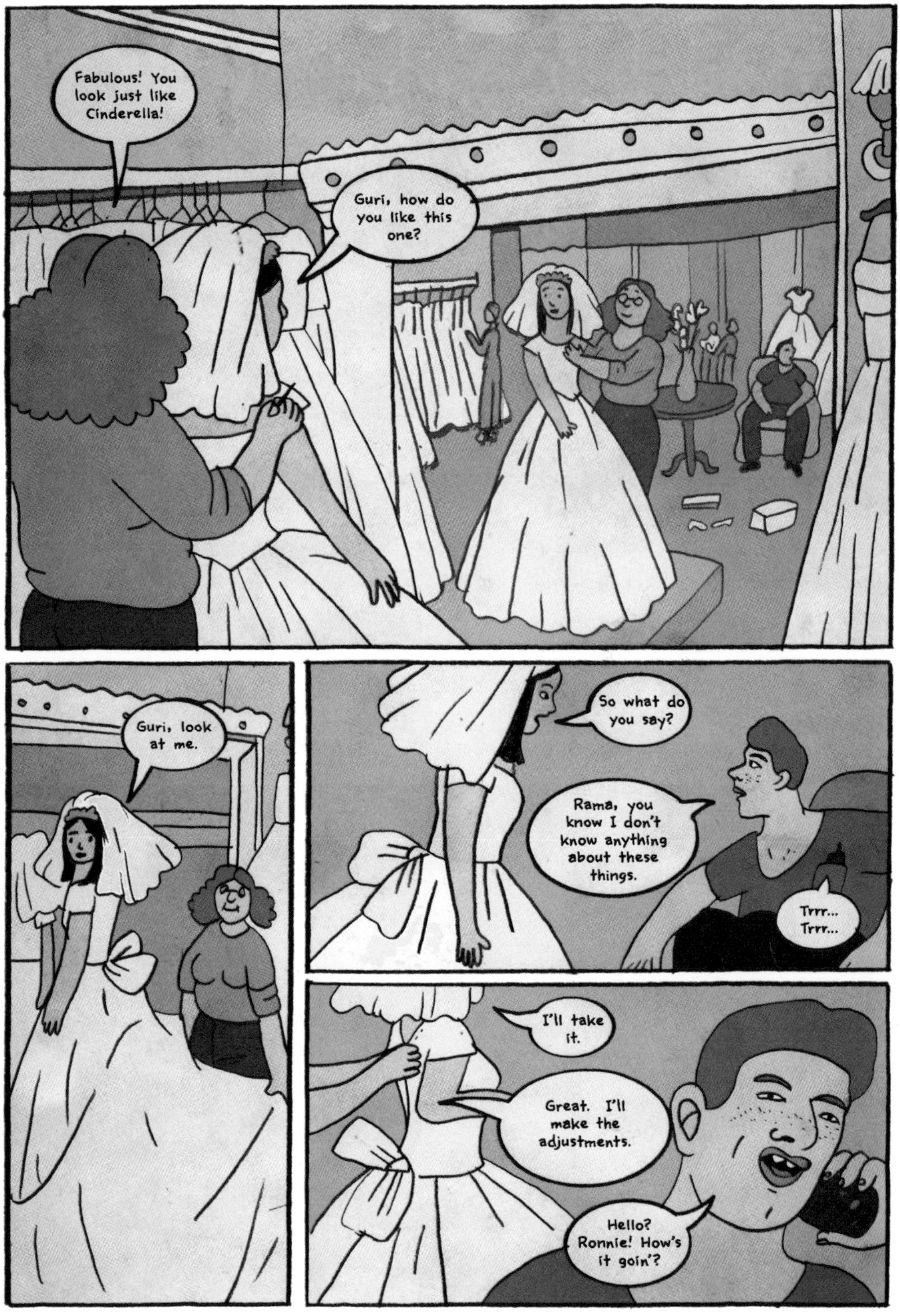
Fabulous! You look just like Cinderella!
Guri, how do you like this one?
Guri, look at me.
So what do you say?
Rama, you know I don't know anything about these things.
Trrr... Trrr...
I'll take it.
Great. I'll make the adjustments.
Hello? Ronnie! How's it goin'?

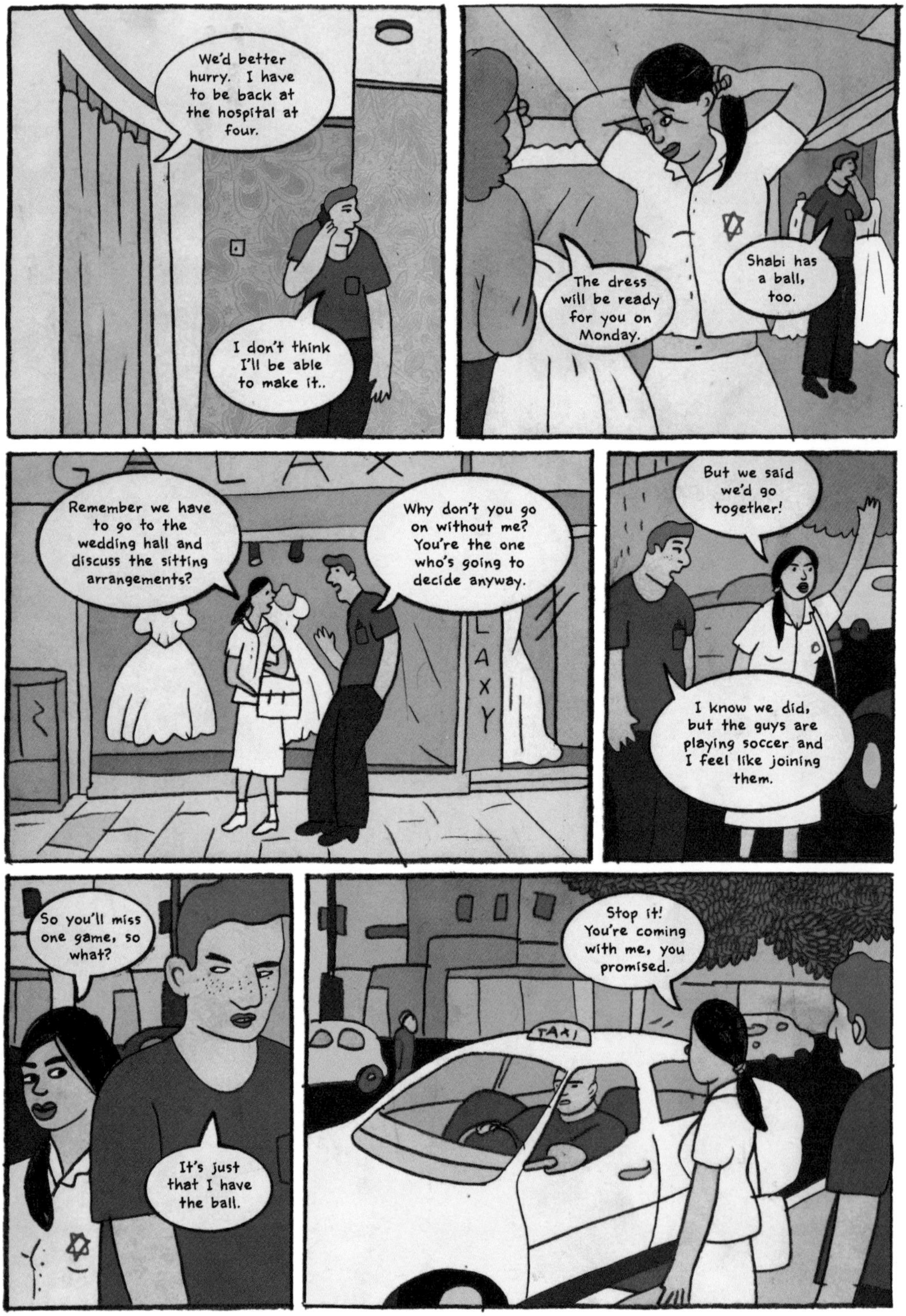
We'd better hurry. I have to be back at the hospital at four.
I don't think I'll be able to make it..
The dress will be ready for you on Monday.
Shabi has a ball, too.
GALAX
Remember we have to go to the wedding hall and discuss the sitting arrangements?
Why don't you go on without me? You're the one who's going to decide anyway.
LAXY
But we said we'd go together!
I know we did, but the guys are playing soccer and I feel like joining them.
So you'll miss one game, so what?
It's just that I have the ball.
Stop it! You're coming with me, you promised.
TAXI

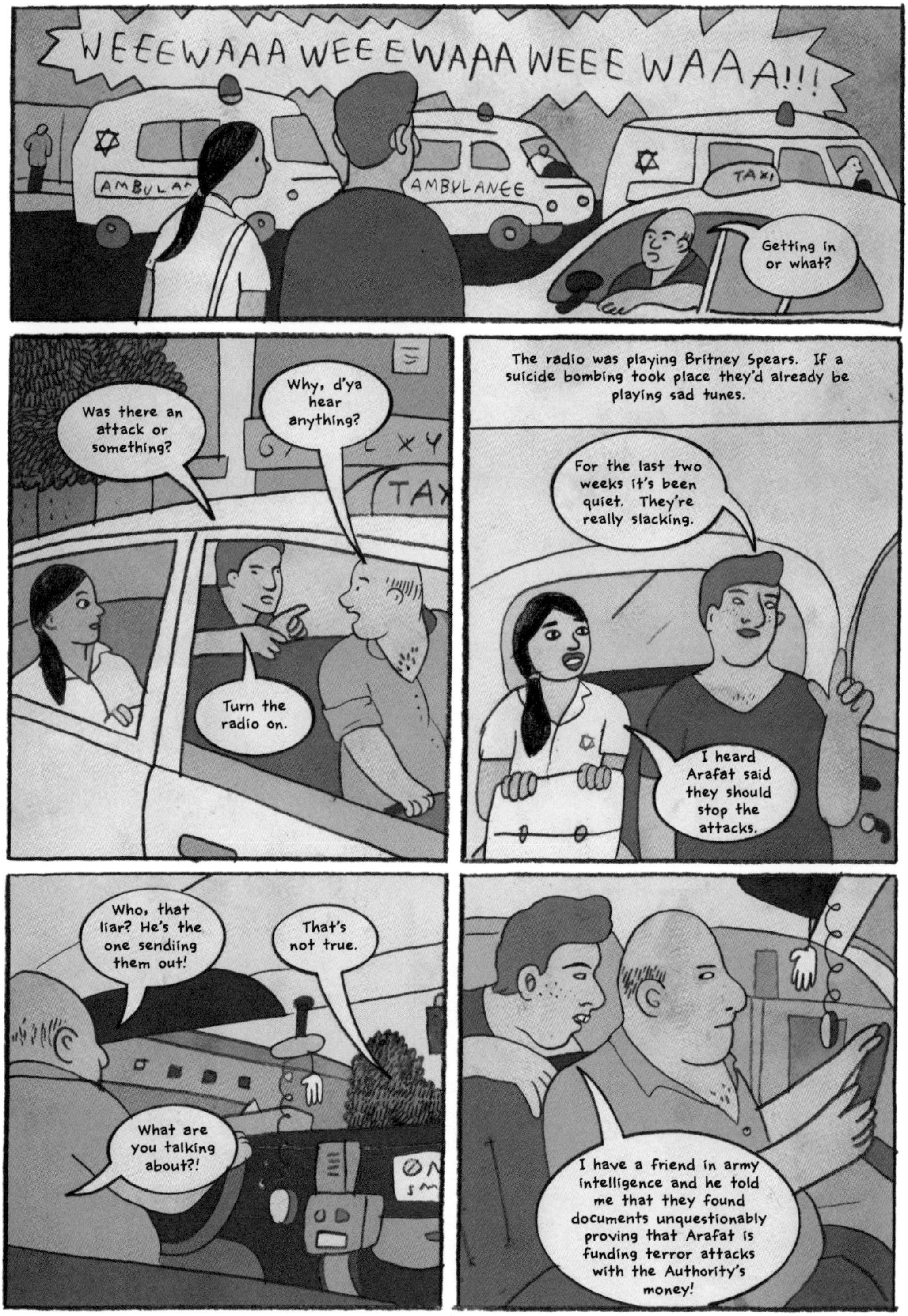
WEEEWAAA WEEEWAAA WEEE WAAA!!!
AMBULAN
AMBULANCE
TAXI
Getting in or what?
Was there an attack or something?
Why, d'ya hear anything?
Turn the radio on.
The radio was playing Britney Spears. If a suicide bombing took place they'd already be playing sad tunes.
For the last two weeks it's been quiet. They're really slacking.
I heard Arafat said they should stop the attacks.
Who, that liar? He's the one sendiing them out!
That's not true.
What are you talking about?!
I have a friend in army intelligence and he told me that they found documents unquestionably proving that Arafat is funding terror attacks with the Authority's money!

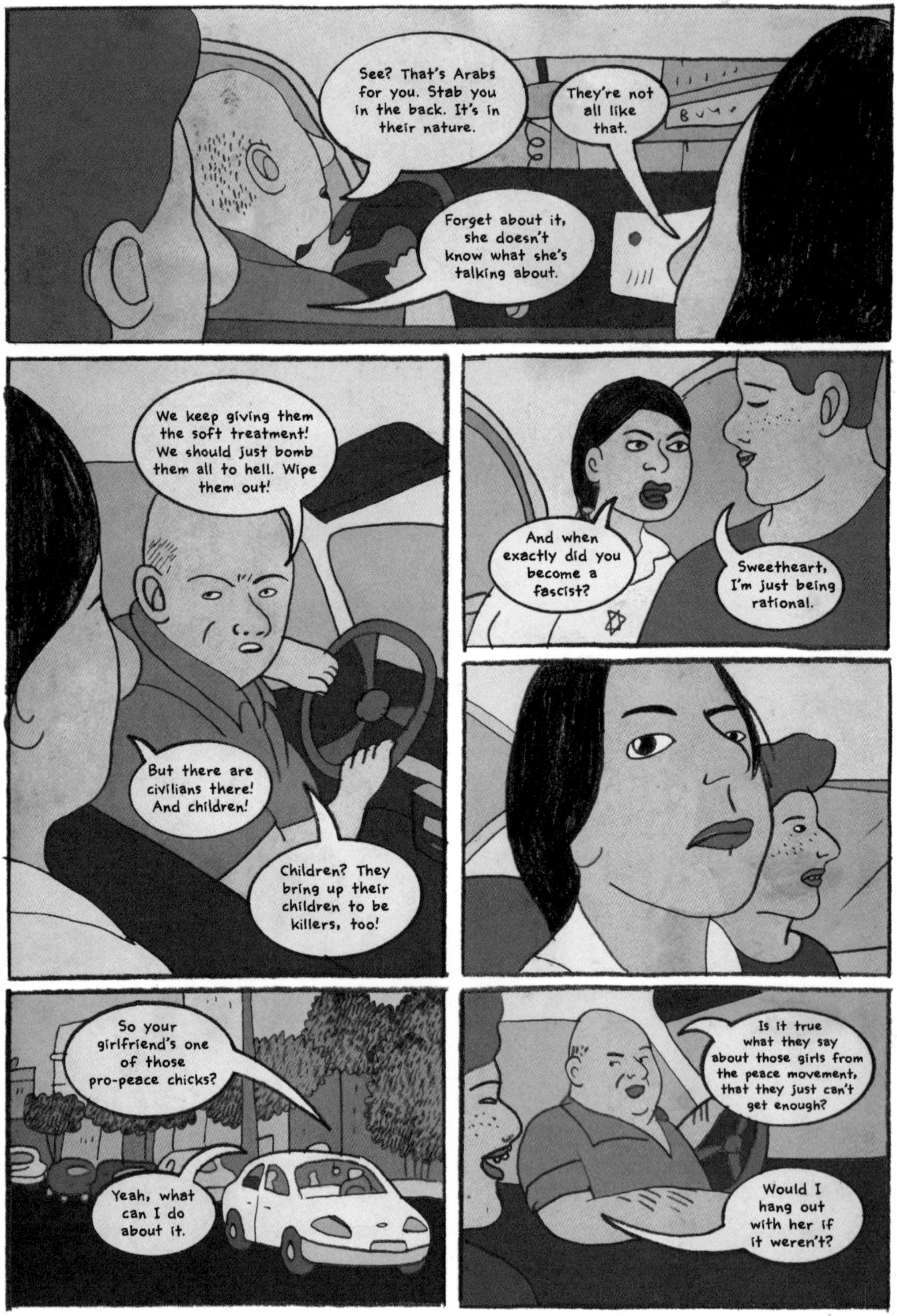
See? That's Arabs for you. Stab you in the back. It's in their nature.
They're not all like that.
Forget about it, she doesn't know what she's talking about.
We keep giving them the soft treatment! We should just bomb them all to hell. Wipe them out!
But there are civilians there! And children!
Children? They bring up their children to be killers, too!
And when exactly did you become a fascist?
Sweetheart, I'm just being rational.
So your girlfriend's one of those pro-peace chicks?
Yeah, what can I do about it.
Is it true what they say about those girls from the peace movement, that they just can't get enough?
Would I hang out with her if it weren't?

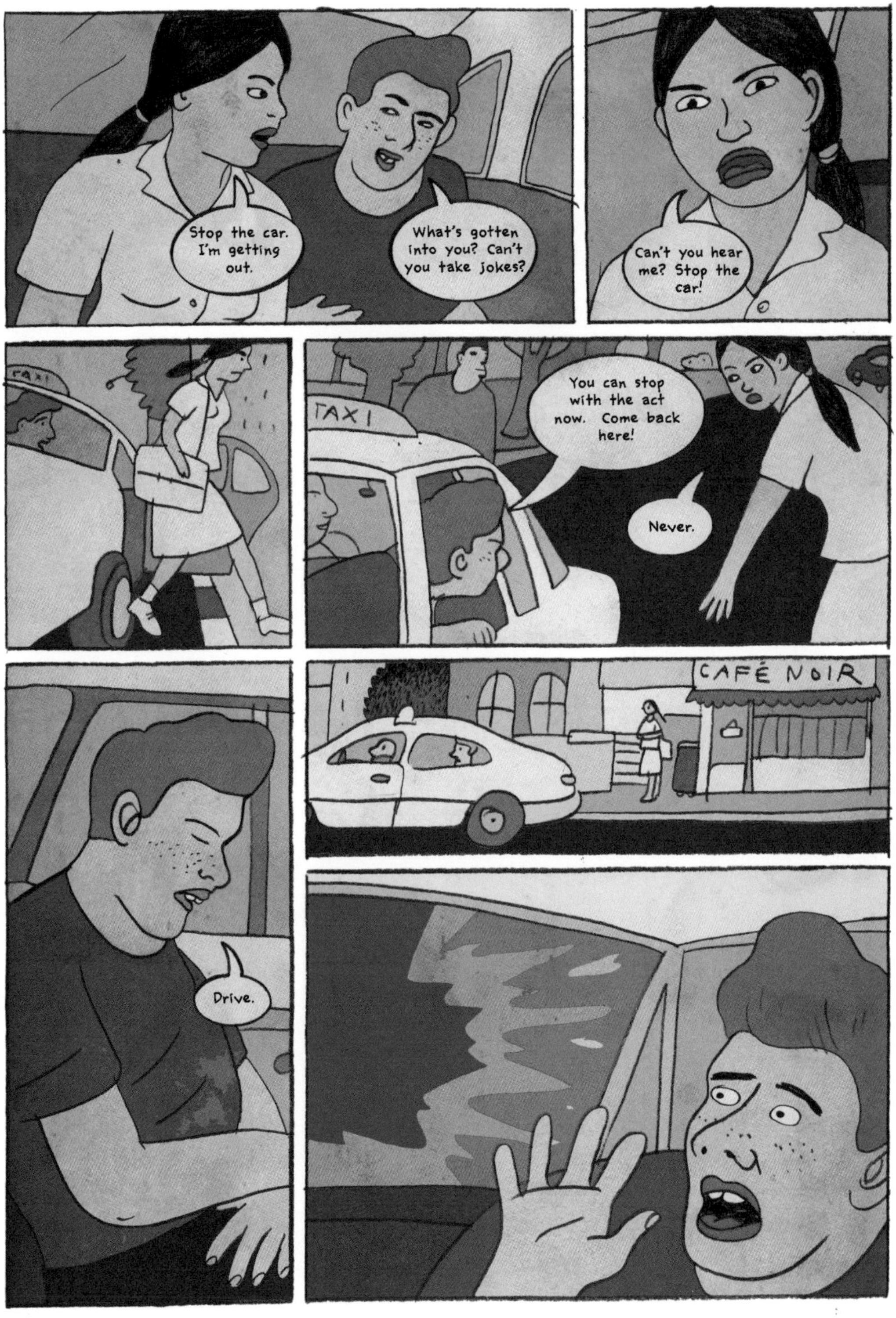
Stop the car. I'm getting out.
What's gotten into you? Can't you take jokes?
Can't you hear me? Stop the car!
TAXI
You can stop with the act now. Come back here!
Never.
CAFÉ NOIR
Drive.

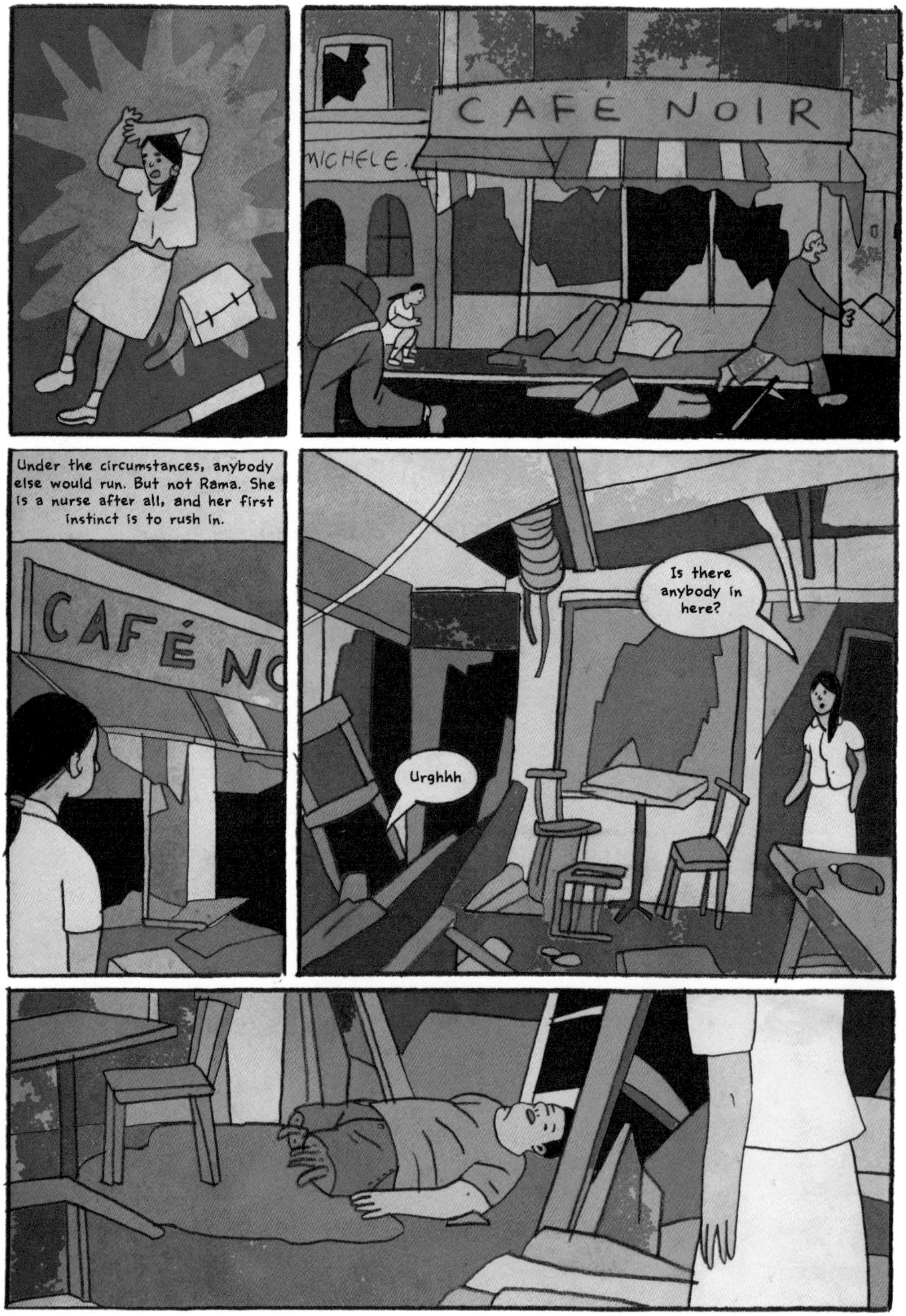
CAFÉ NOIR
MICHELE.
Under the circumstances, anybody else would run. But not Rama. She is a nurse after all, and her first instinct is to rush in.
CAFÉ NO
Is there anybody in here?
Urghhh

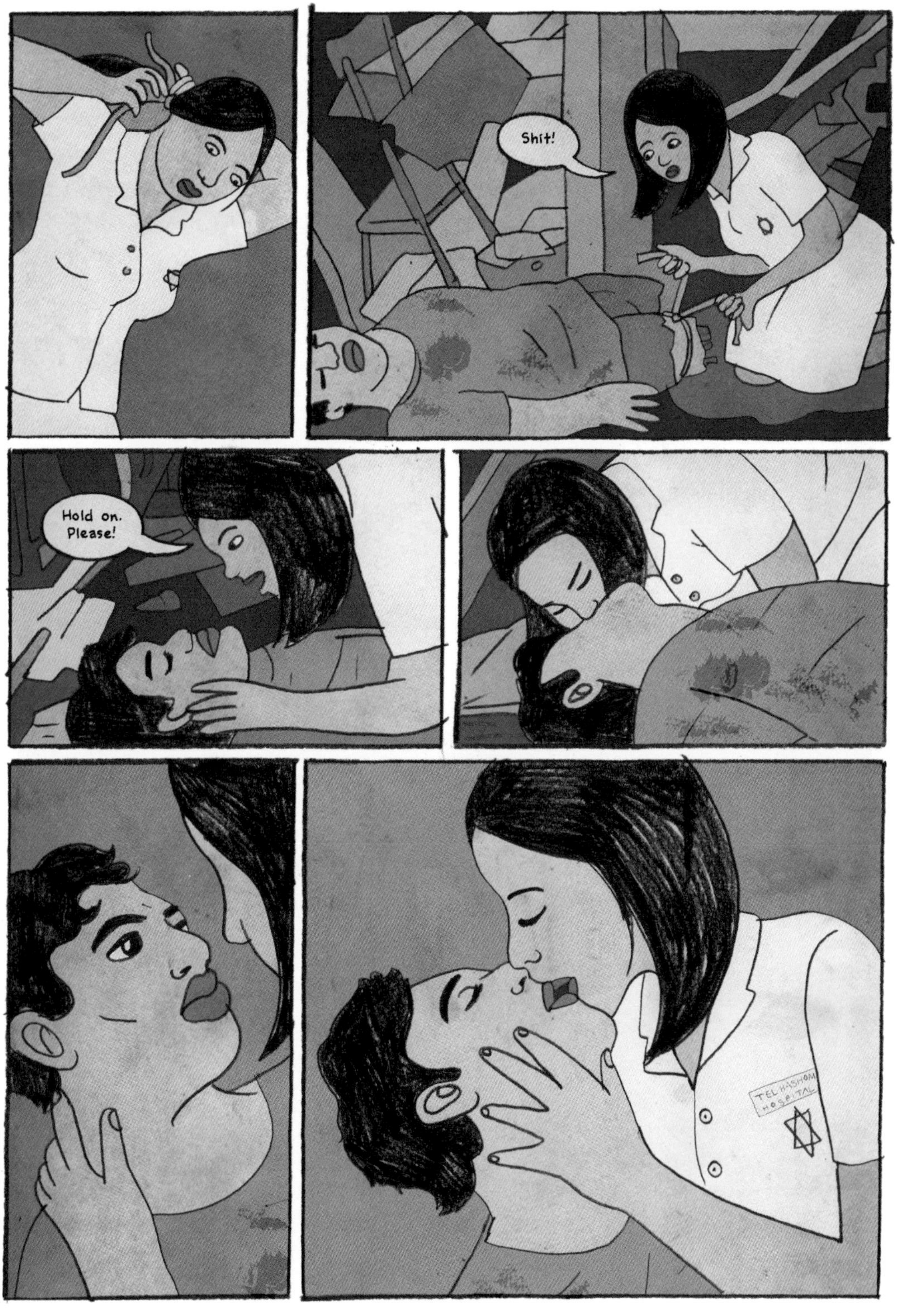

Shit!
Hold on. Please!
TEL HASHOMER HOSPITAL

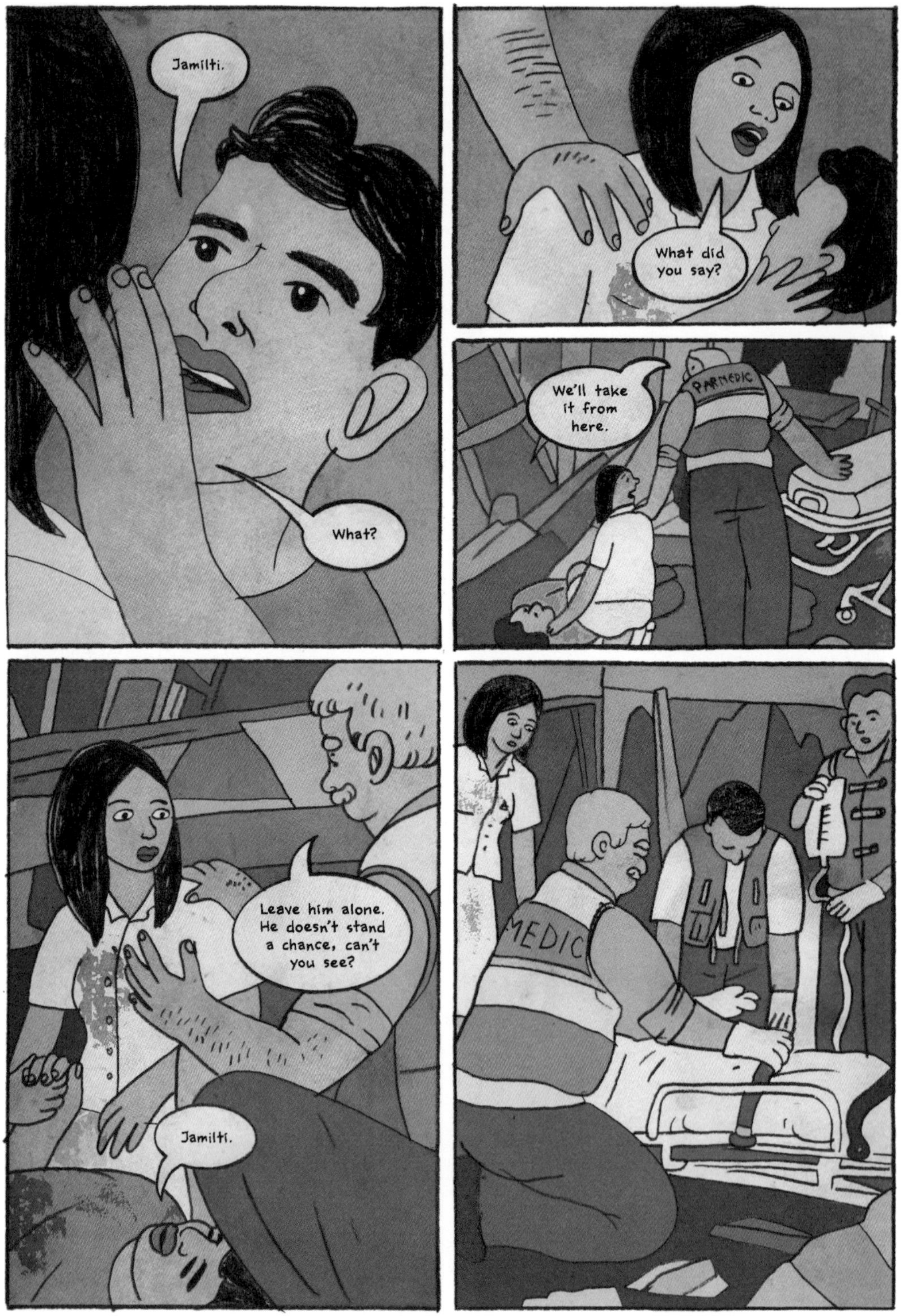
Jamilti.
What?
What did you say?
We'll take it from here.
PARMEDIC
Leave him alone. He doesn't stand a chance, can't you see?
Jamilti.
MEDIC

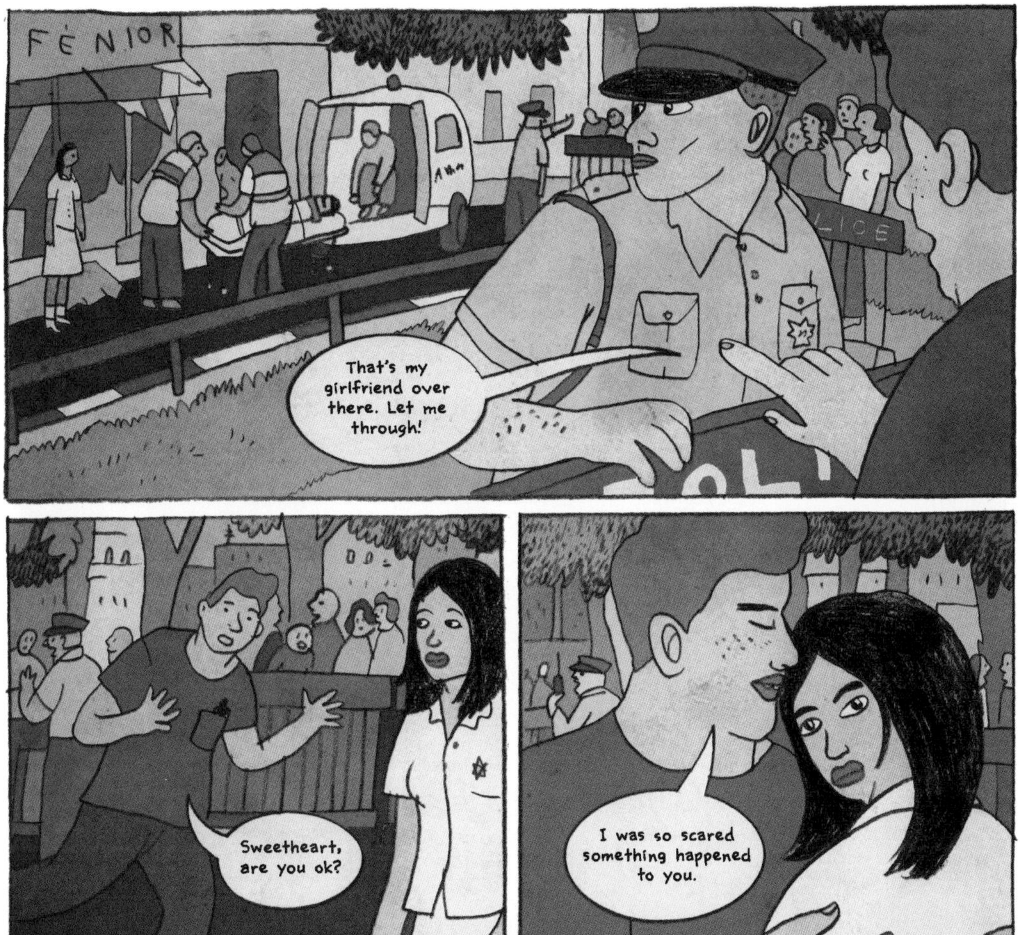
That's my girlfriend over there. Let me through!
Sweetheart, are you ok?
I was so scared something happened to you.
Evening.
The news is on. Let's see what they say about our attack.

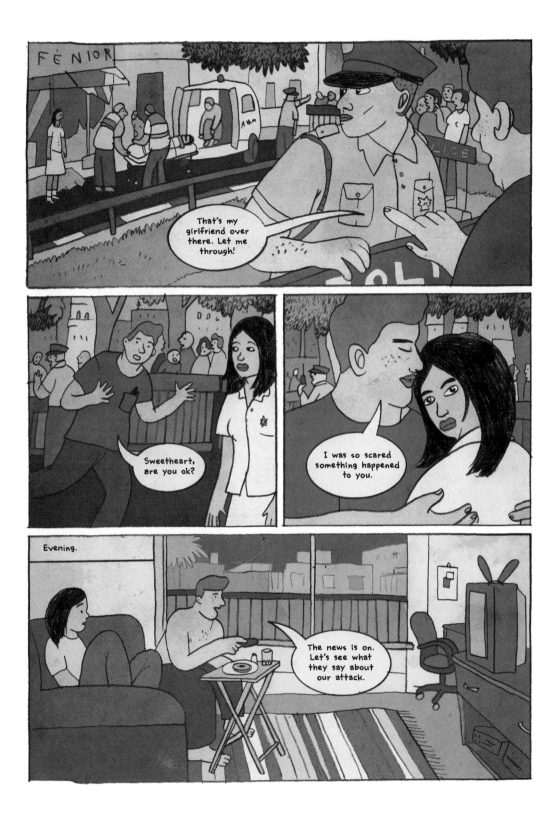

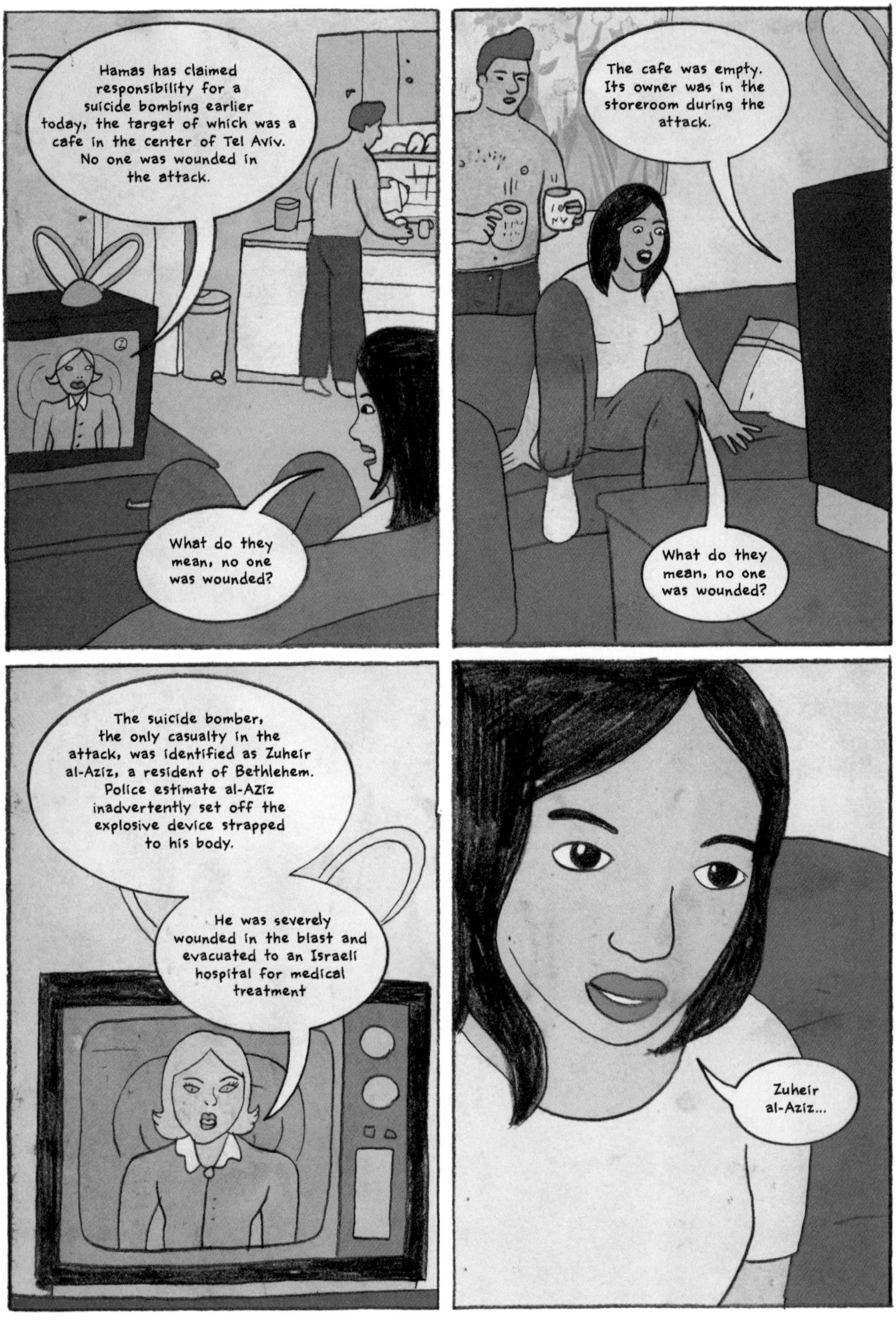
Hamas has claimed responsibility for a suicide bombing earlier today, the target of which was a cafe in the center of Tel Aviv. No one was wounded in the attack.
What do they mean, no one was wounded?
The cafe was empty. Its owner was in the storeroom during the attack.
What do they mean, no one was wounded?
The suicide bomber, the only casualty in the attack, was identified as Zuheir al-Aziz, a resident of Bethlehem. Police estimate al-Aziz inadvertently set off the explosive device strapped to his body.
He was severely wounded in the blast and evacuated to an Israeli hospital for medical treatment
Zuheir al-Aziz...

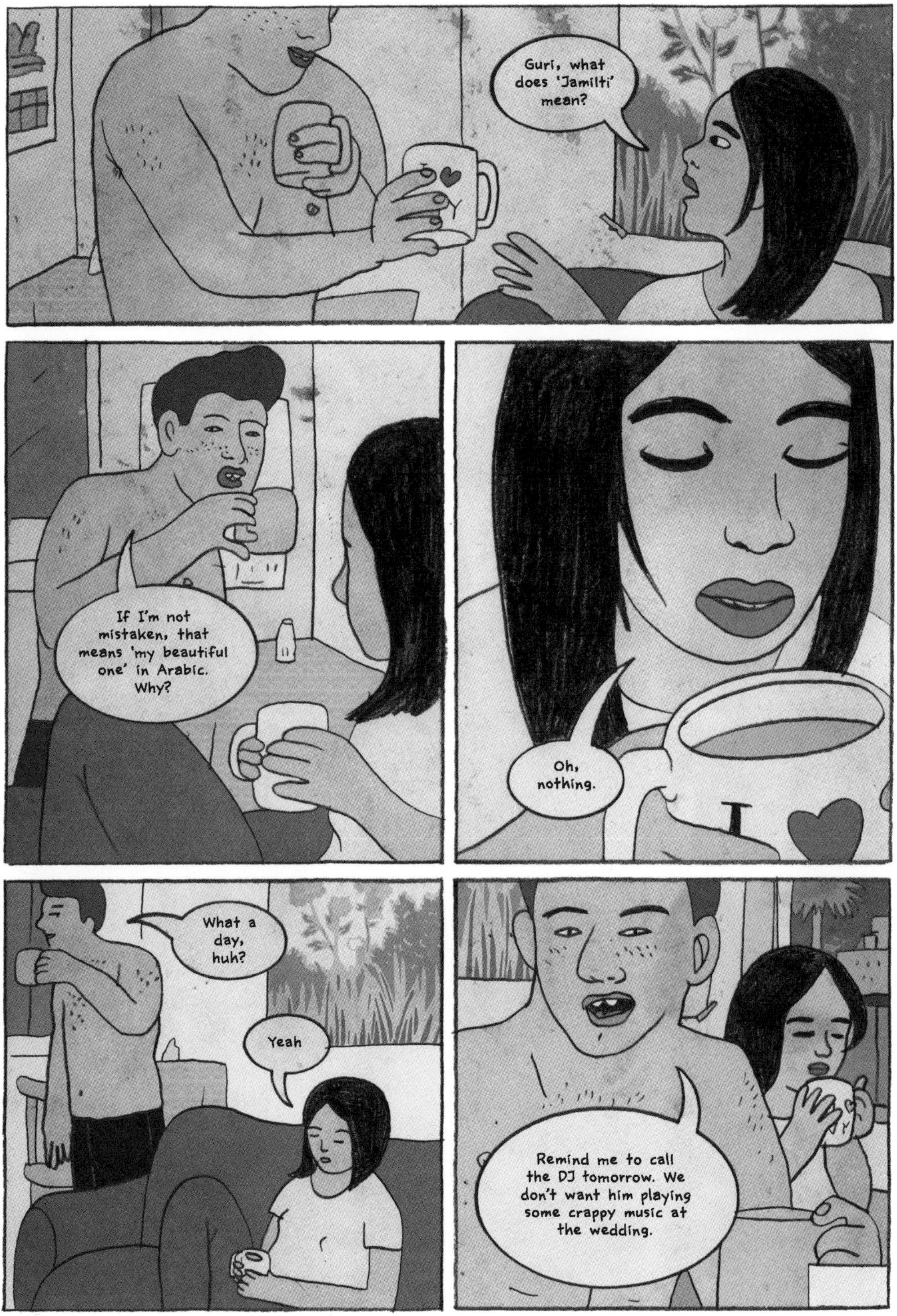
Guri, what does 'Jamilti' mean?
If I'm not mistaken, that means 'my beautiful one' in Arabic. Why?
Oh, nothing.
What a day, huh?
Yeah
Remind me to call the DJ tomorrow. We don't want him playing some crappy music at the wedding.

ENERGY BLOCKAGE

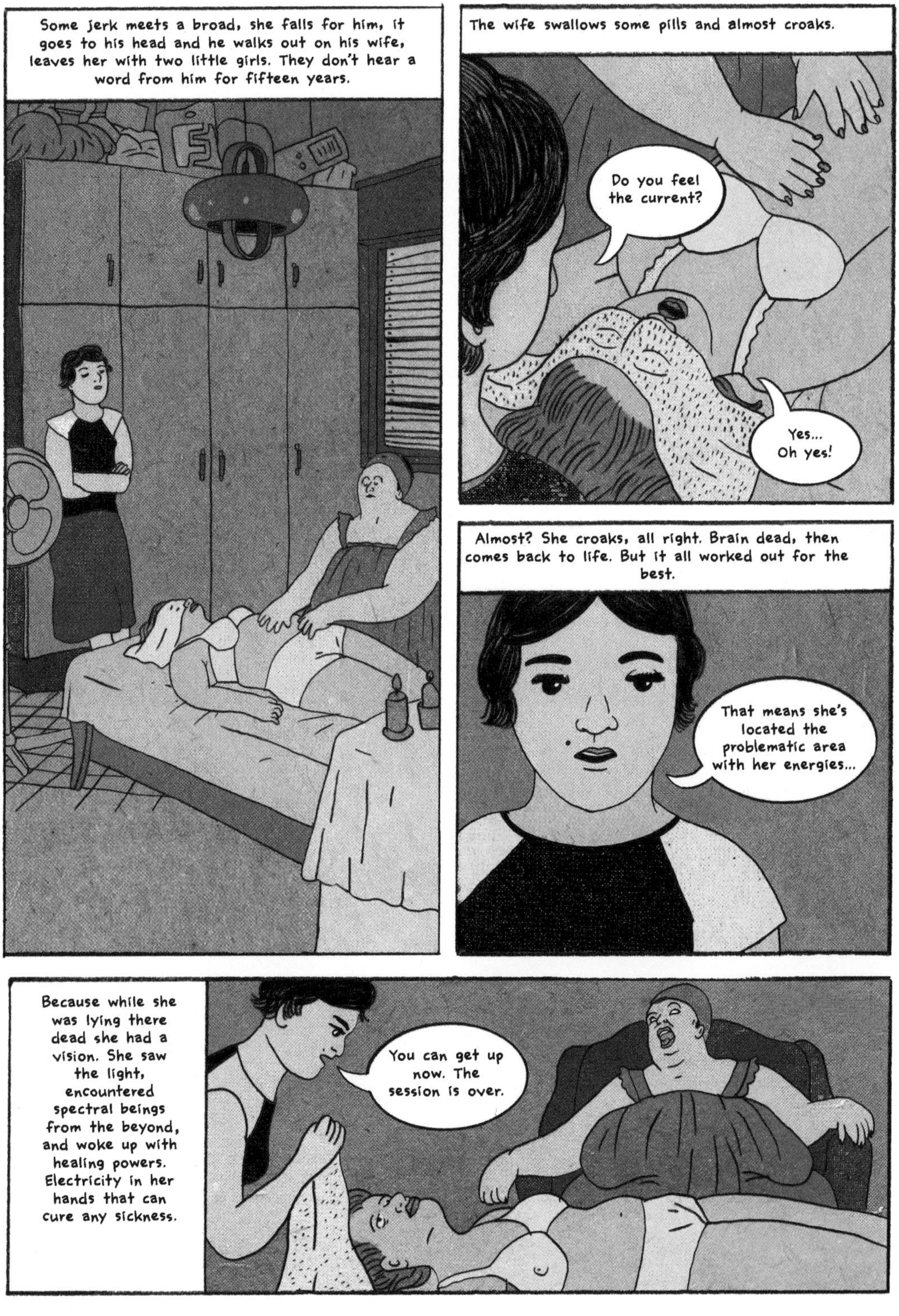
Some jerk meets a broad, she falls for him, it goes to his head and he walks out on his wife, leaves her with two little girls. They don't hear a word from him for fifteen years.
The wife swallows some pills and almost croaks.
Do you feel the current?
Yes... Oh yes!
Almost? She croaks, all right. Brain dead, then comes back to life. But it all worked out for the best.
That means she's located the problematic area with her energies...
Because while she was lying there dead she had a vision. She saw the light, encountered spectral beings from the beyond, and woke up with healing powers. Electricity in her hands that can cure any sickness.
You can get up now. The session is over.

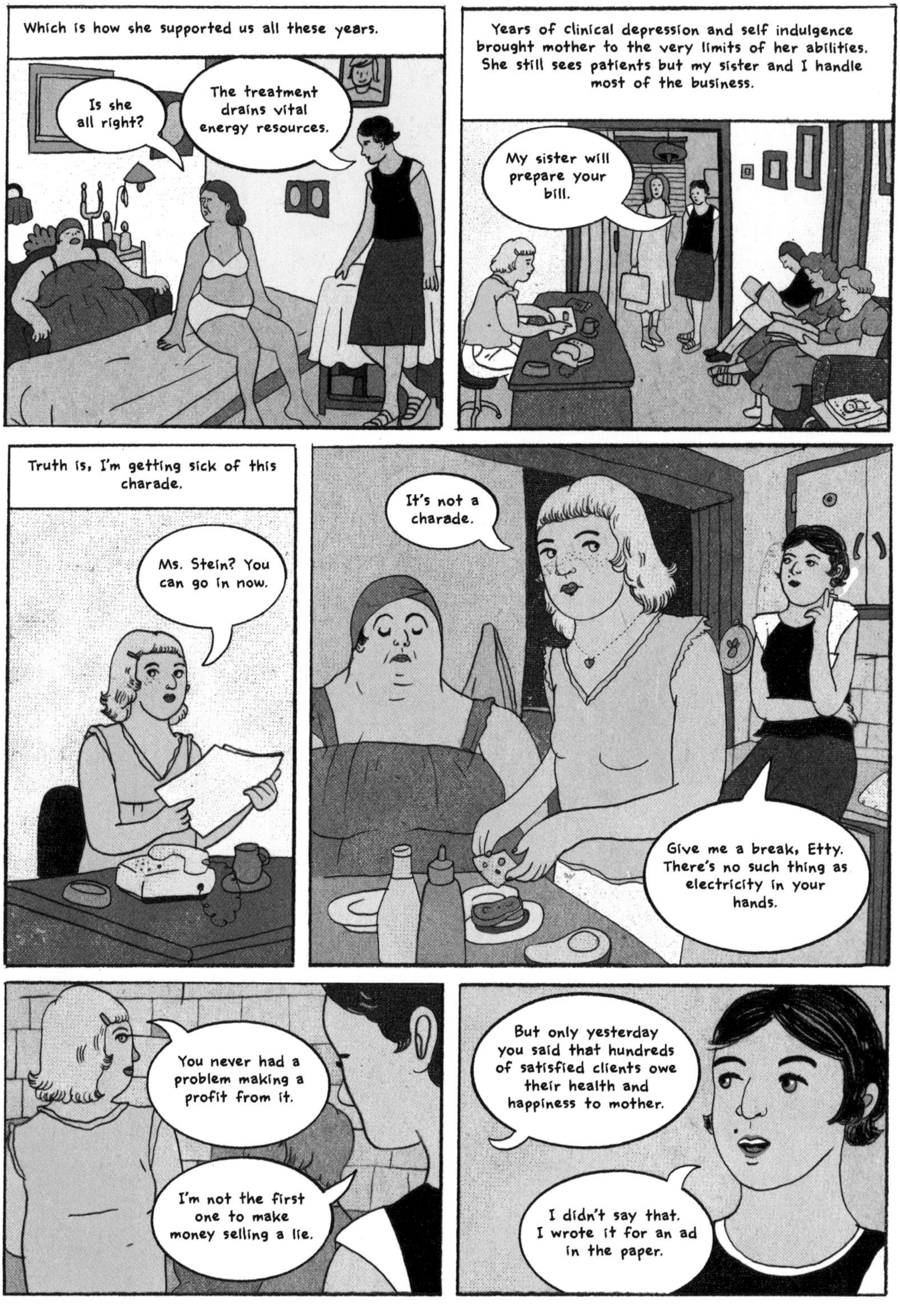
Which is how she supported us all these years.
Is she all right?
The treatment drains vital energy resources.
Years of clinical depression and self indulgence brought mother to the very limits of her abilities. She still sees patients but my sister and I handle most of the business.
My sister will prepare your bill.
Truth is, I'm getting sick of this charade.
Ms. Stein? You can go in now.
It's not a charade.
Give me a break, Etty. There's no such thing as electricity in your hands.
You never had a problem making a profit from it.
I'm not the first one to make money selling a lie.
But only yesterday you said that hundreds of satisfied clients owe their health and happiness to mother.
I didn't say that. I wrote it for an ad in the paper.

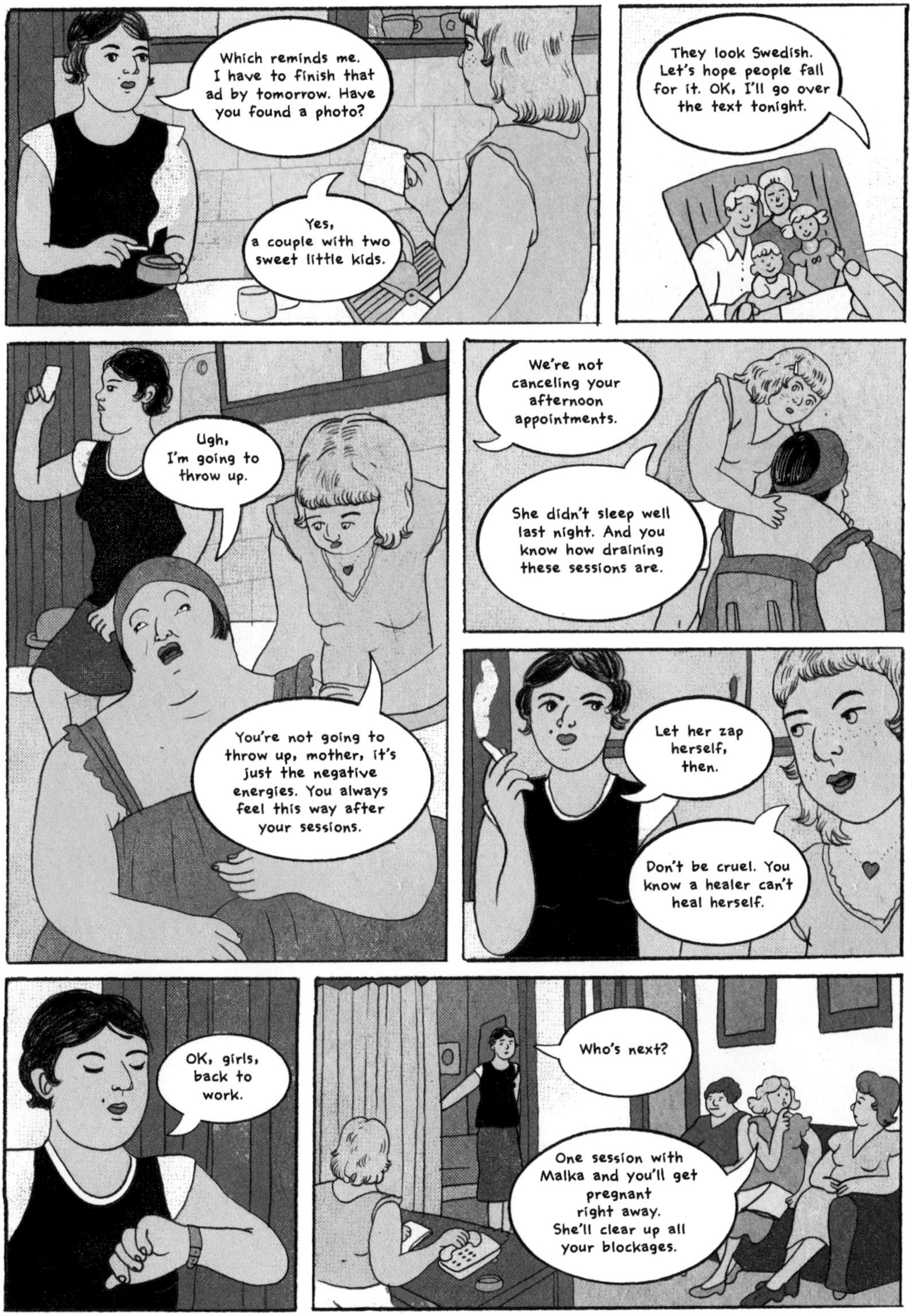
Which reminds me. I have to finish that ad by tomorrow. Have you found a photo?
Yes, a couple with two sweet little kids.
They look Swedish. Let's hope people fall for it. OK, I'll go over the text tonight.
Ugh, I'm going to throw up.
You're not going to throw up, mother, it's just the negative energies. You always feel this way after your sessions.
We're not canceling your afternoon appointments.
She didn't sleep well last night. And you know how draining these sessions are.
Let her zap herself, then.
Don't be cruel. You know a healer can't heal herself.
OK, girls, back to work.
Who's next?
One session with Malka and you'll get pregnant right away. She'll clear up all your blockages.

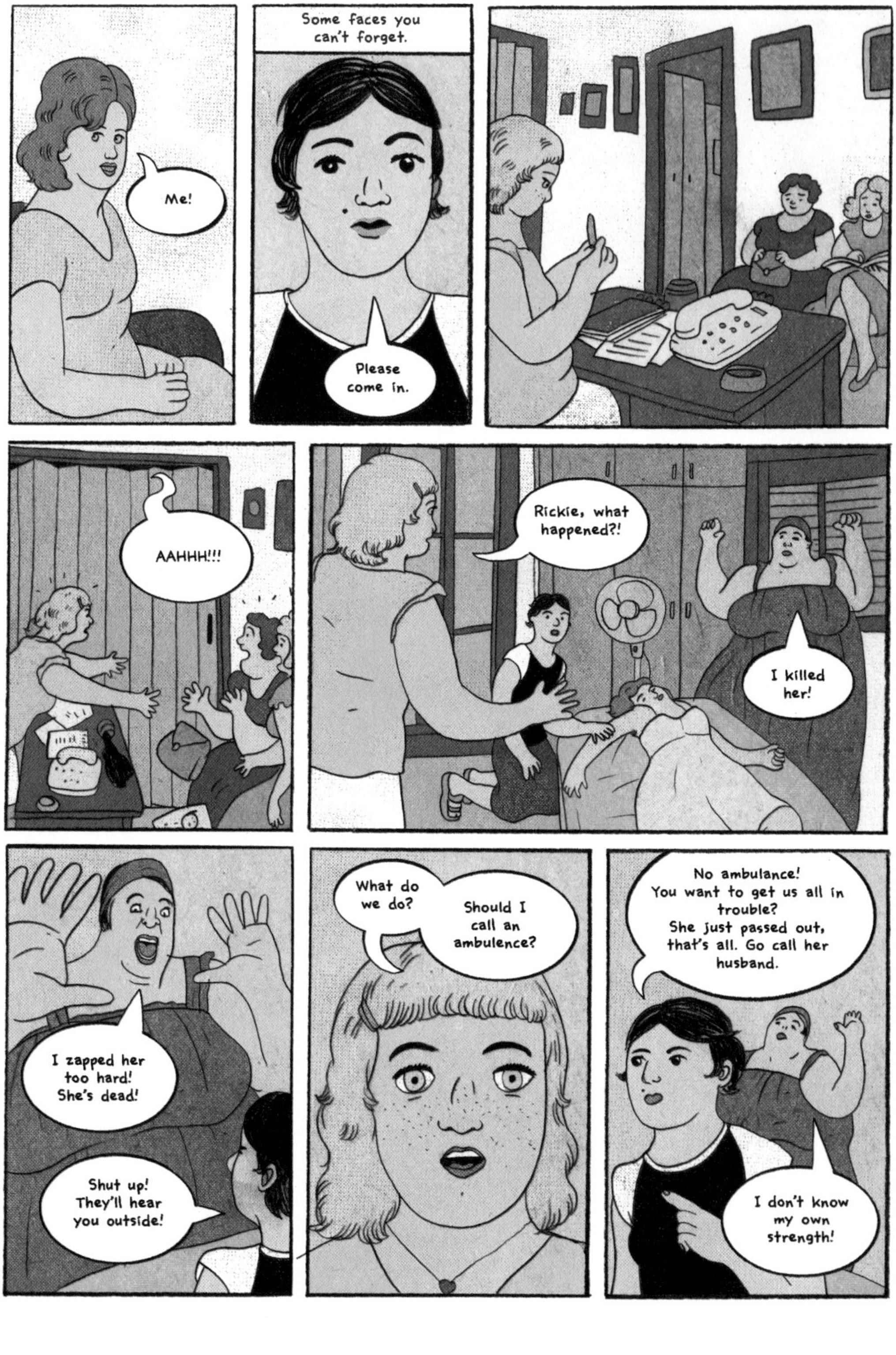
Me!
Some faces you can't forget.
Please come in.
AAHHH!!!
Rickie, what happened?!
I killed her!
I zapped her too hard! She's dead!
Shut up! They'll hear you outside!
What do we do?
Should I call an ambulence?
No ambulance! You want to get us all in trouble? She just passed out, that's all. Go call her husband.
I don't know my own strength!

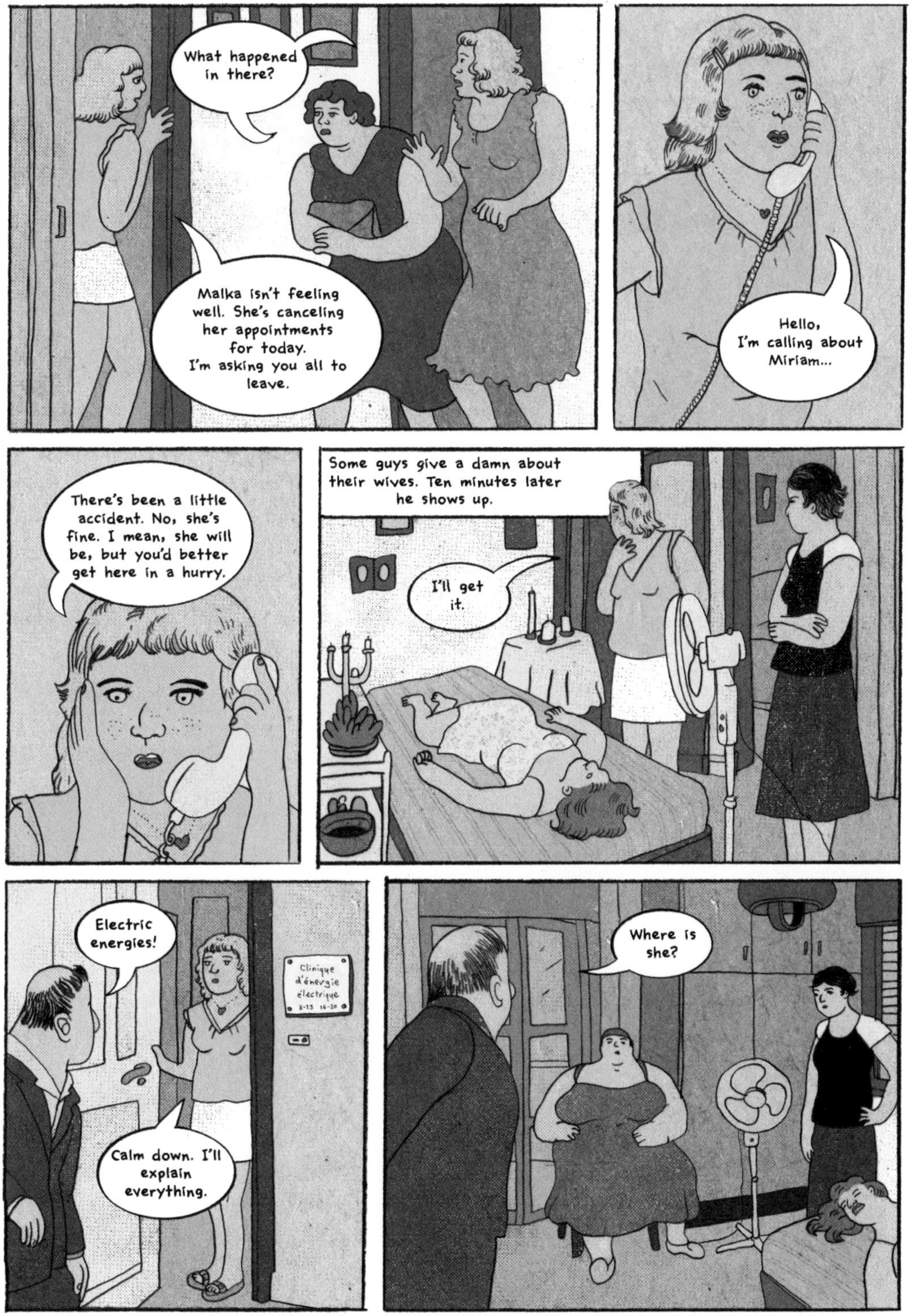
What happened in there?
Malka isn't feeling well. She's canceling her appointments for today. I'm asking you all to leave.
Hello, I'm calling about Miriam...
There's been a little accident. No, she's fine. I mean, she will be, but you'd better get here in a hurry.
Some guys give a damn about their wives. Ten minutes later he shows up.
I'll get it.
Electric energies!
Clinique d'énergie électrique 8-13 16-20
Calm down. I'll explain everything.
Where is she?

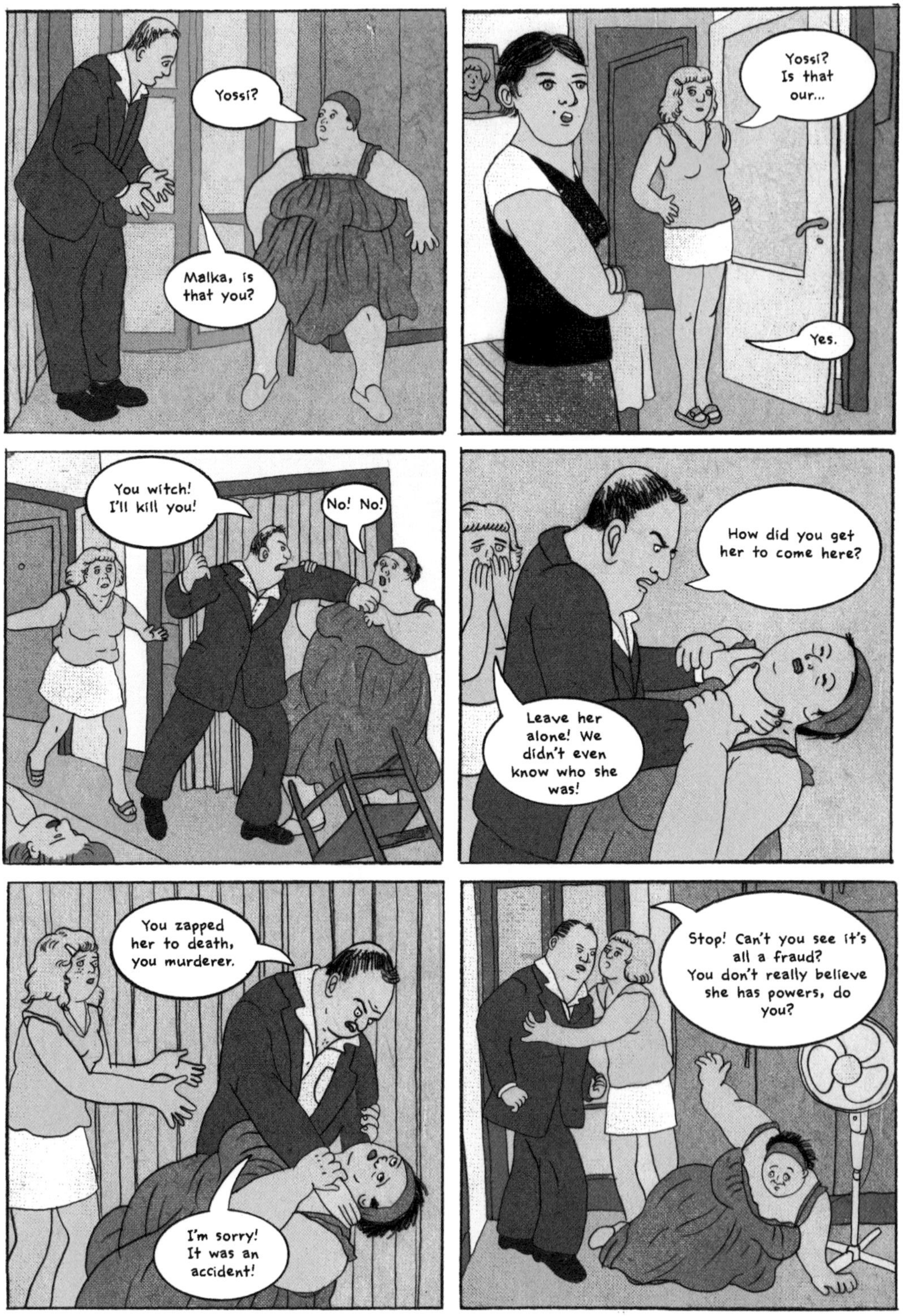
Yossi?
Malka, is that you?
Yossi? Is that our...
Yes.
You witch! I'll kill you!
No! No!
How did you get her to come here?
Leave her alone! We didn't even know who she was!
You zapped her to death, you murderer.
I'm sorry! It was an accident!
Stop! Can't you see it's all a fraud? You don't really believe she has powers, do you?

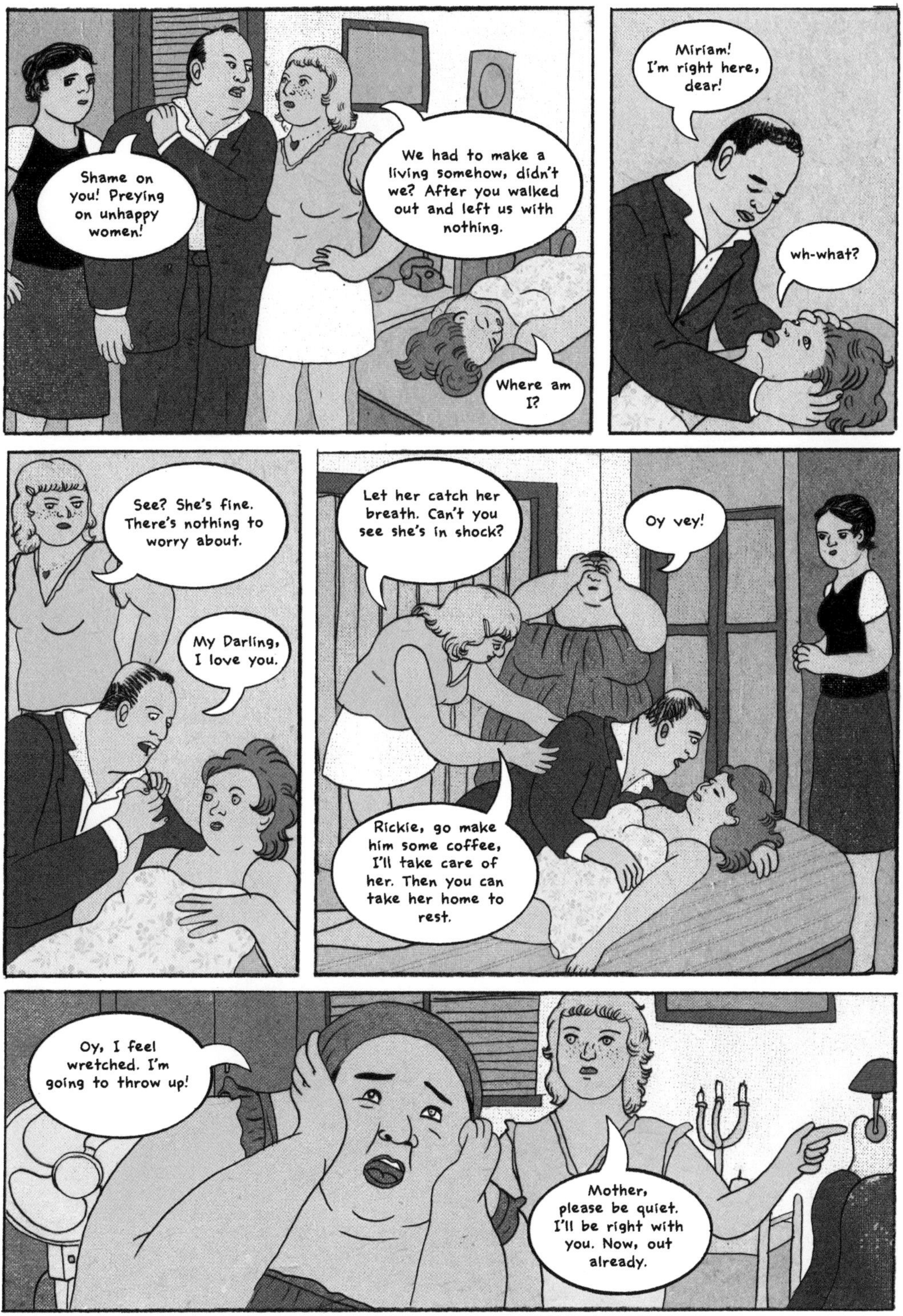
Shame on you! Preying on unhappy women!
We had to make a living somehow, didn't we? After you walked out and left us with nothing.
Where am I?
Miriam! I'm right here, dear!
wh-what?
See? She's fine. There's nothing to worry about.
My Darling, I love you.
Let her catch her breath. Can't you see she's in shock?
Oy vey!
Rickie, go make him some coffee, I'll take care of her. Then you can take her home to rest.
Oy, I feel wretched. I'm going to throw up!
Mother, please be quiet. I'll be right with you. Now, out already.

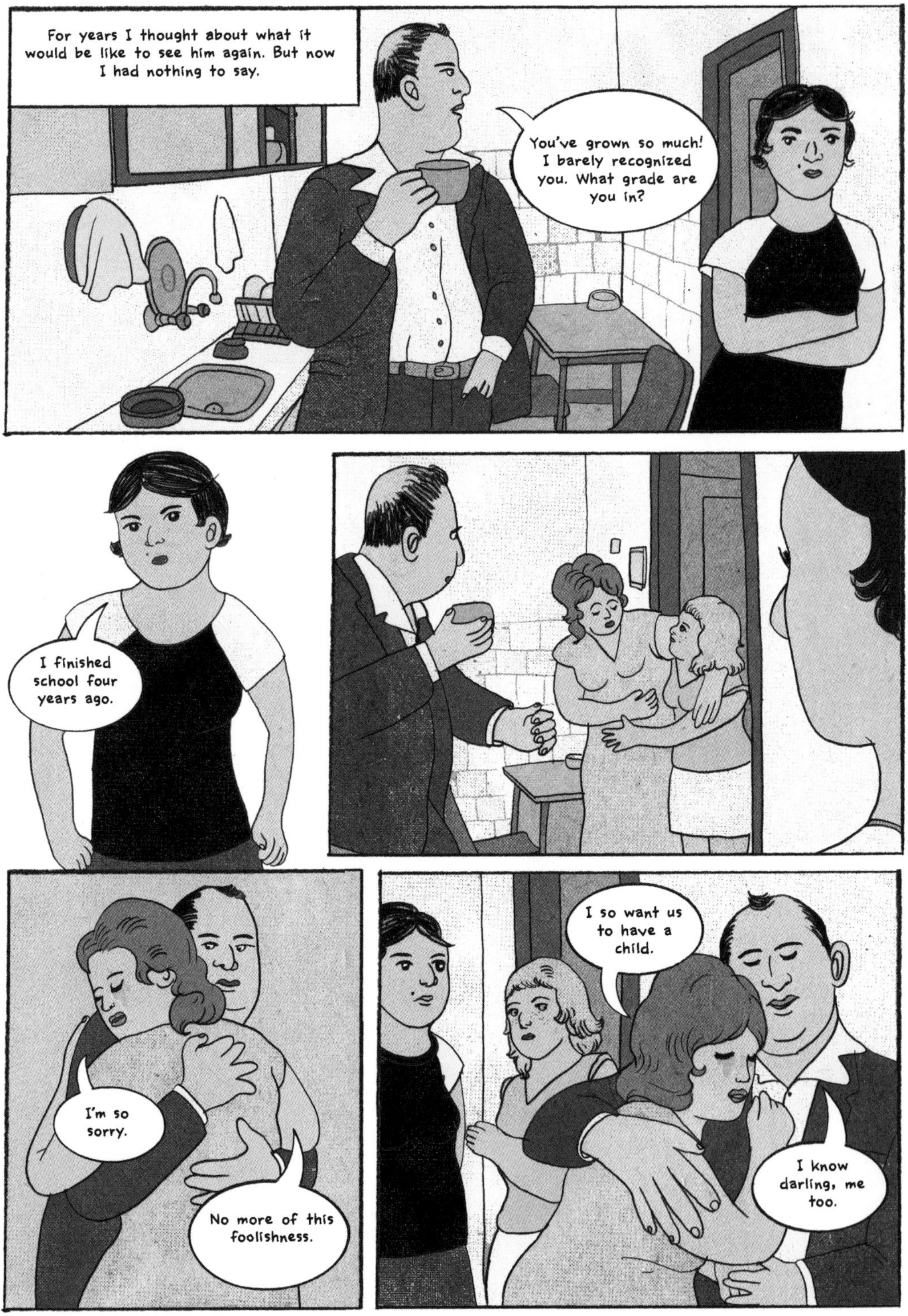
For years I thought about what it would be like to see him again. But now I had nothing to say.
You've grown so much! I barely recognized you. What grade are you in?
I finished school four years ago.
I'm so sorry.
No more of this foolishness.
I so want us to have a child.
I know darling, me too.

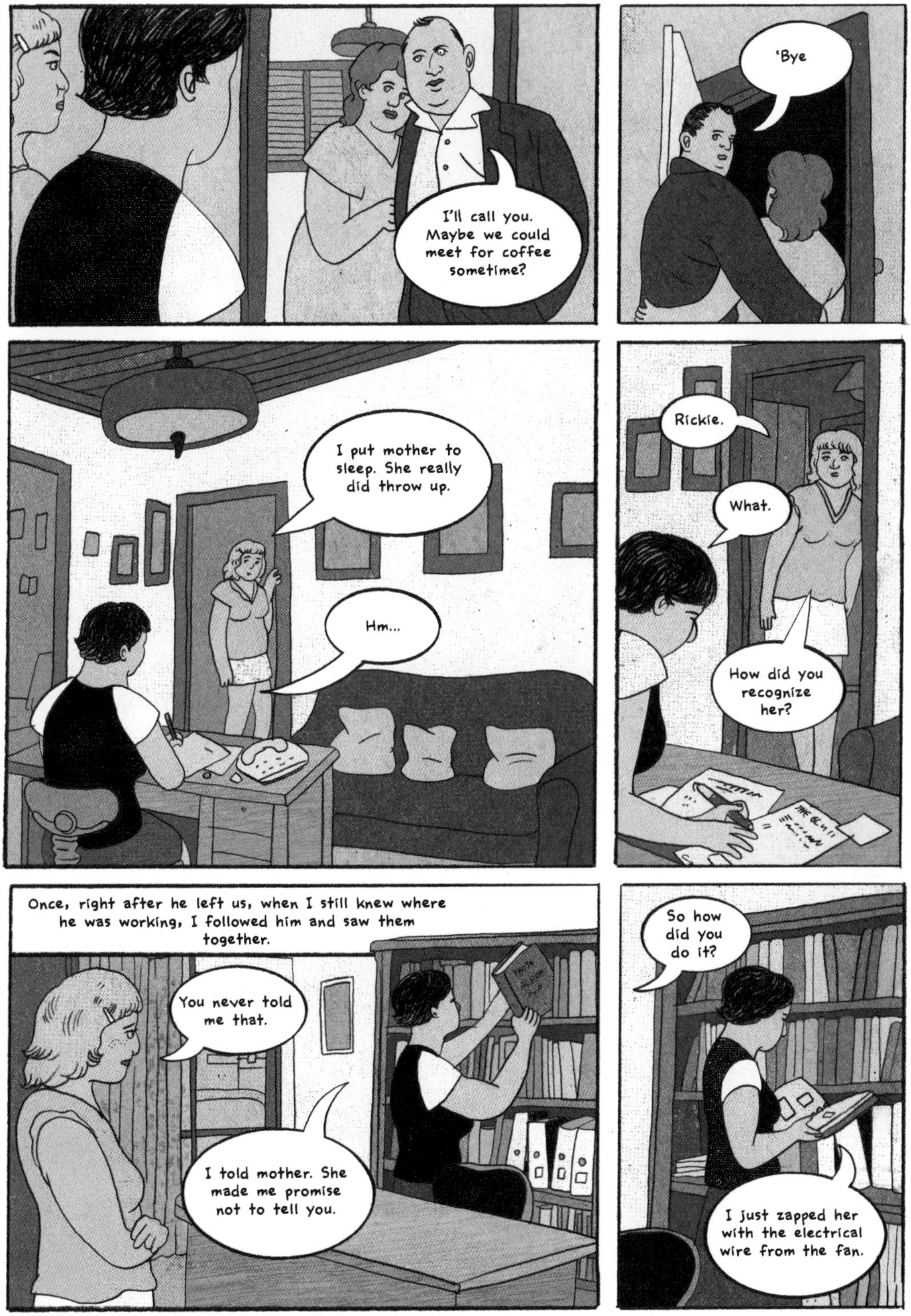
I'll call you. Maybe we could meet for coffee sometime?
'Bye
I put mother to sleep. She really did throw up.
Hm...
Rickie.
What.
How did you recognize her?
Once, right after he left us, when I still knew where he was working, I followed him and saw them together.
You never told me that.
I told mother. She made me promise not to tell you.
So how did you do it?
I just zapped her with the electrical wire from the fan.

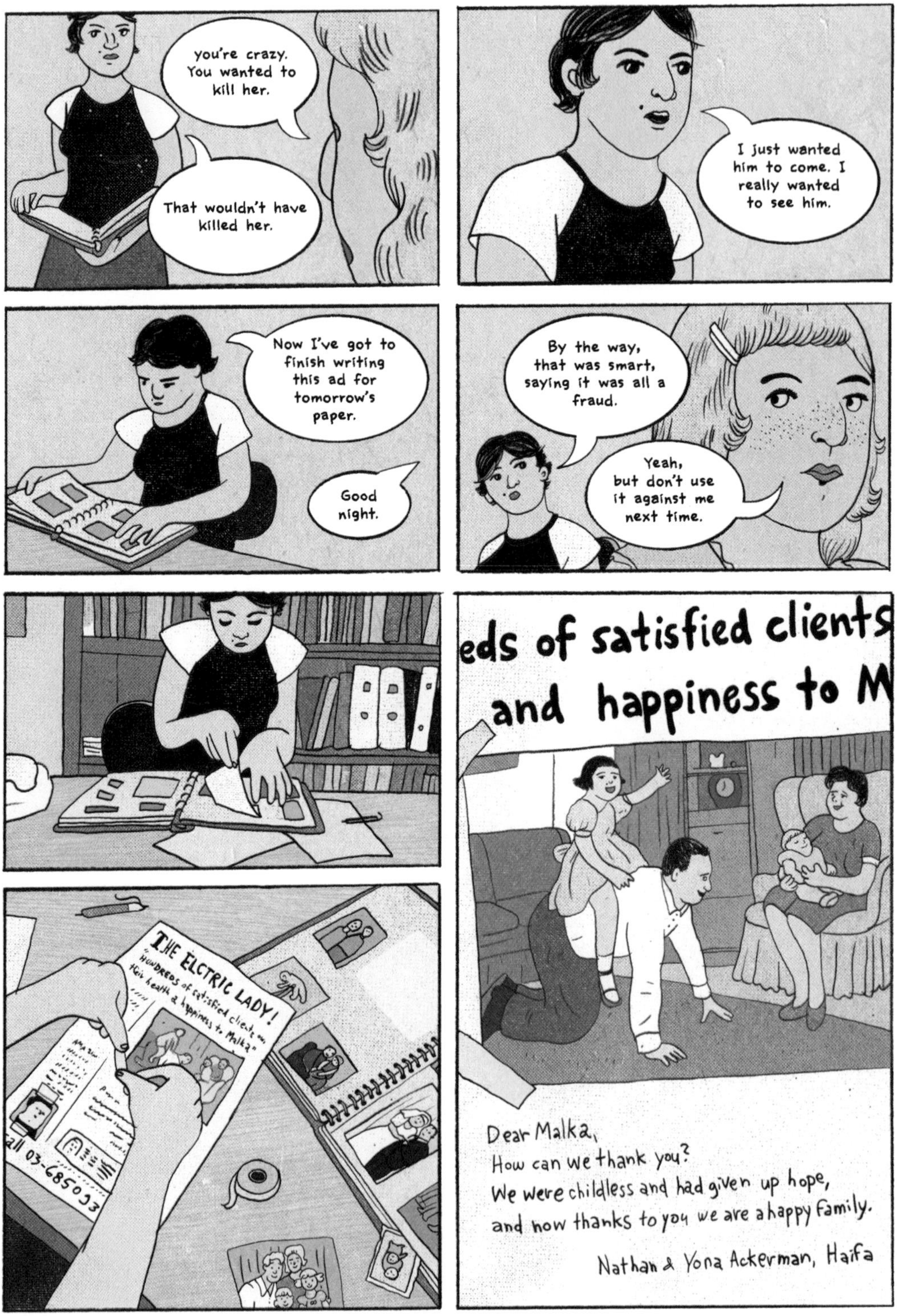
you're crazy. You wanted to kill her.
That wouldn't have killed her.
I just wanted him to come. I really wanted to see him.
Now I've got to finish writing this ad for tomorrow's paper.
Good night.
By the way, that was smart, saying it was all a fraud.
Yeah, but don't use it against me next time.
THE ELCTRIC LADY!
eds of satisfied clients
and happiness to M
Dear Malka,
How can we thank you?
We were childless and had given up hope,
and now thanks to you we are a happy family.
Nathan & Yona Ackerman, Haifa

BYGONE

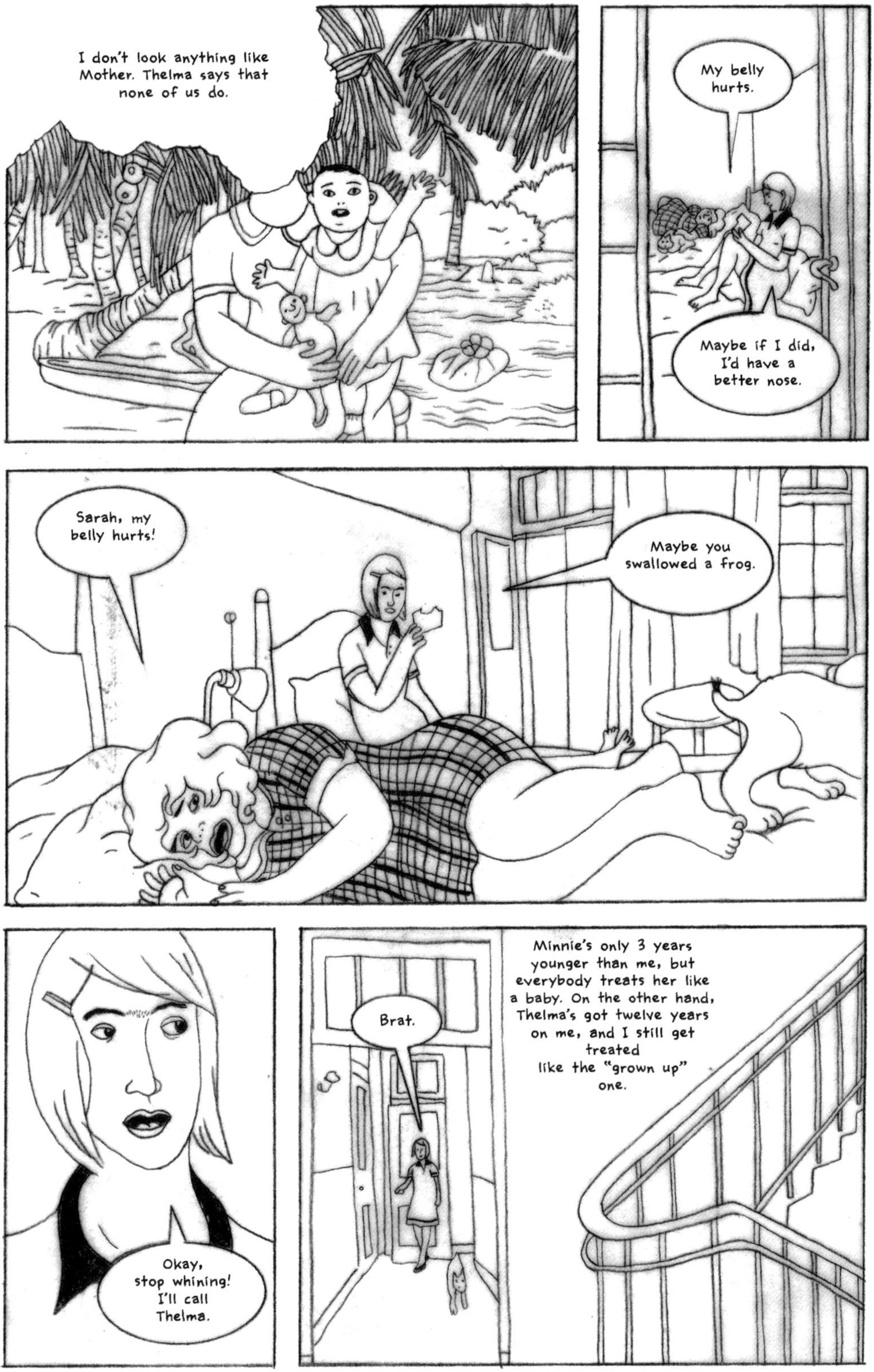
I don't look anything like Mother. Thelma says that none of us do.
My belly hurts.
Maybe if I did, I'd have a better nose.
Sarah, my belly hurts!
Maybe you swallowed a frog.
Okay, stop whining! I'll call Thelma.
Brat.
Minnie's only 3 years younger than me, but everybody treats her like a baby. On the other hand, Thelma's got twelve years on me, and I still get treated like the "grown up" one.

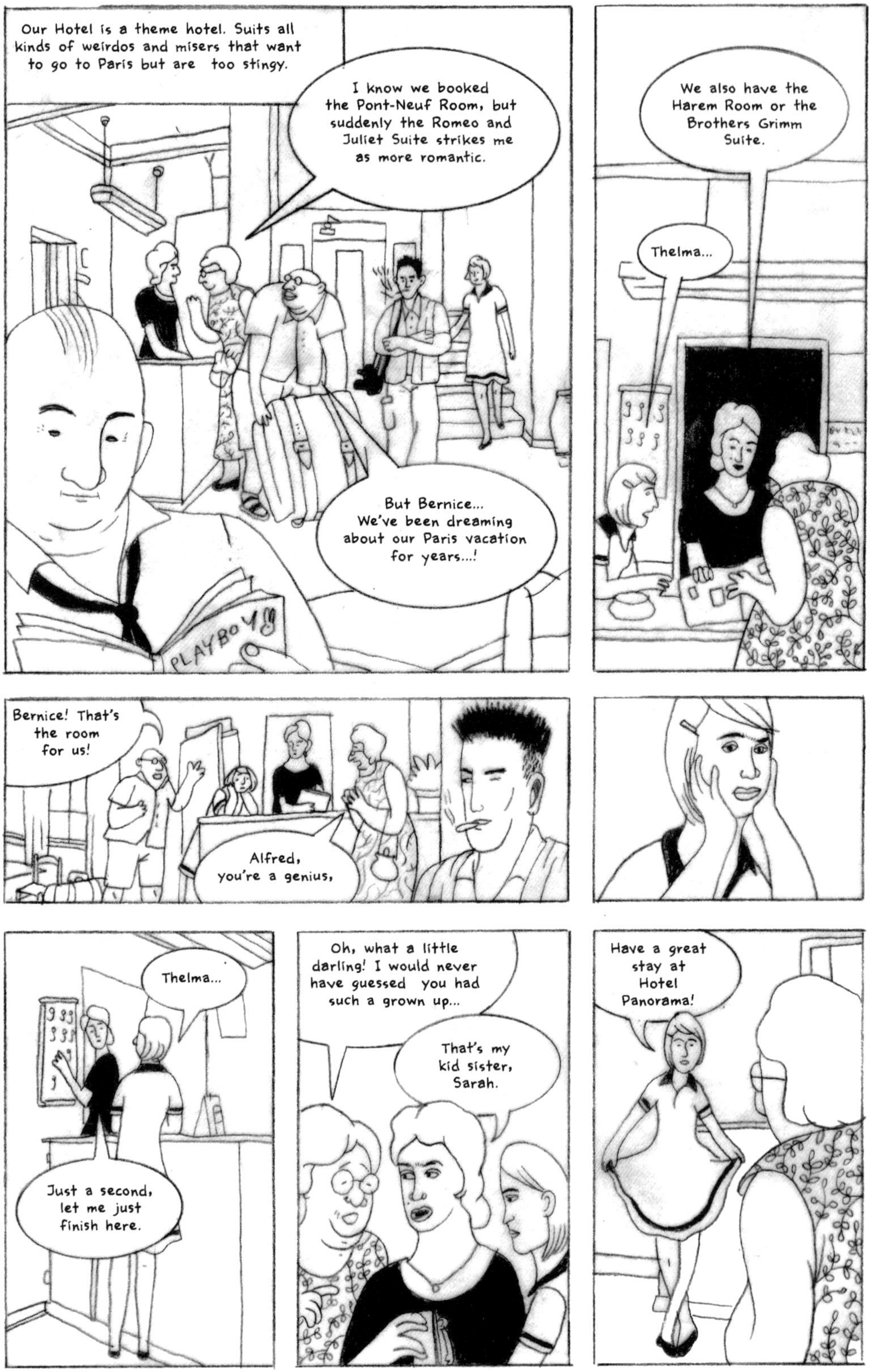
Our Hotel is a theme hotel. Suits all kinds of weirdos and misers that want to go to Paris but are too stingy.
I know we booked the Pont-Neuf Room, but suddenly the Romeo and Juliet Suite strikes me as more romantic.
But Bernice... We've been dreaming about our Paris vacation for years...!
PLAYBOY
We also have the Harem Room or the Brothers Grimm Suite.
Thelma...
Bernice! That's the room for us!
Alfred, you're a genius,
Thelma...
Just a second, let me just finish here.
Oh, what a little darling! I would never have guessed you had such a grown up...
That's my kid sister, Sarah.
Have a great stay at Hotel Panorama!

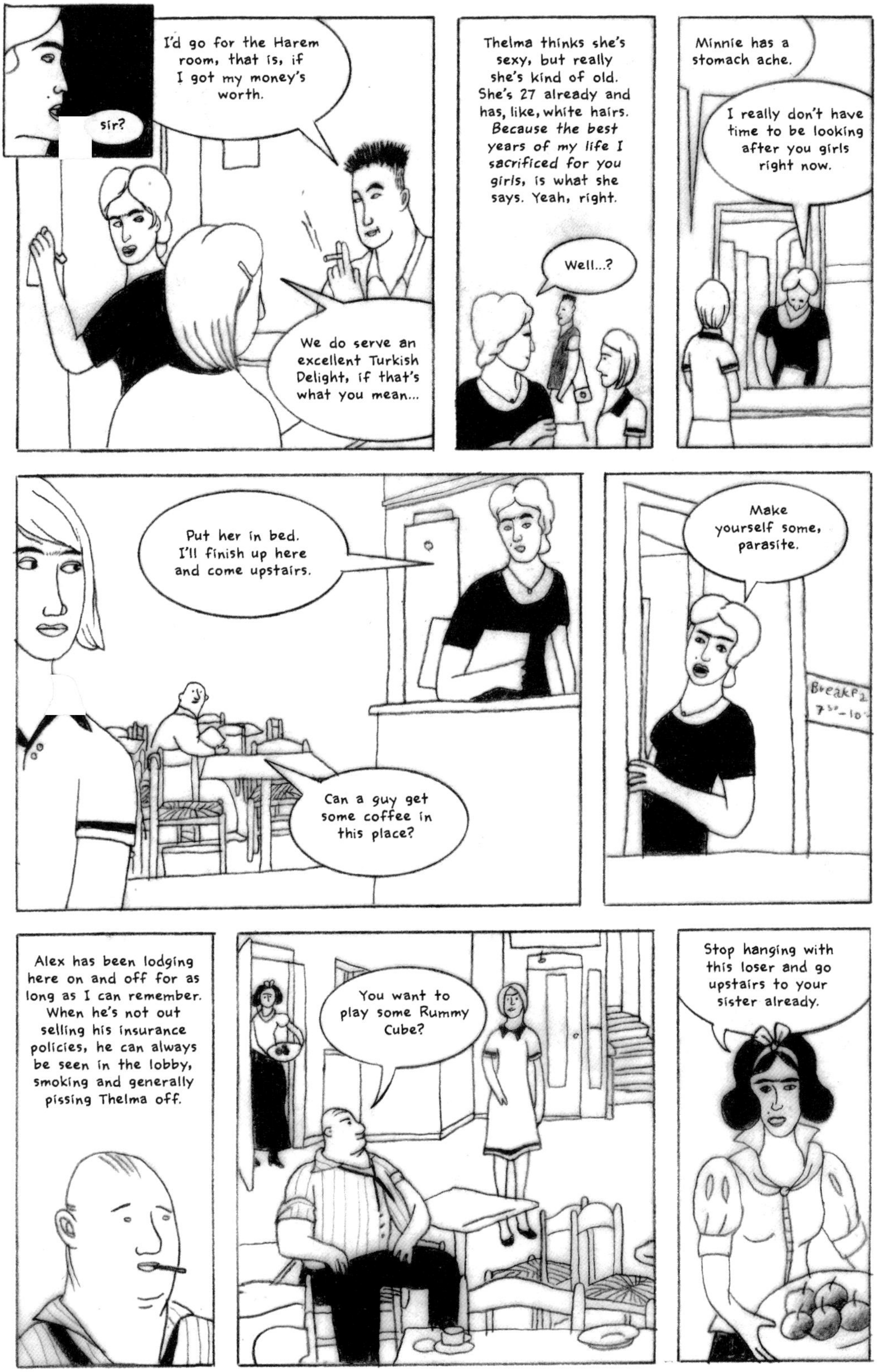
sir?
I'd go for the Harem room, that is, if I got my money's worth.
We do serve an excellent Turkish Delight, if that's what you mean...
Thelma thinks she's sexy, but really she's kind of old. She's 27 already and has, like, white hairs. *Because the best years of my life I sacrificed for you girls,* is what she says. Yeah, right.
Well...?
Minnie has a stomach ache.
I really don't have time to be looking after you girls right now.
Put her in bed. I'll finish up here and come upstairs.
Can a guy get some coffee in this place?
Make yourself some, parasite.
Alex has been lodging here on and off for as long as I can remember. When he's not out selling his insurance policies, he can always be seen in the lobby, smoking and generally pissing Thelma off.
You want to play some Rummy Cube?
Stop hanging with this loser and go upstairs to your sister already.

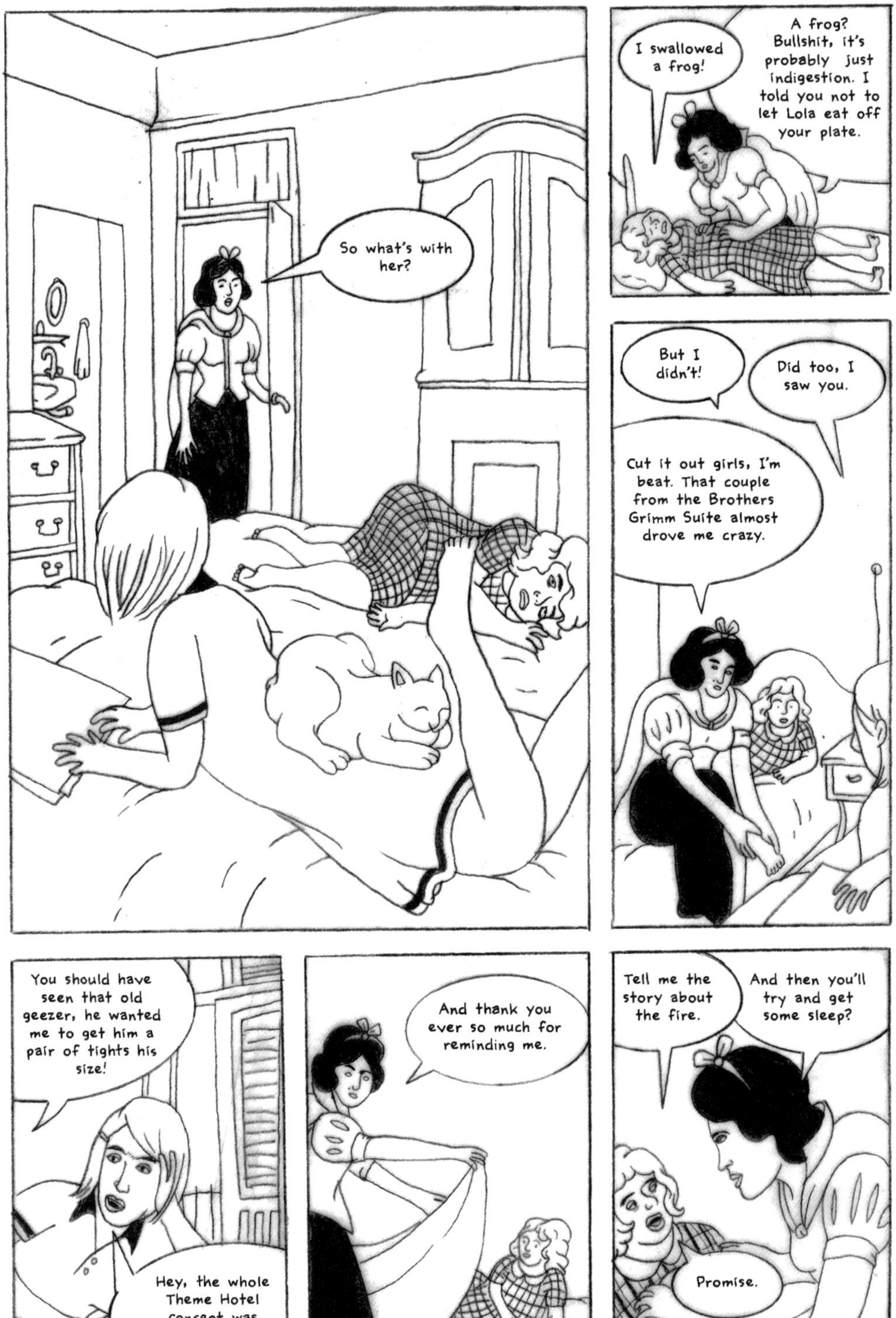
So what's with her?
I swallowed a frog!
A frog? Bullshit, it's probably just indigestion. I told you not to let Lola eat off your plate.
But I didn't!
Did too, I saw you.
Cut it out girls, I'm beat. That couple from the Brothers Grimm Suite almost drove me crazy.
You should have seen that old geezer, he wanted me to get him a pair of tights his size!
Hey, the whole Theme Hotel concept was yours in the first place.
And thank you ever so much for reminding me.
Tell me the story about the fire.
And then you'll try and get some sleep?
Promise.

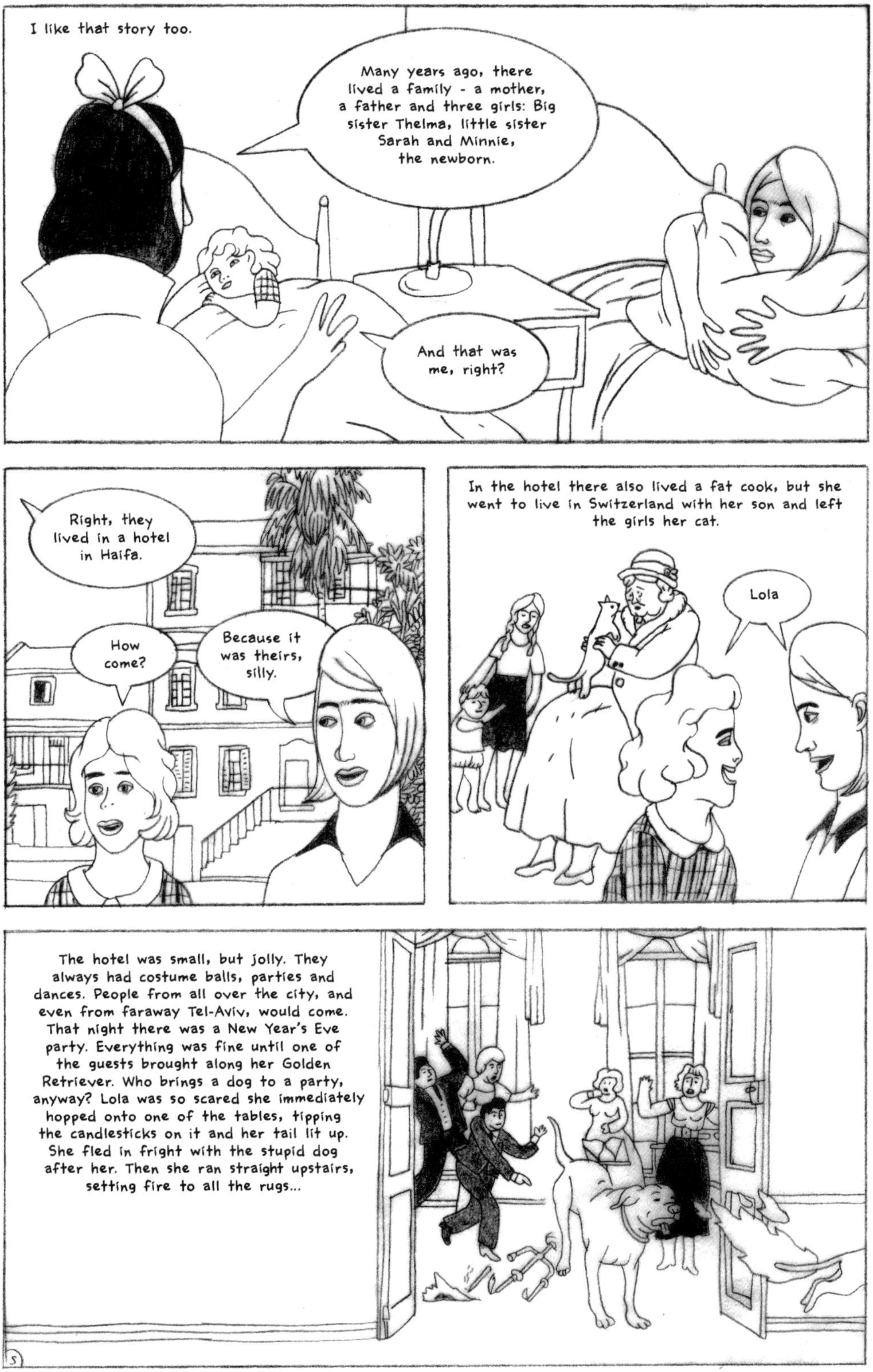
I like that story too.
Many years ago, there lived a family - a mother, a father and three girls: Big sister Thelma, little sister Sarah and Minnie, the newborn.
And that was me, right?
Right, they lived in a hotel in Haifa.
How come?
Because it was theirs, silly.
In the hotel there also lived a fat cook, but she went to live in Switzerland with her son and left the girls her cat.
Lola
The hotel was small, but jolly. They always had costume balls, parties and dances. People from all over the city, and even from faraway Tel-Aviv, would come. That night there was a New Year's Eve party. Everything was fine until one of the guests brought along her Golden Retriever. Who brings a dog to a party, anyway? Lola was so scared she immediately hopped onto one of the tables, tipping the candlesticks on it and her tail lit up. She fled in fright with the stupid dog after her. Then she ran straight upstairs, setting fire to all the rugs...

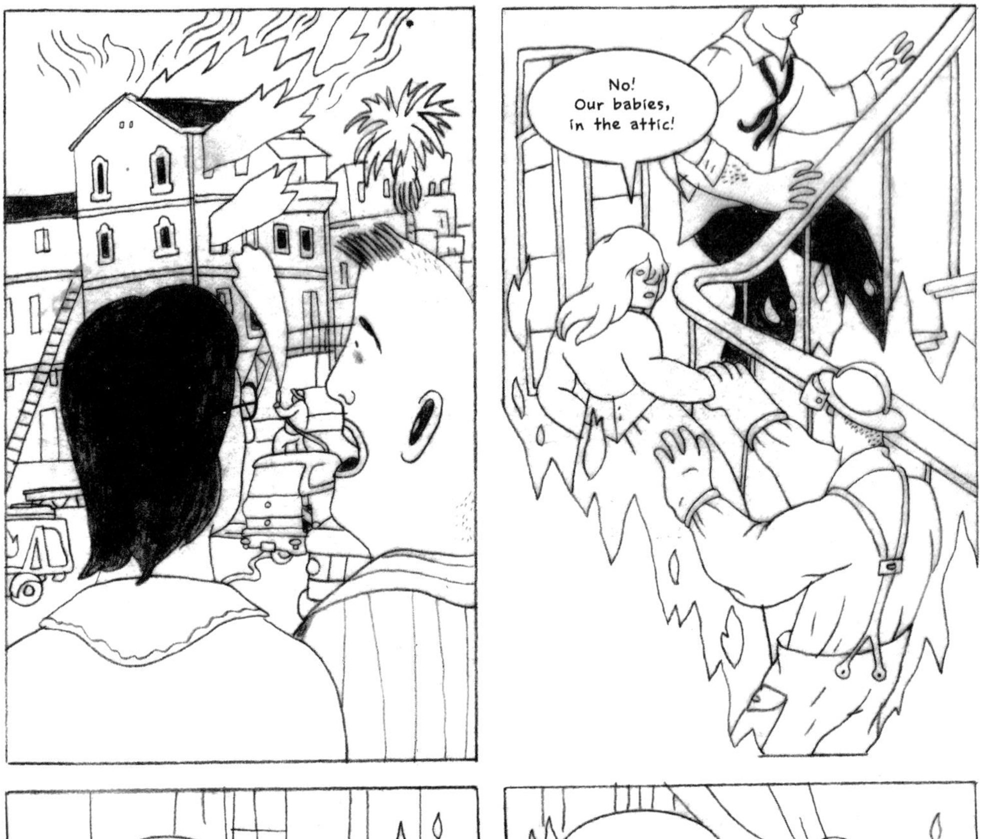
No! Our babies, in the attic!
Sarah, Thelma!
Over here, save the children!

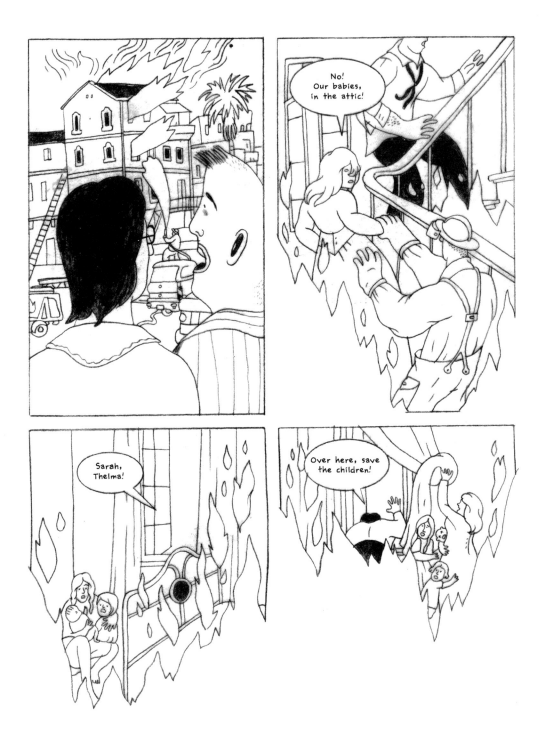

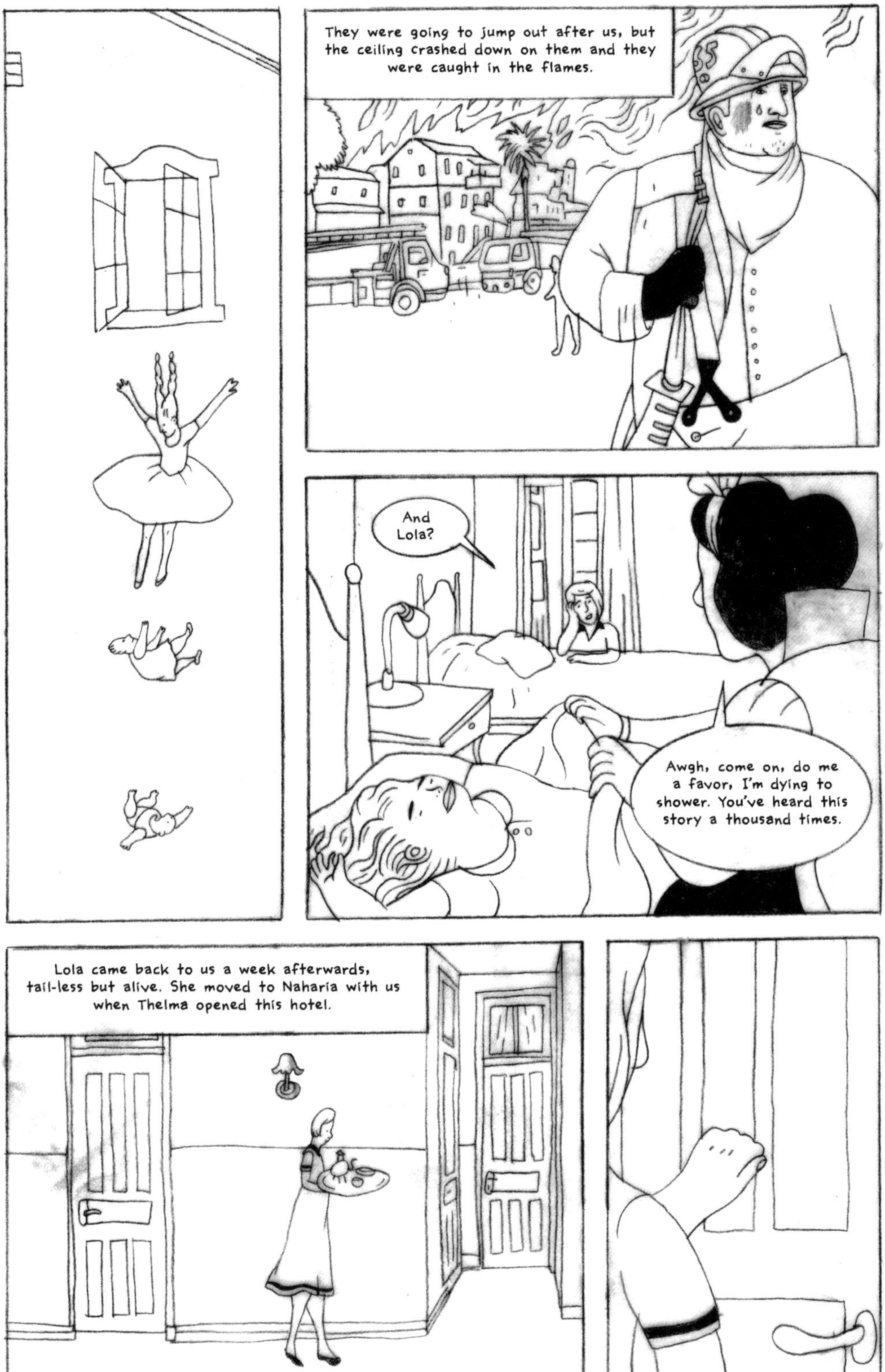
They were going to jump out after us, but the ceiling crashed down on them and they were caught in the flames.
And Lola?
Awgh, come on, do me a favor, I'm dying to shower. You've heard this story a thousand times.
Lola came back to us a week afterwards, tail-less but alive. She moved to Naharia with us when Thelma opened this hotel.

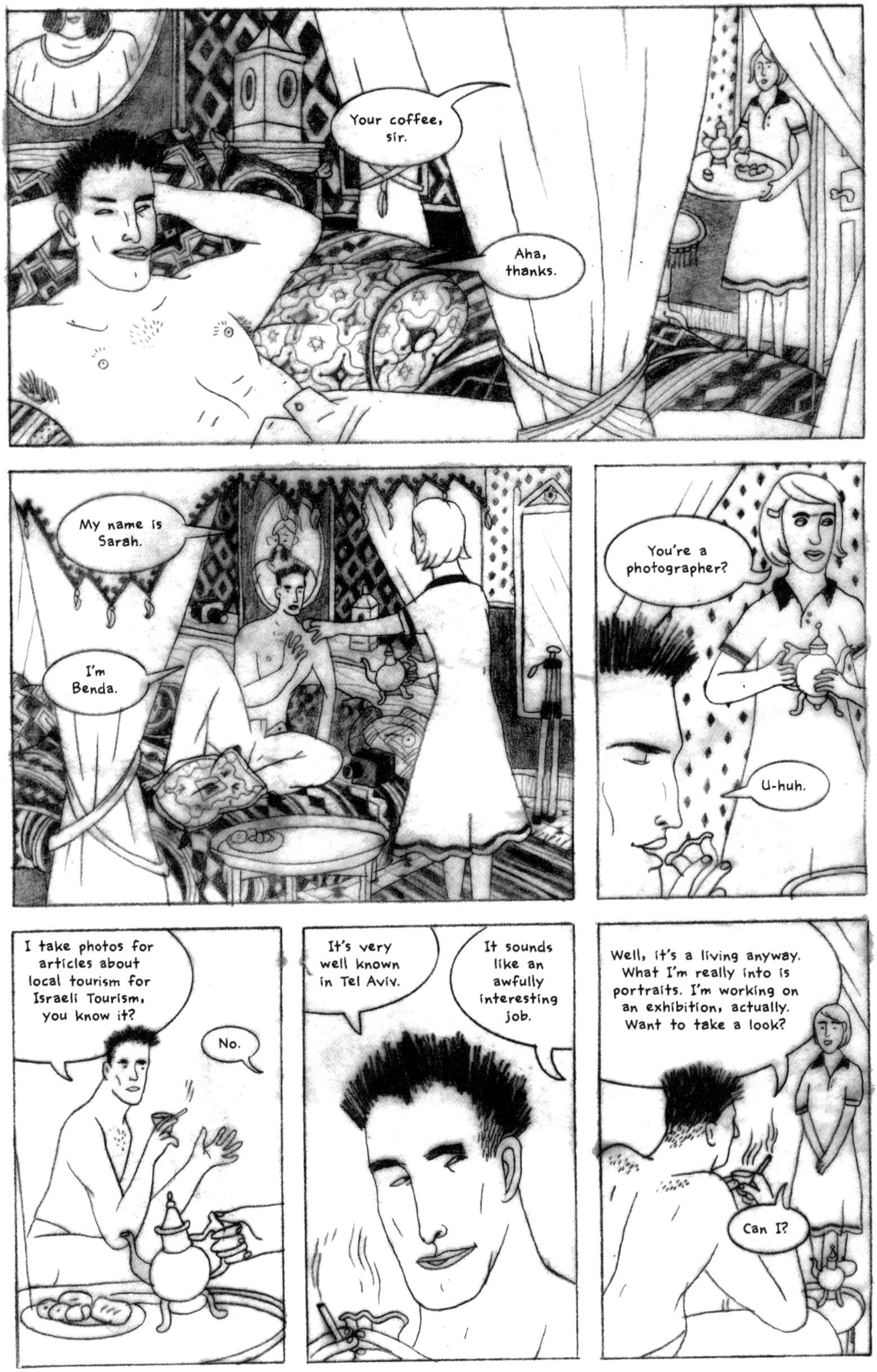
Your coffee, sir.
Aha, thanks.
My name is Sarah.
I'm Benda.
You're a photographer?
U-huh.
I take photos for articles about local tourism for Israeli Tourism, you know it?
No.
It's very well known in Tel Aviv.
It sounds like an awfully interesting job.
Well, it's a living anyway. What I'm really into is portraits. I'm working on an exhibition, actually. Want to take a look?
Can I?

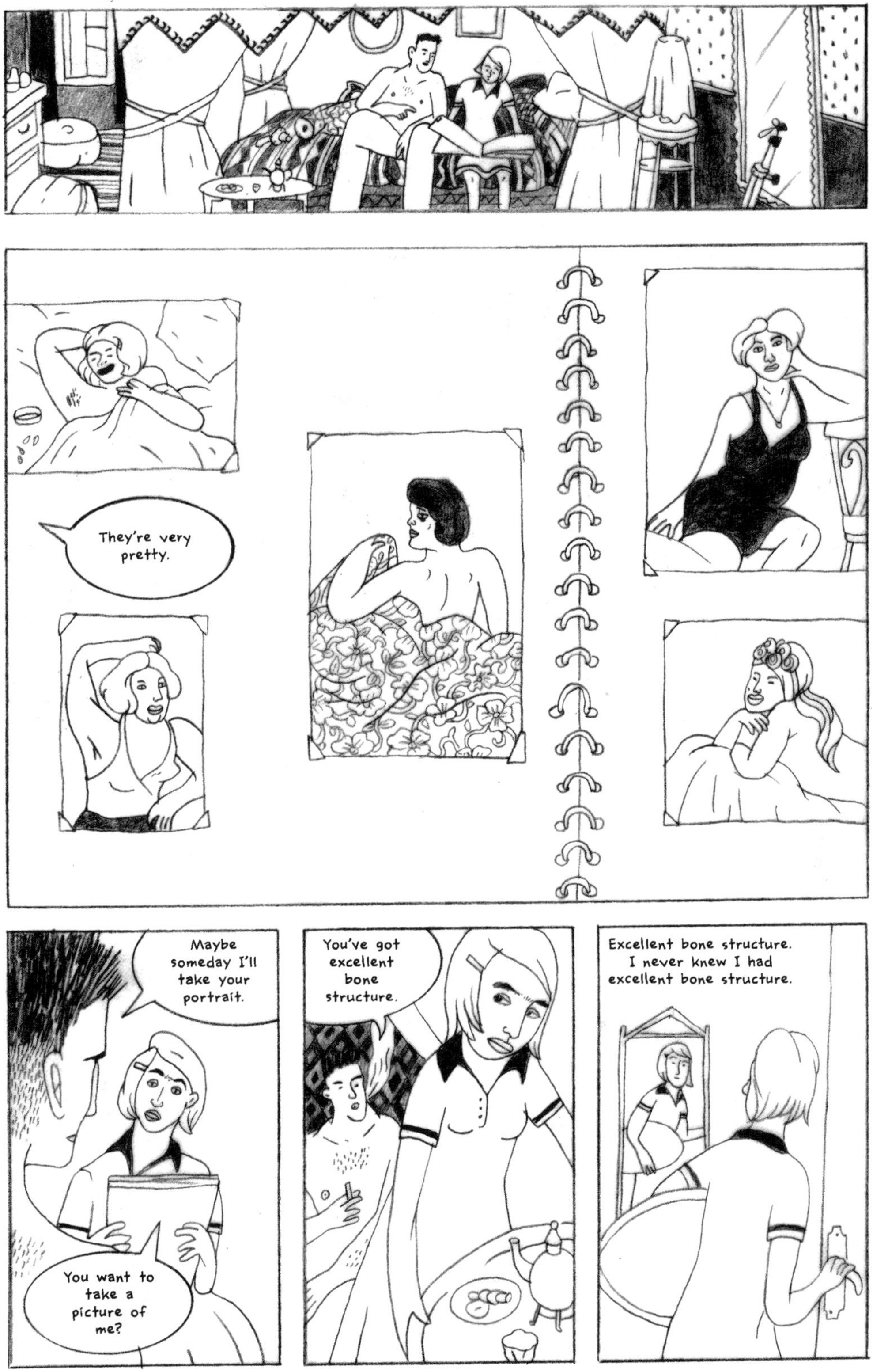
They're very pretty.
Maybe someday I'll take your portrait.
You want to take a picture of me?
You've got excellent bone structure.
Excellent bone structure. I never knew I had excellent bone structure.

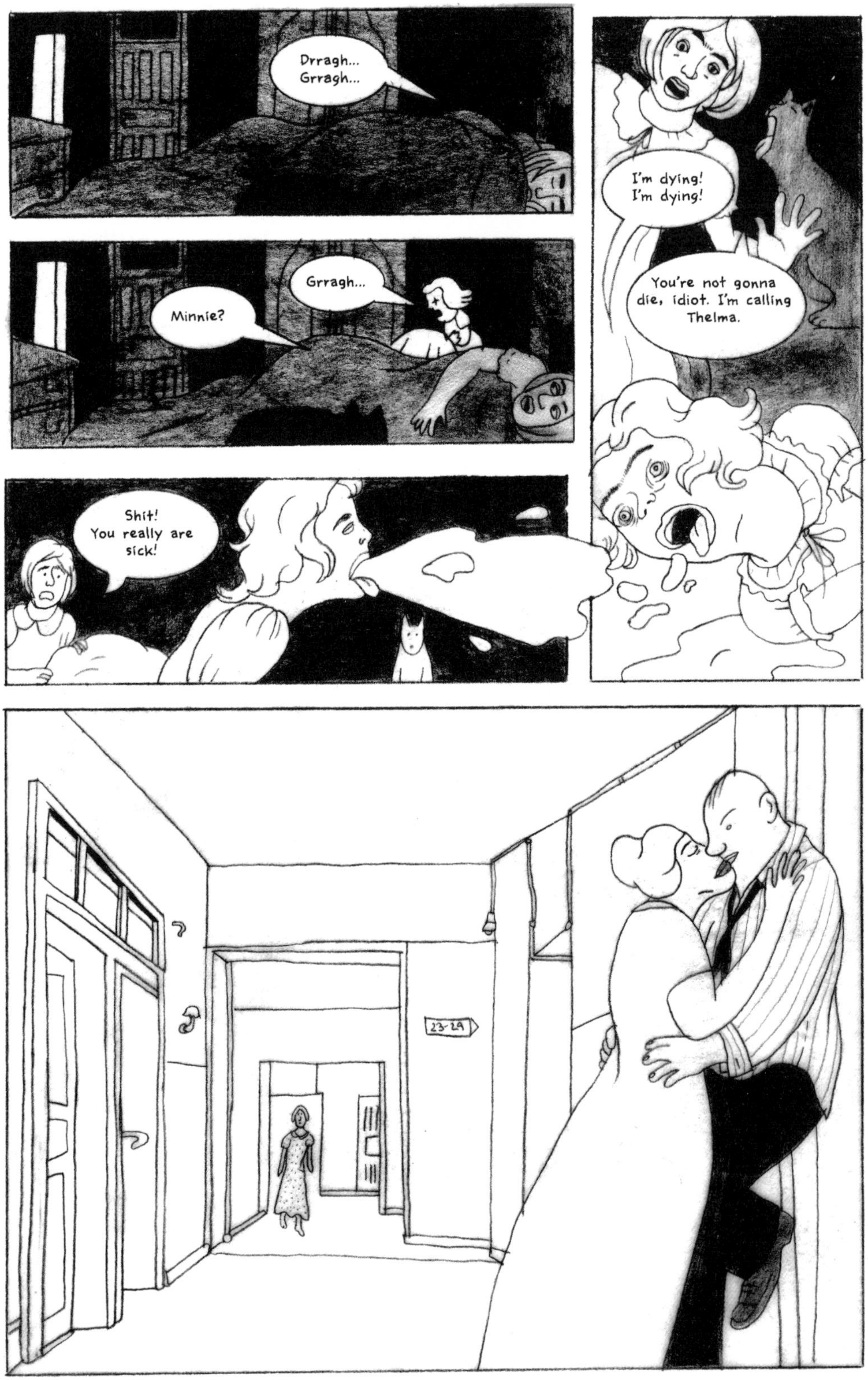
Drragh...
Grragh...
Minnie?
Grragh...
Shit! You really are sick!
I'm dying! I'm dying!
You're not gonna die, idiot. I'm calling Thelma.
23-29

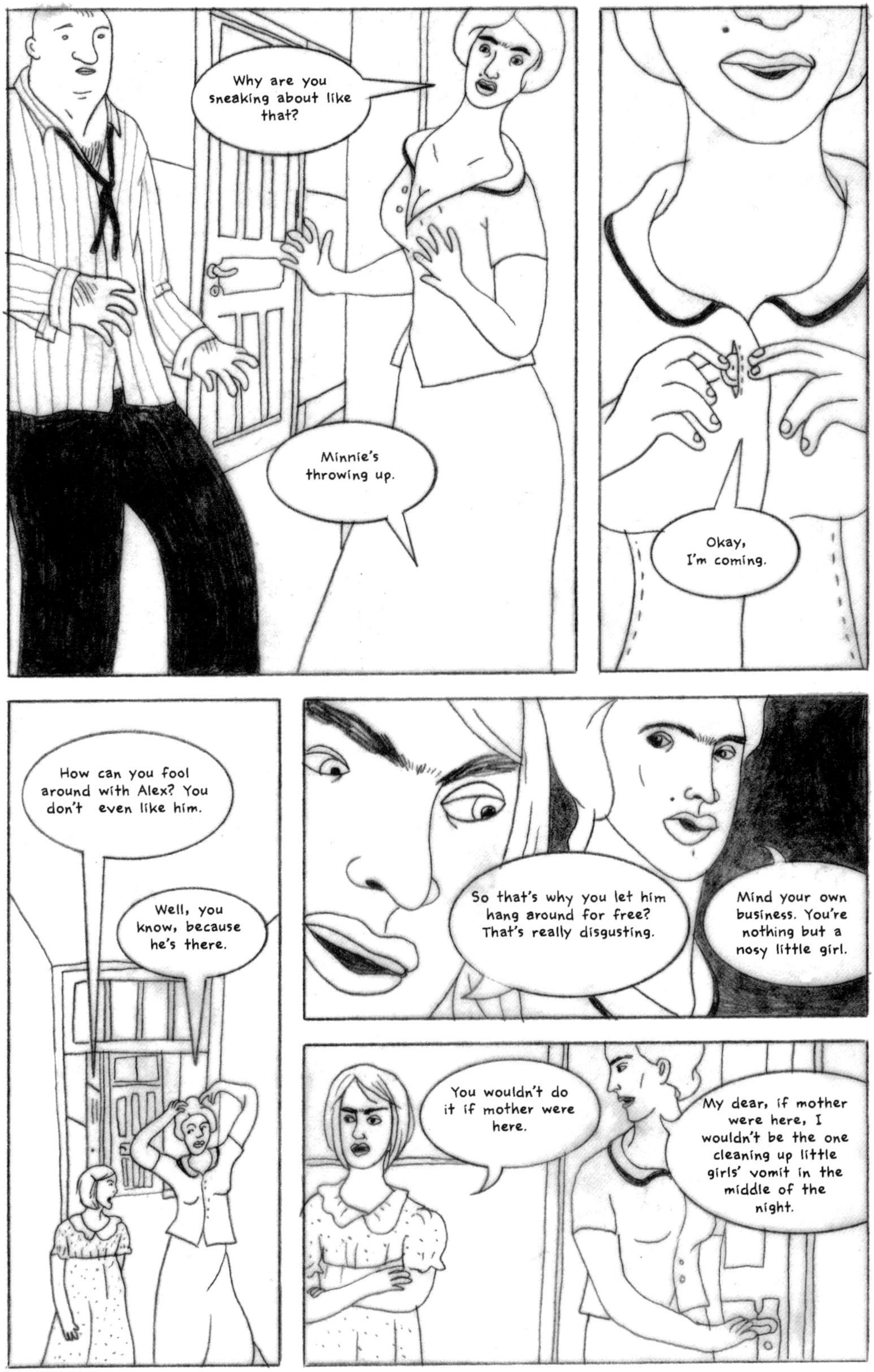
Why are you sneaking about like that?
Minnie's throwing up.
Okay, I'm coming.
How can you fool around with Alex? You don't even like him.
Well, you know, because he's there.
So that's why you let him hang around for free? That's really disgusting.
Mind your own business. You're nothing but a nosy little girl.
You wouldn't do it if mother were here.
My dear, if mother were here, I wouldn't be the one cleaning up little girls' vomit in the middle of the night.

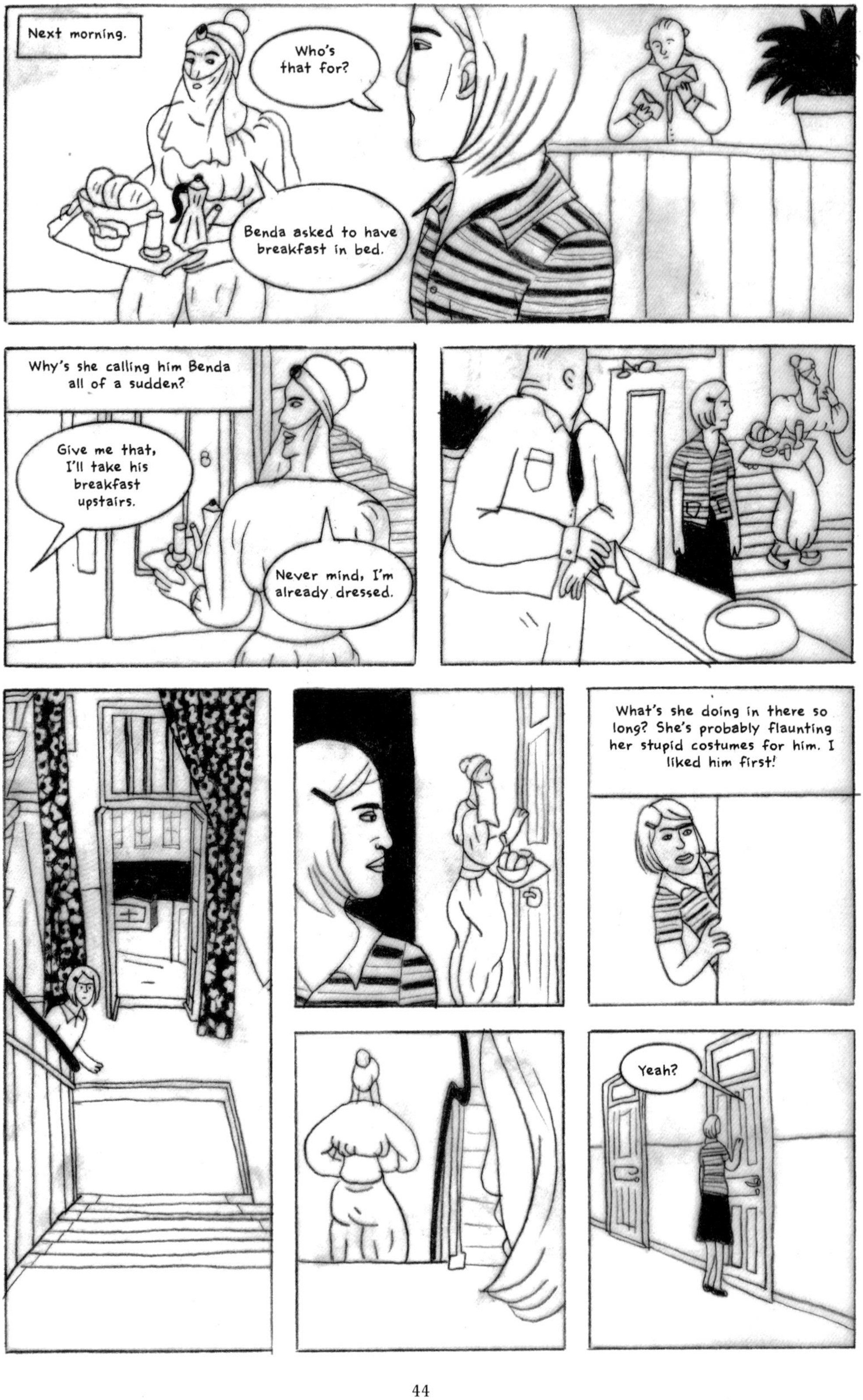

Next morning.
Who's that for?
Benda asked to have breakfast in bed.
Why's she calling him Benda all of a sudden?
Give me that, I'll take his breakfast upstairs.
Never mind, I'm already dressed.
What's she doing in there so long? She's probably flaunting her stupid costumes for him. I liked him first!
Yeah?

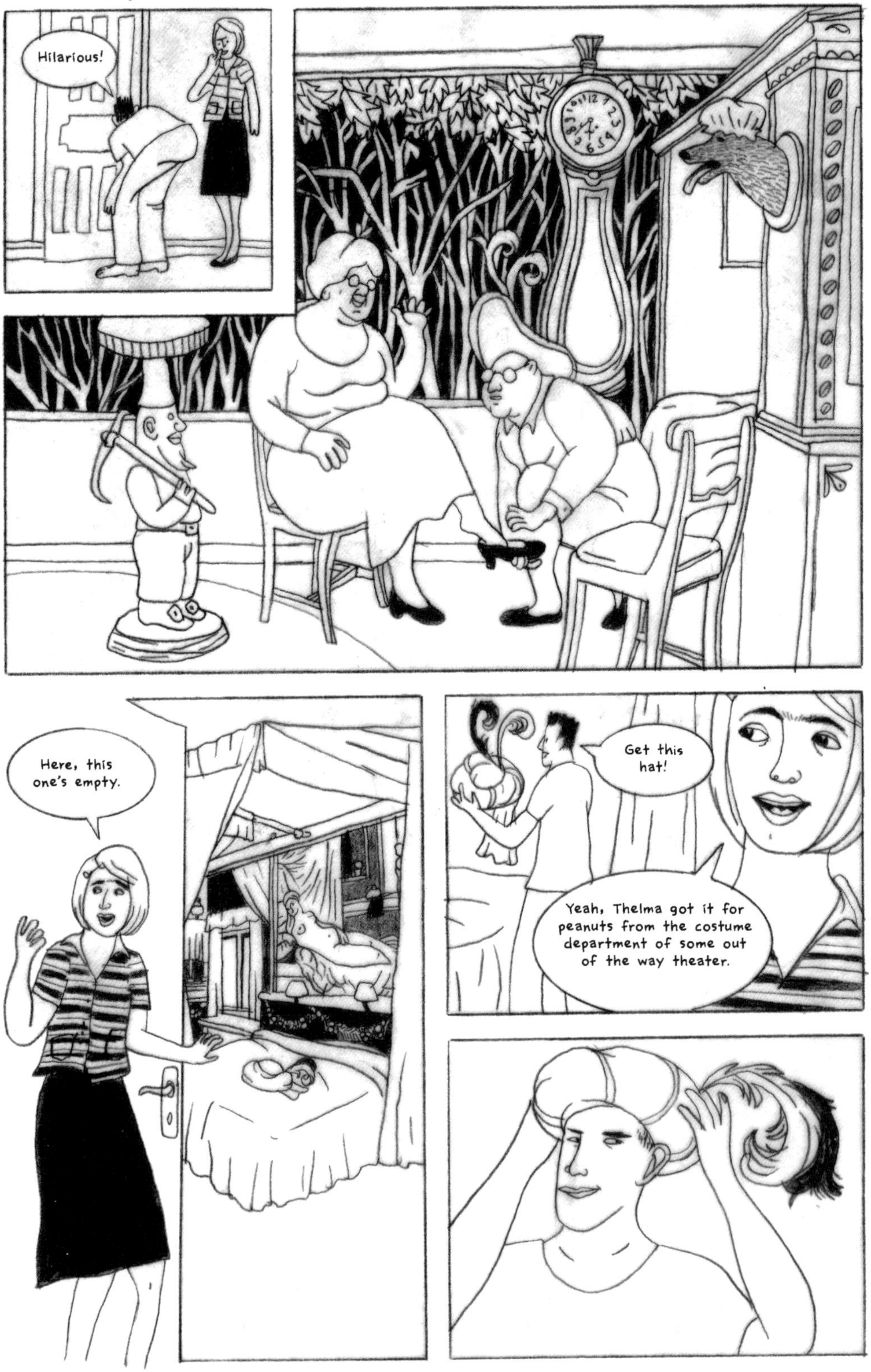
Hilarious!
Here, this one's empty.
Get this hat!
Yeah, Thelma got it for peanuts from the costume department of some out of the way theater.

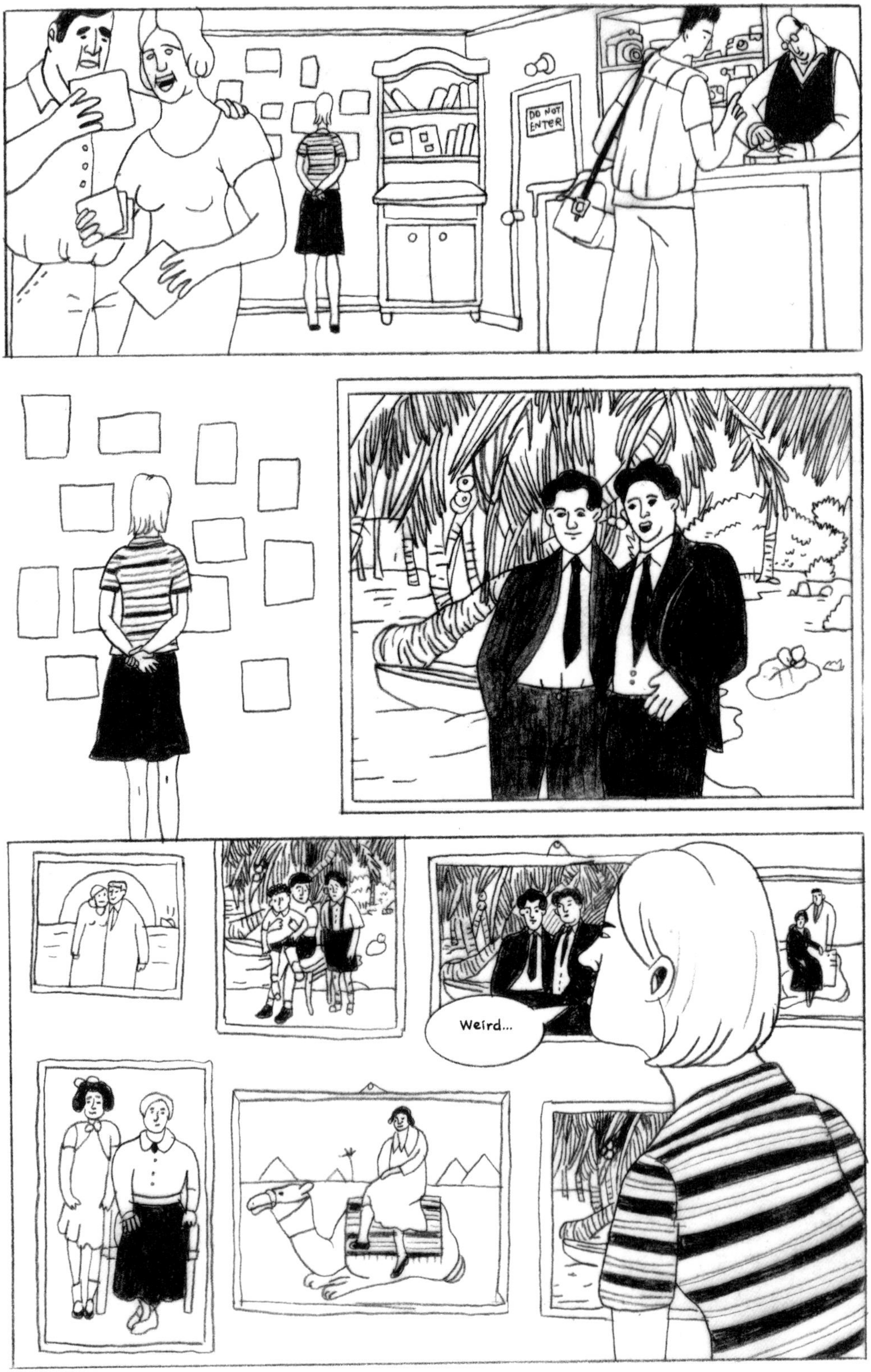
DO NOT ENTER
Weird...

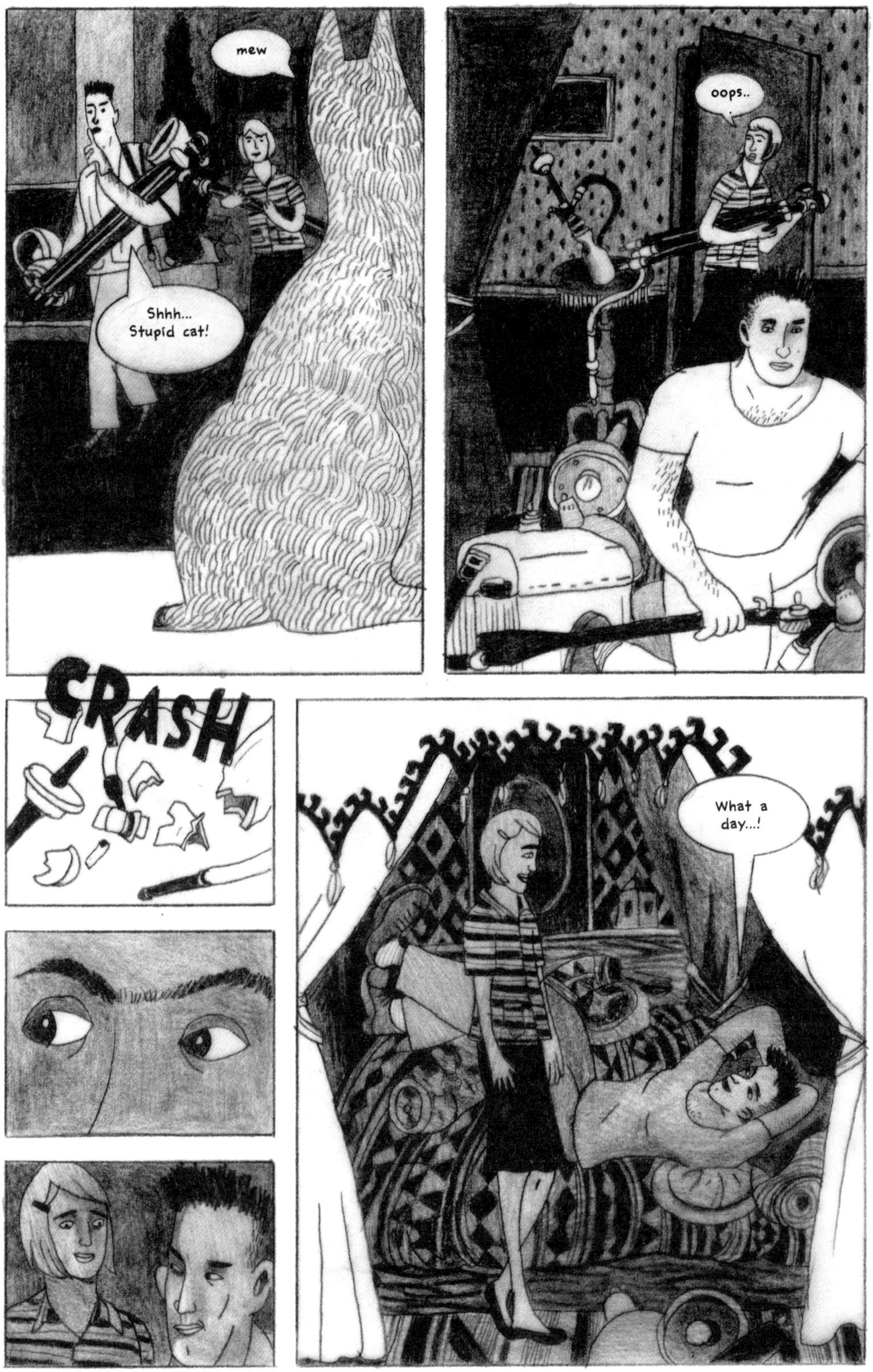
mew
Shhh... Stupid cat!
oops..
CRASH
What a day...!

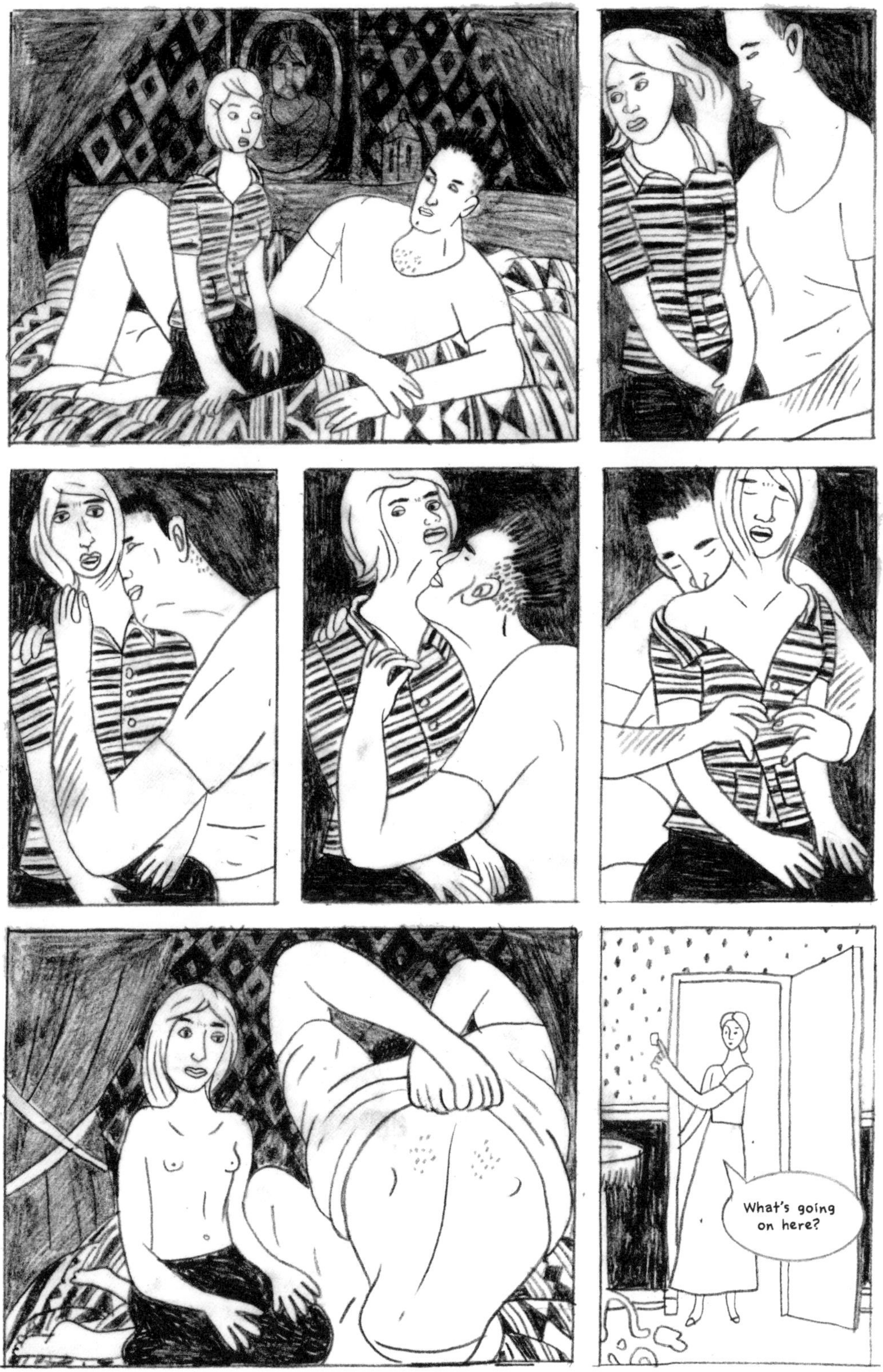
What's going on here?

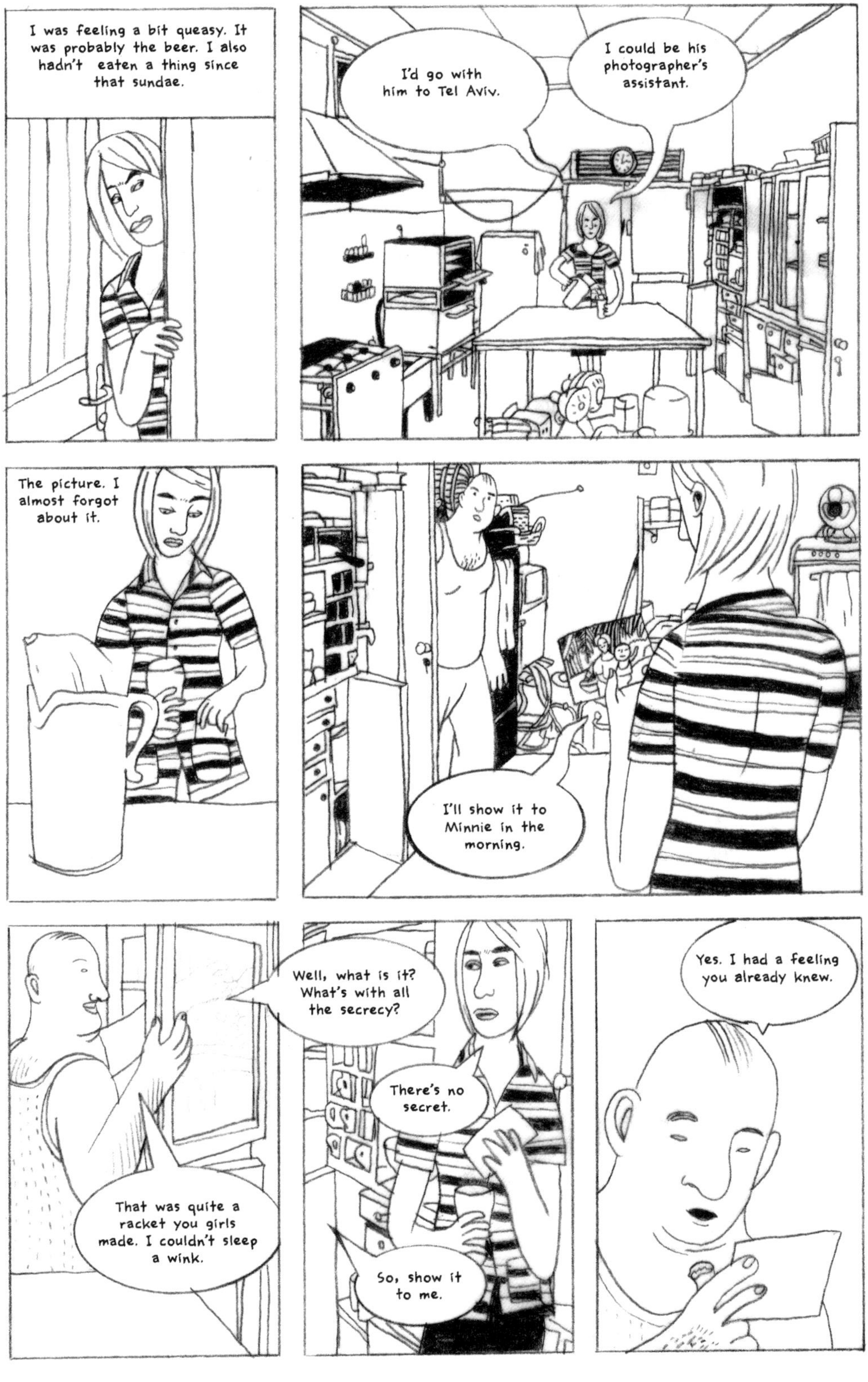
I was feeling a bit queasy. It was probably the beer. I also hadn't eaten a thing since that sundae.
I'd go with him to Tel Aviv.
I could be his photographer's assistant.
The picture. I almost forgot about it.
I'll show it to Minnie in the morning.
That was quite a racket you girls made. I couldn't sleep a wink.
Well, what is it? What's with all the secrecy?
There's no secret.
So, show it to me.
Yes. I had a feeling you already knew.

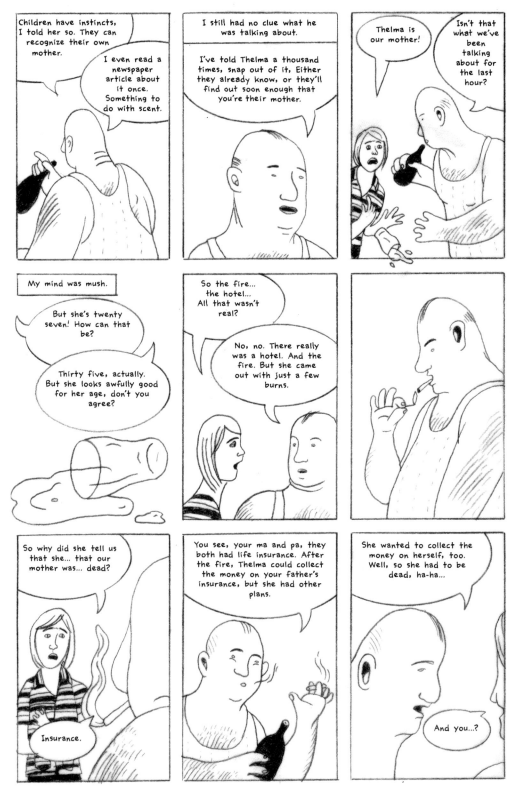

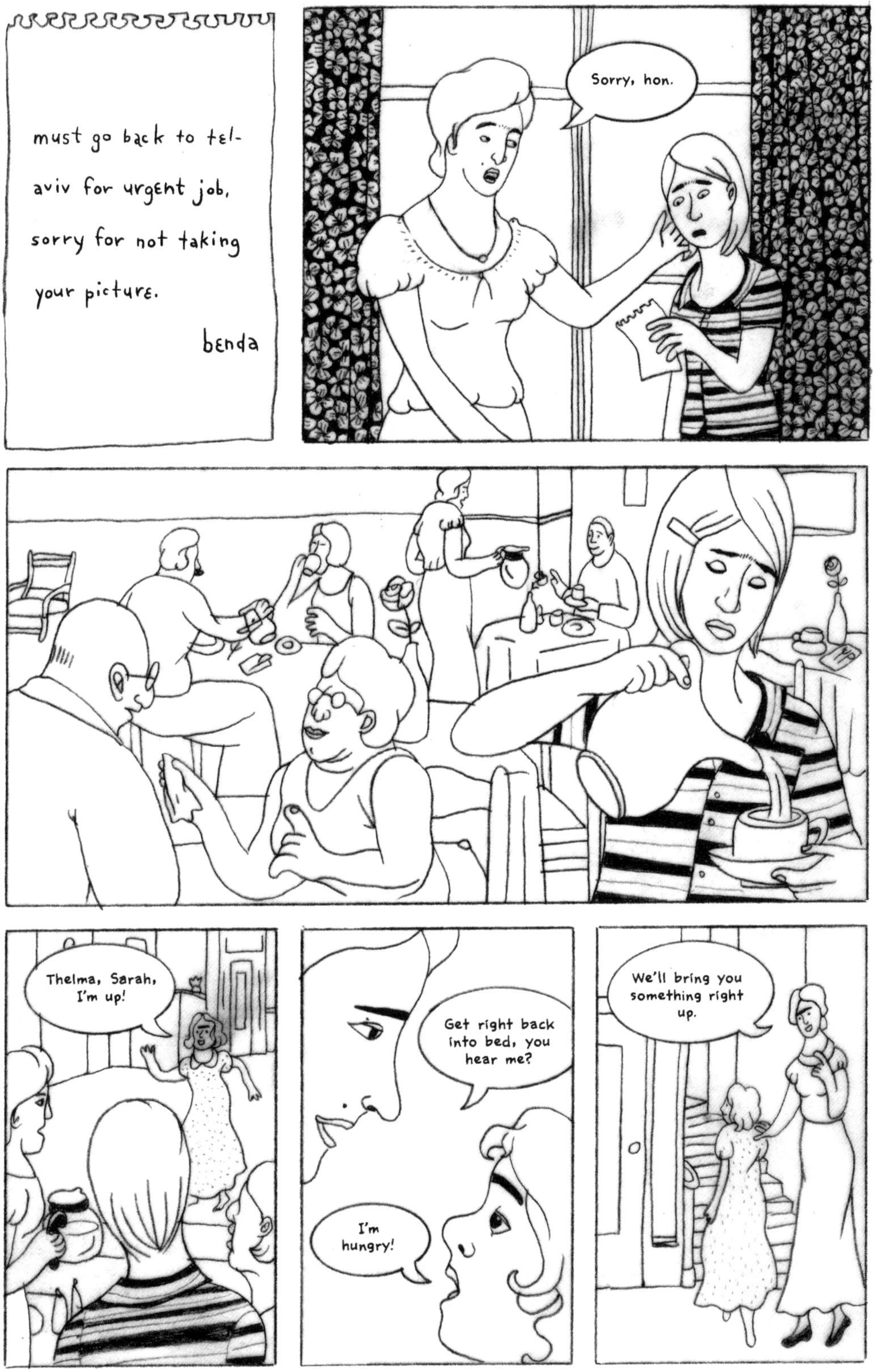
must go back to tel-aviv for urgent job, sorry for not taking your picture.
benda
Sorry, hon.
Thelma, Sarah, I'm up!
Get right back into bed, you hear me?
I'm hungry!
We'll bring you something right up.

THE PANTY KILLER

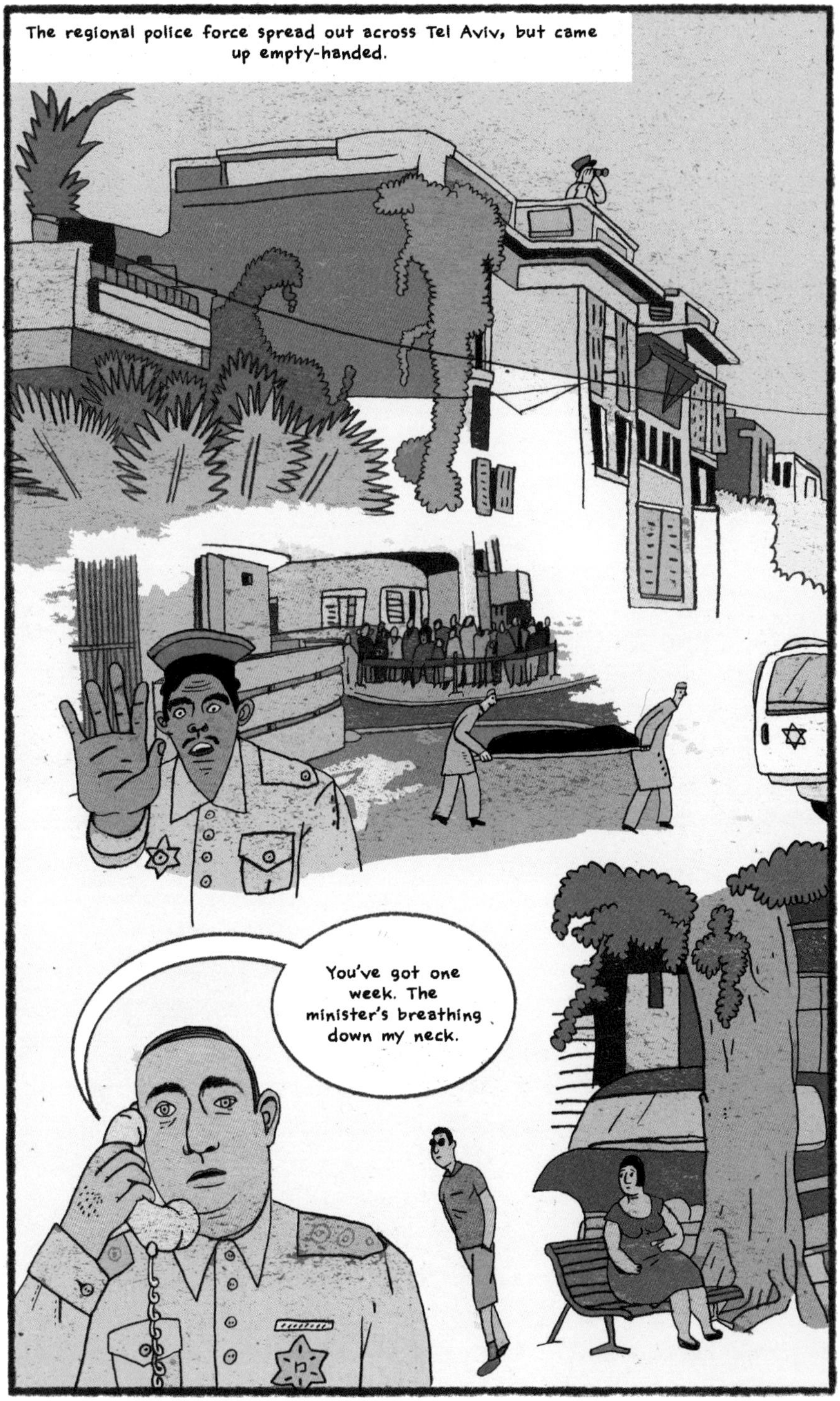
The regional police force spread out across Tel Aviv, but came up empty-handed.
You've got one week. The minister's breathing down my neck.

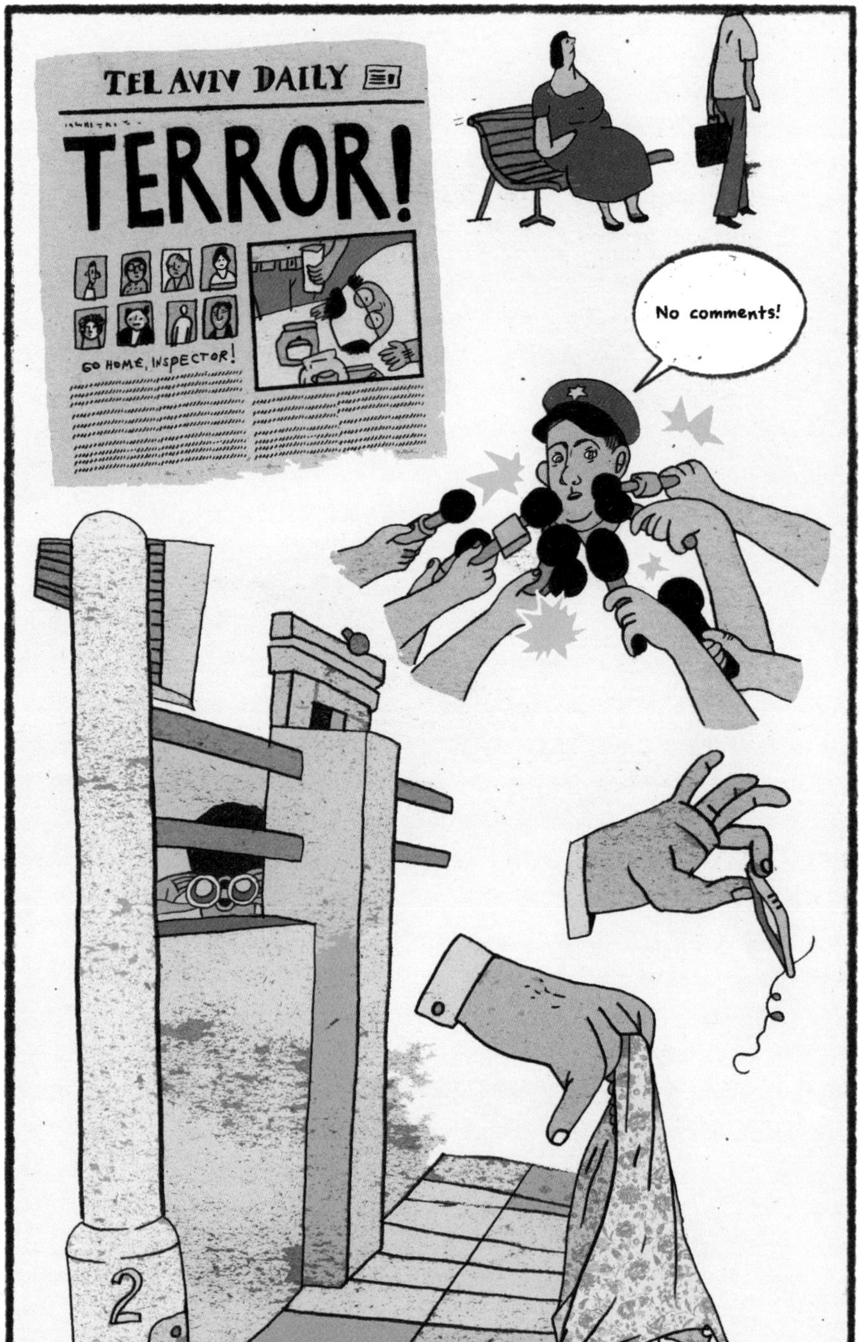
TEL AVIV DAILY
TERROR!
GO HOME, INSPECTOR!
No comments!
2

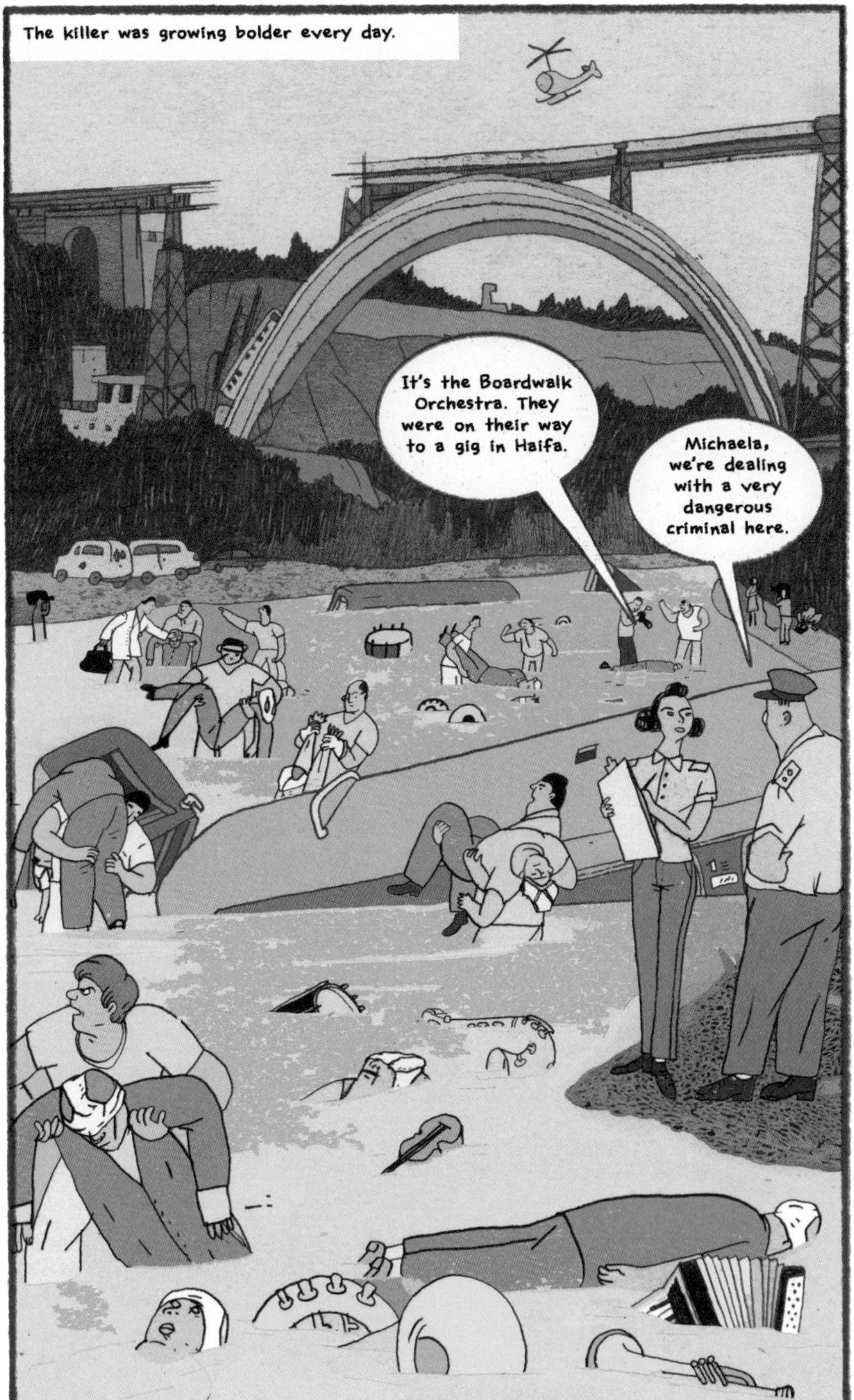
The killer was growing bolder every day.
It's the Boardwalk Orchestra. They were on their way to a gig in Haifa.
Michaela, we're dealing with a very dangerous criminal here.

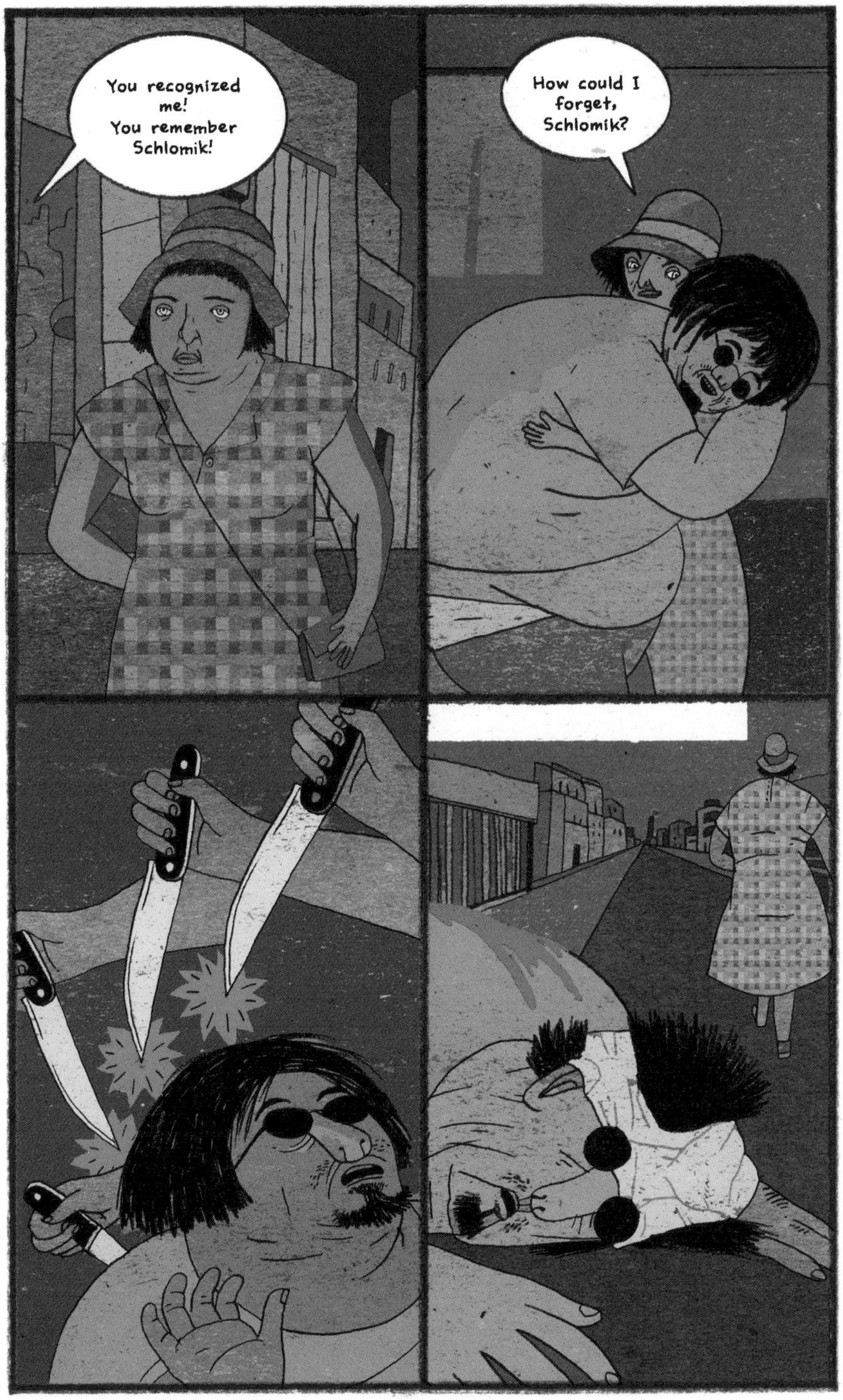
You recognized me! You remember Schlomik!
How could I forget, Schlomik?

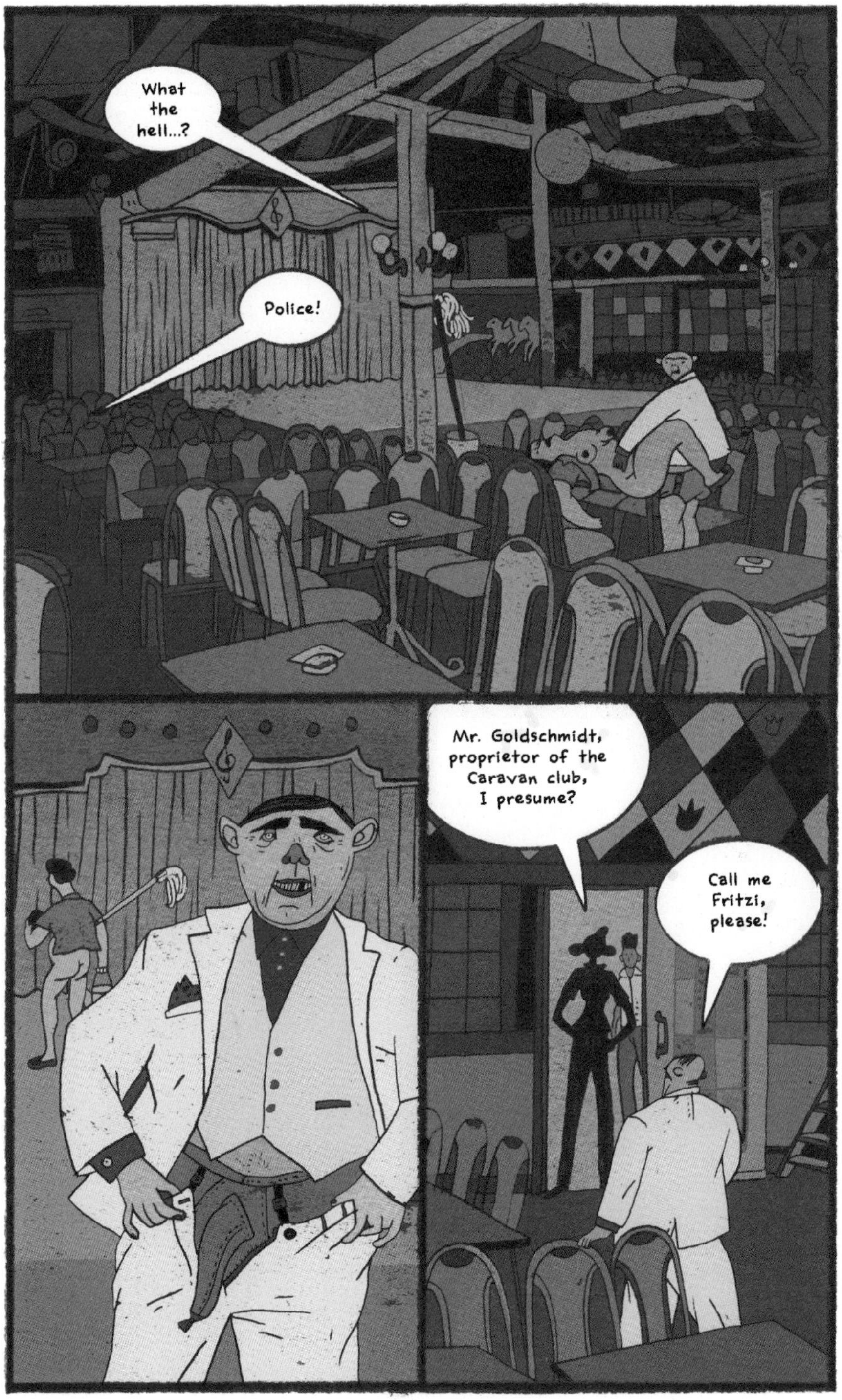
What the hell...?
Police!
Mr. Goldschmidt, proprietor of the Caravan club, I presume?
Call me Fritzi, please!

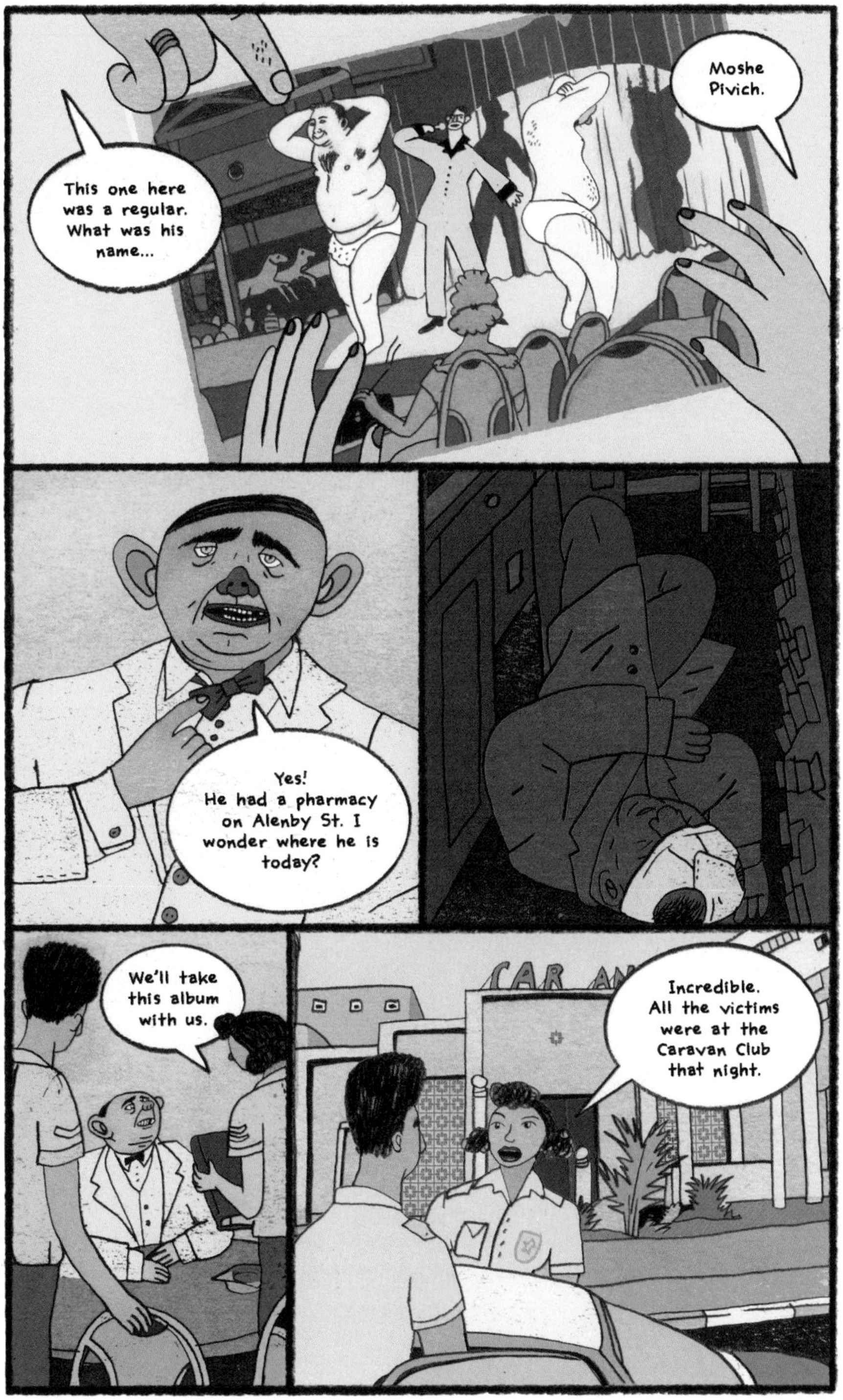
This one here was a regular. What was his name...
Moshe Pivich.
Yes! He had a pharmacy on Alenby St. I wonder where he is today?
We'll take this album with us.
CAR
Incredible. All the victims were at the Caravan Club that night.

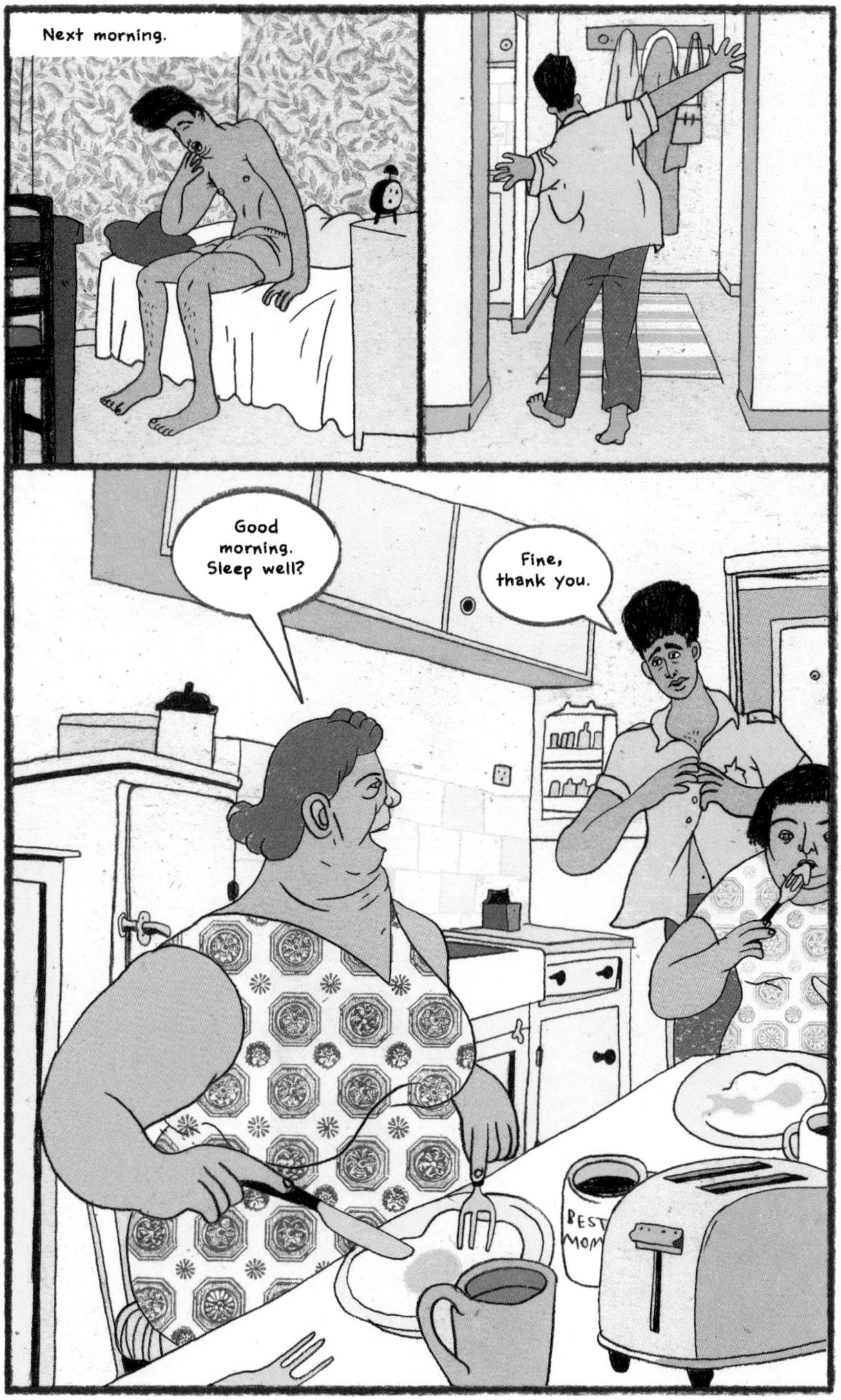
Next morning.
Good morning. Sleep well?
Fine, thank you.
BEST MOM

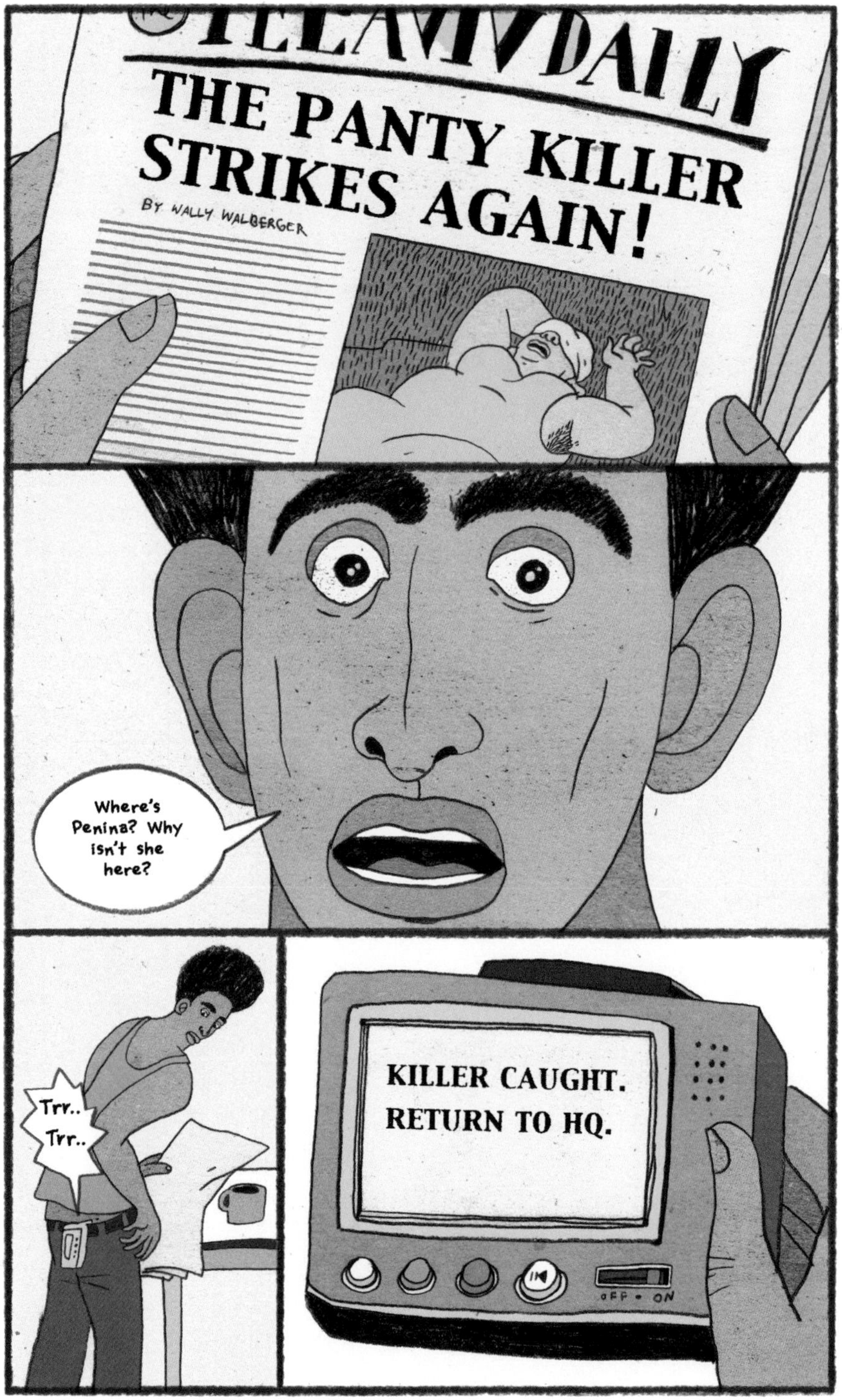
TEL AVIV DAILY
THE PANTY KILLER STRIKES AGAIN!
BY WALLY WALBERGER
Where's Penina? Why isn't she here?
Trr.. Trr..
KILLER CAUGHT. RETURN TO HQ.
OFF • ON

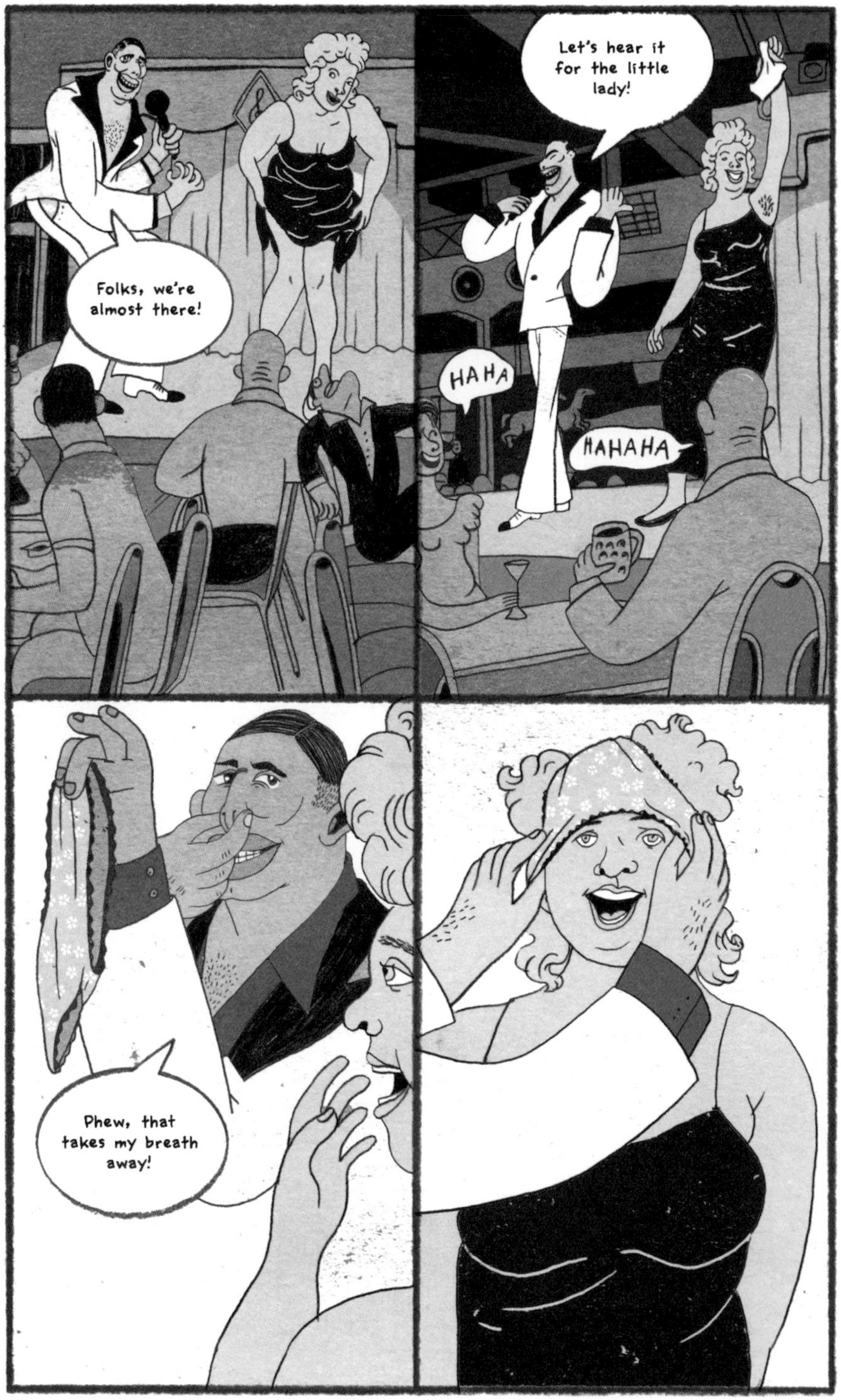
Folks, we're almost there!
Let's hear it for the little lady!
HAHA
HAHAHA
Phew, that takes my breath away!

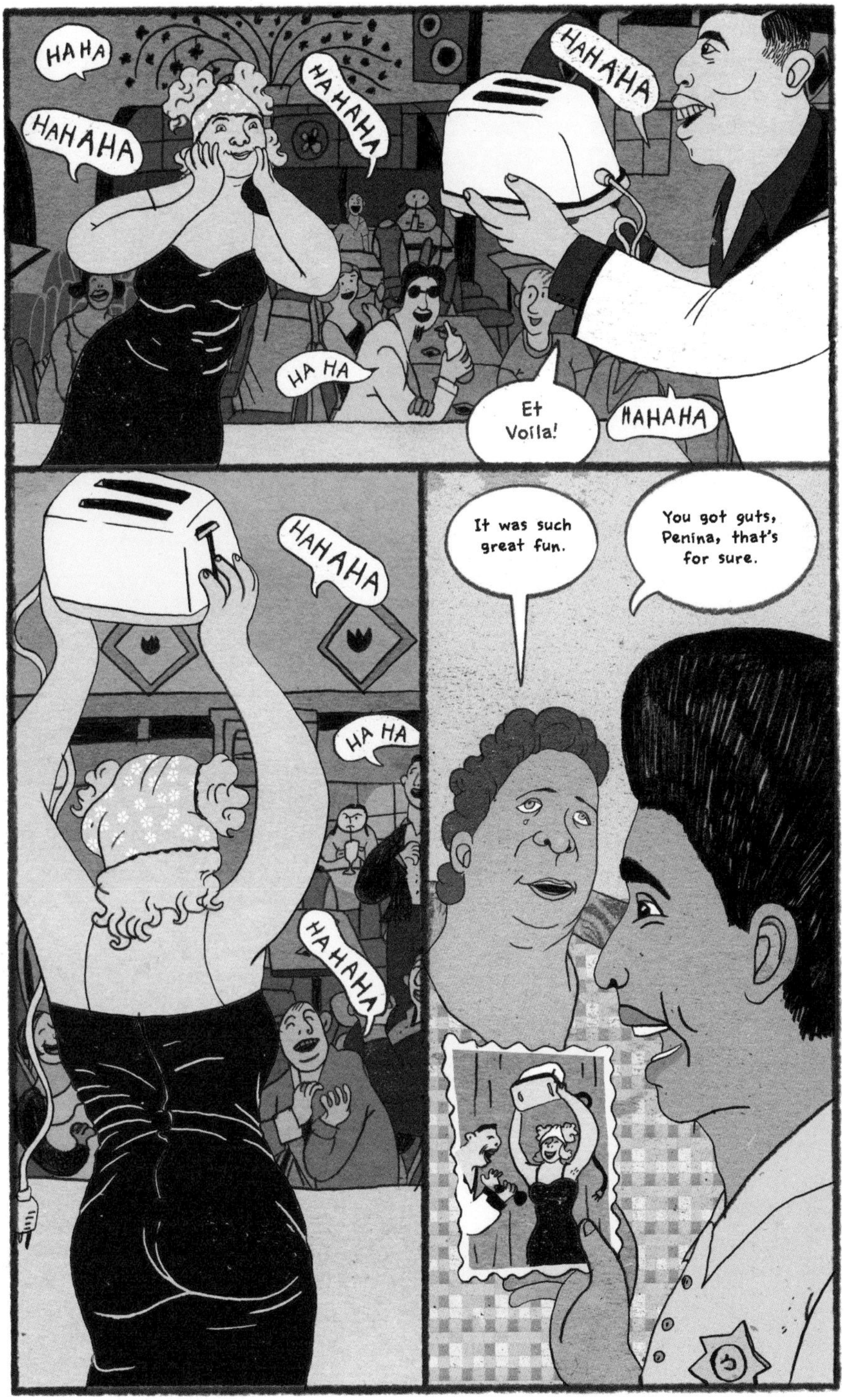
HAHA
HAHAHA
HAHAHA
HAHAHA
HA HA
Et Voila!
HAHAHA
HAHAHA
HA HA
HAHAHA
It was such great fun.
You got guts, Penina, that's for sure.

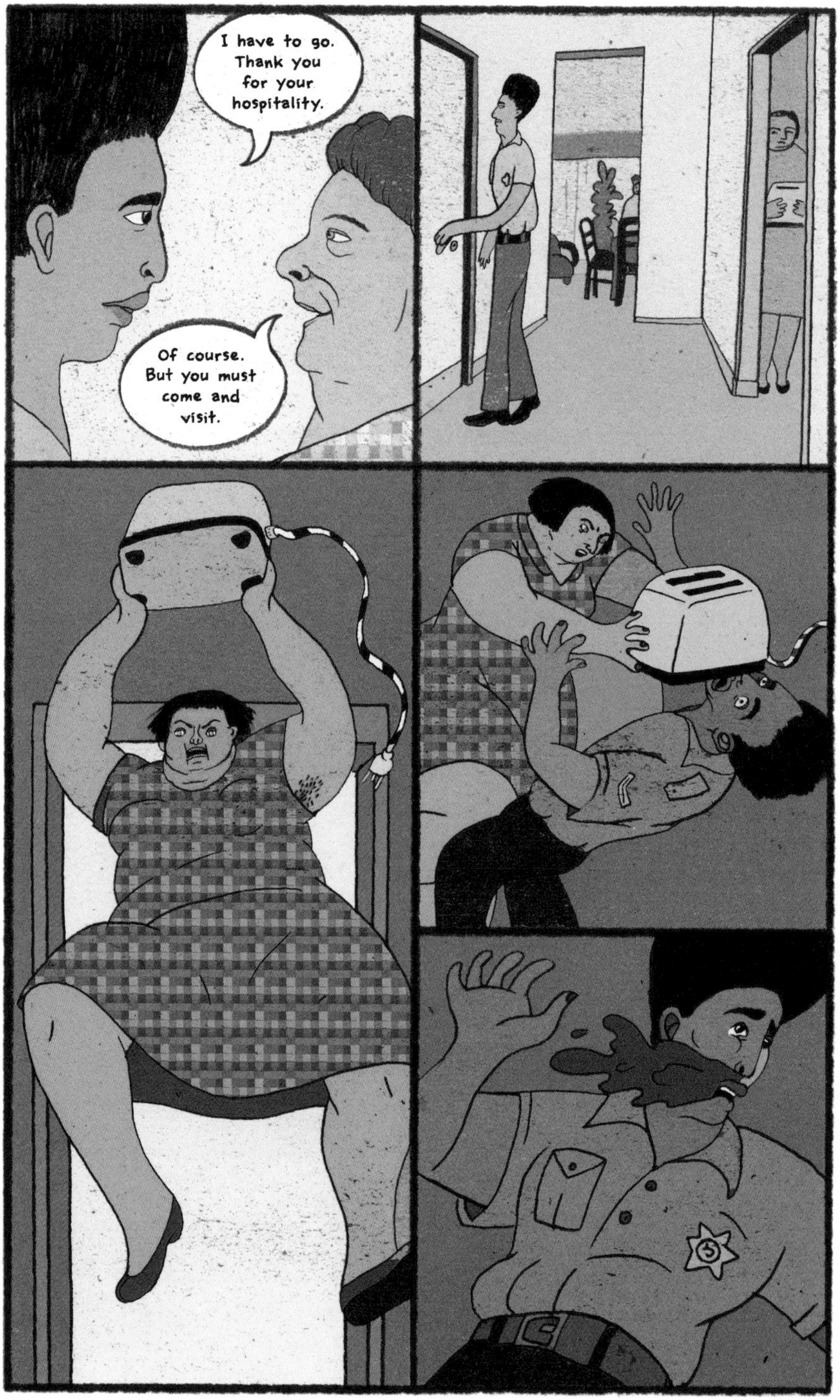
I have to go. Thank you for your hospitality.
Of course. But you must come and visit.

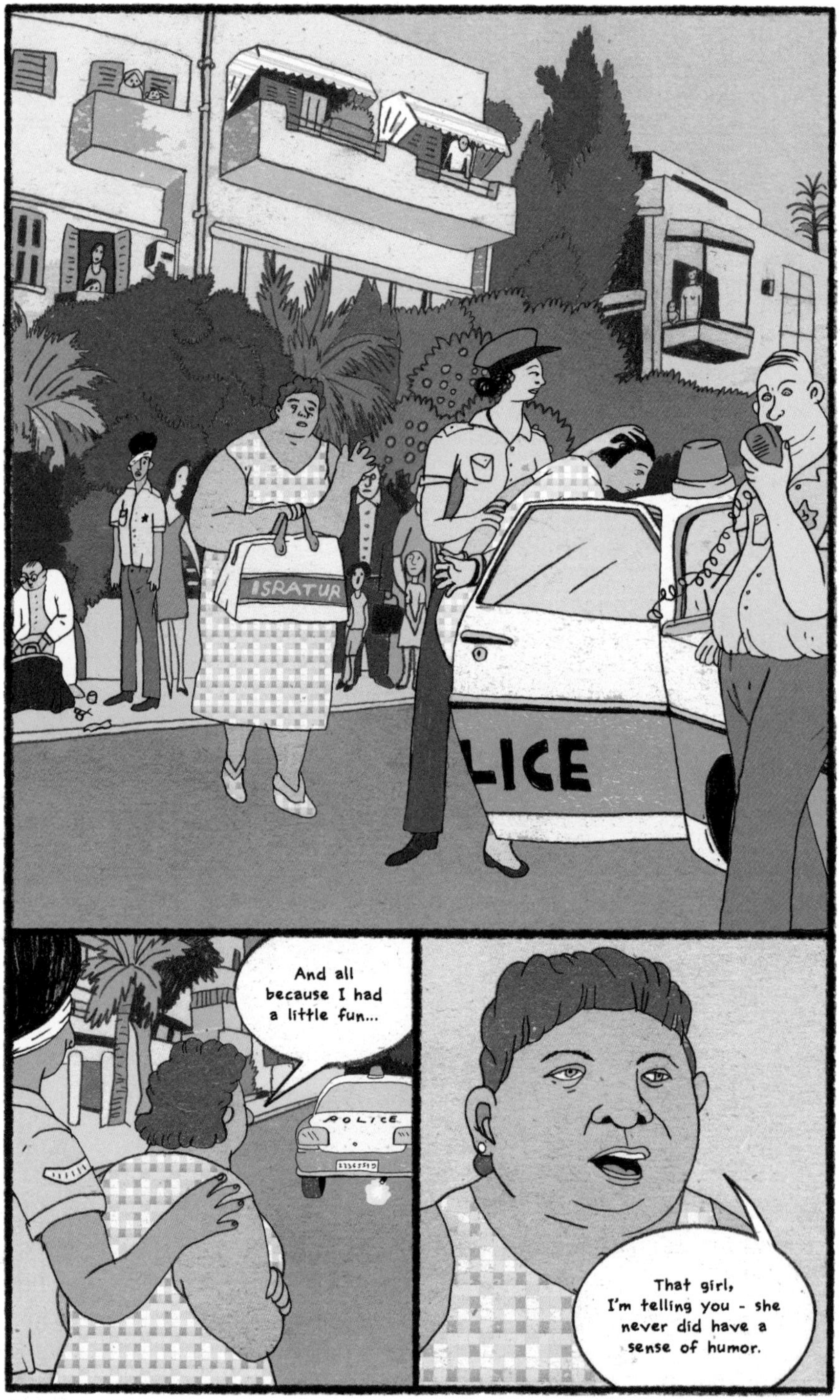
ISRATUR
LICE
POLICE
And all because I had a little fun...
That girl, I'm telling you - she never did have a sense of humor.

HOMECOMING

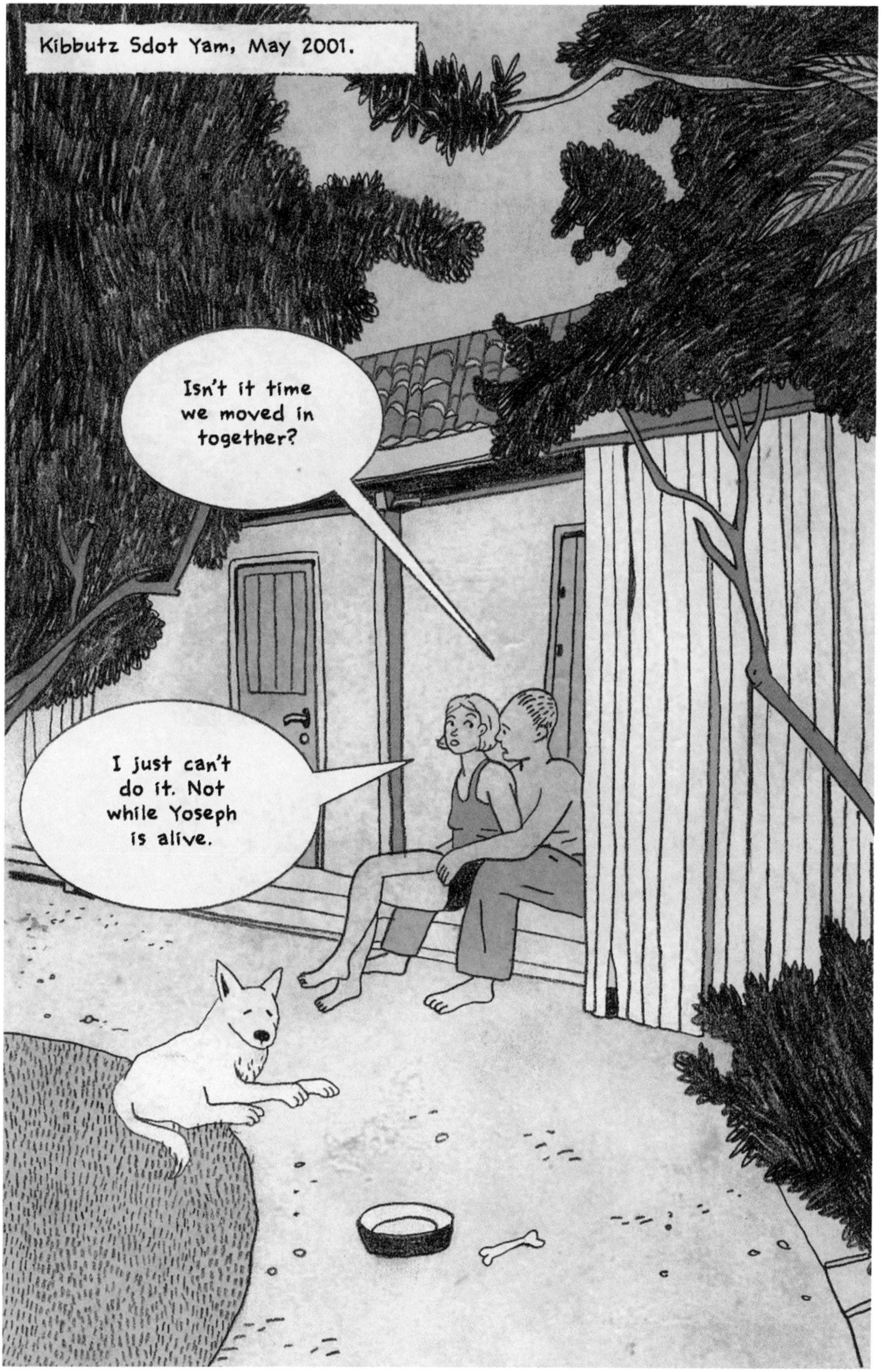
Kibbutz Sdot Yam, May 2001.
Isn't it time we moved in together?
I just can't do it. Not while Yoseph is alive.

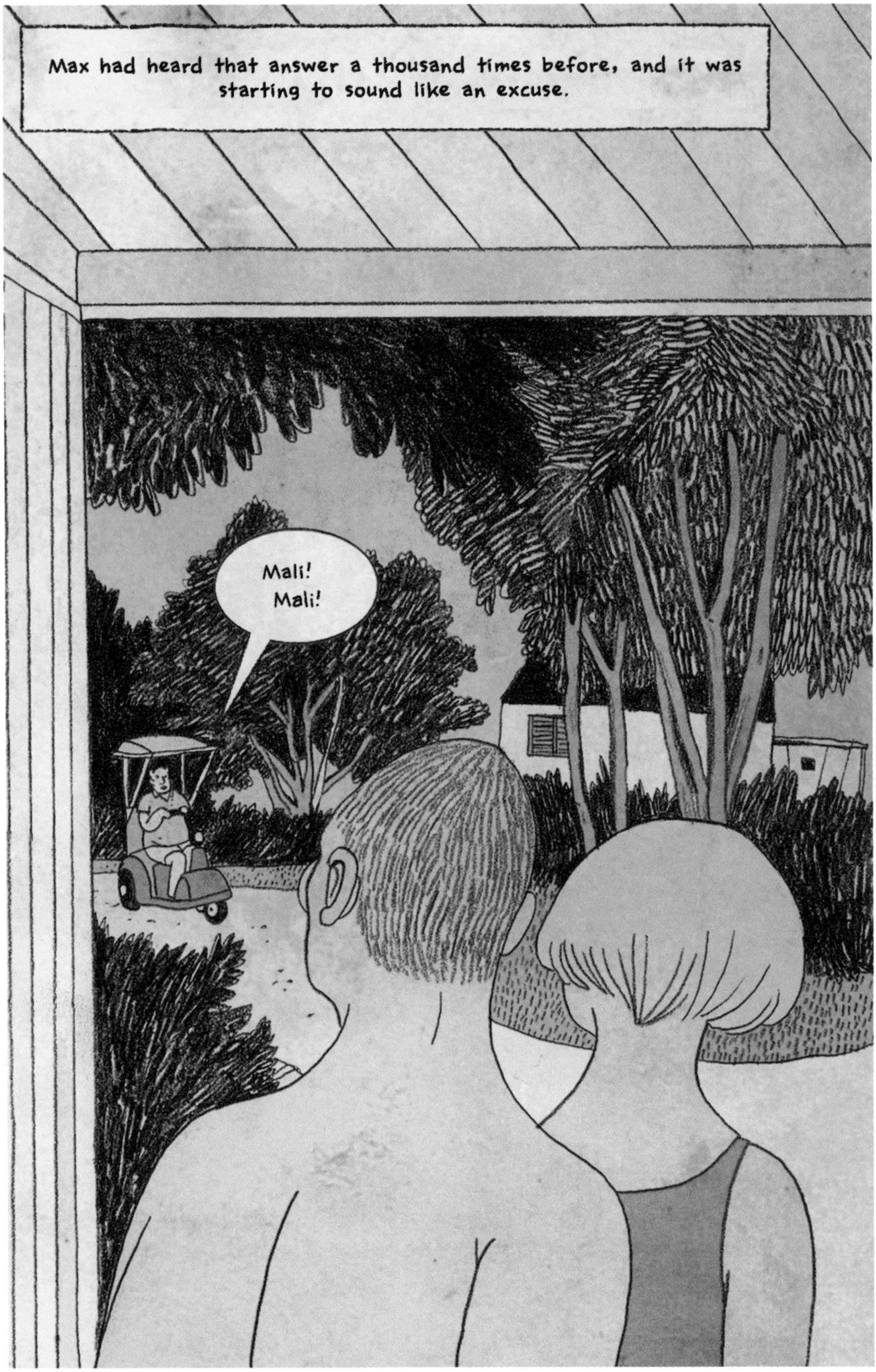
Max had heard that answer a thousand times before, and it was starting to sound like an excuse.
Mali! Mali!

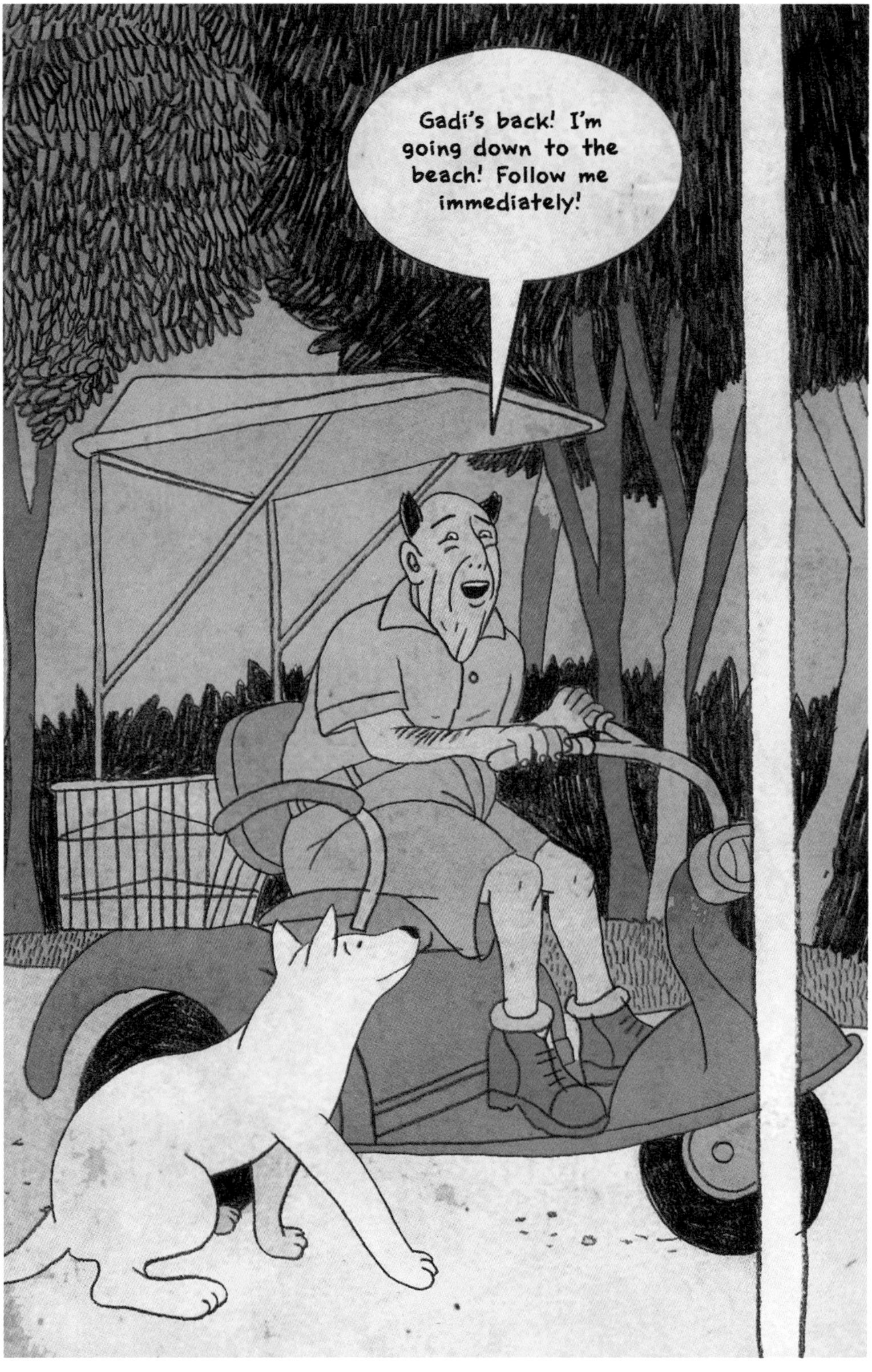
Gadi's back! I'm going down to the beach! Follow me immediately!

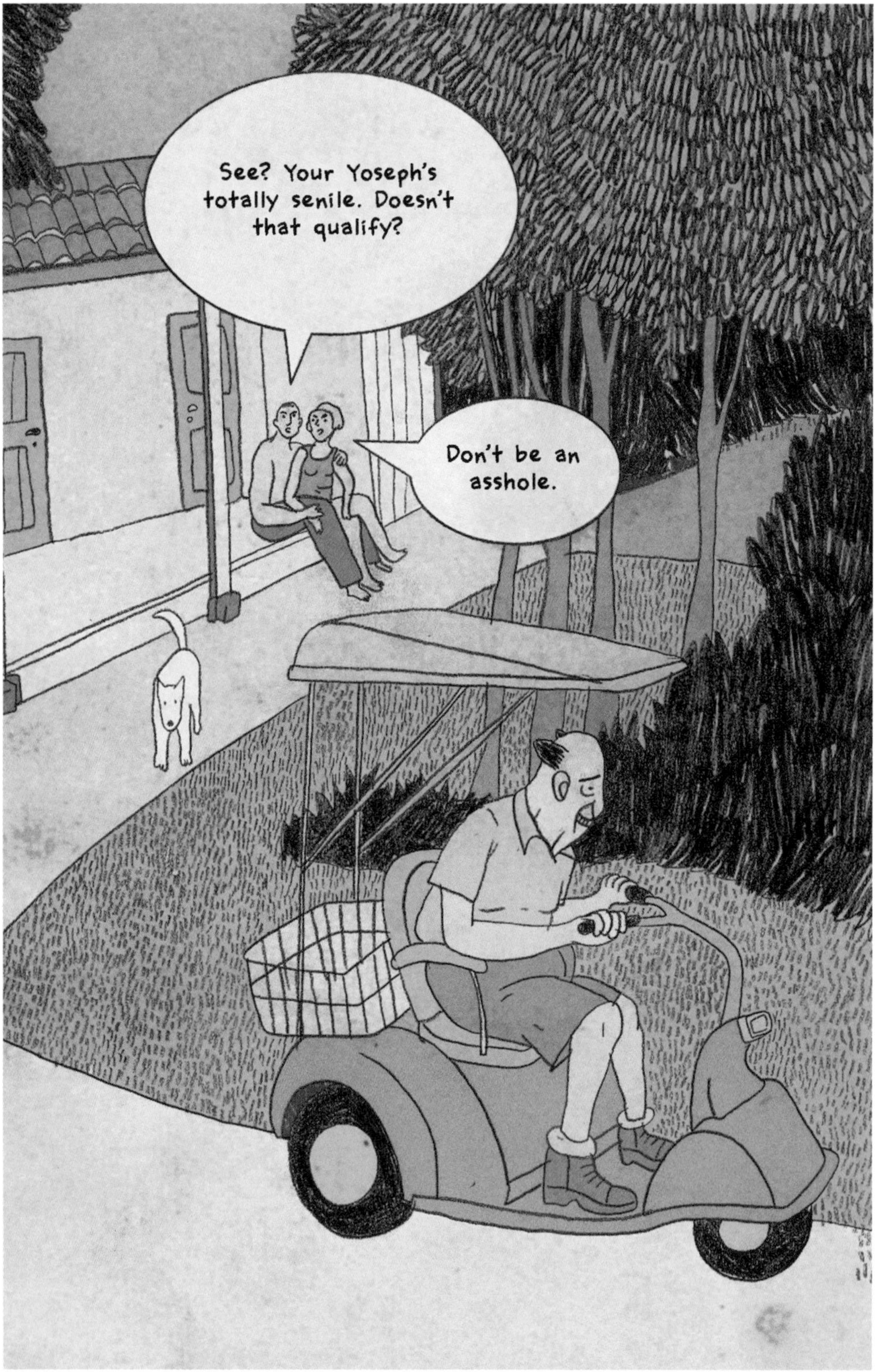
See? Your Yoseph's totally senile. Doesn't that qualify?
Don't be an asshole.

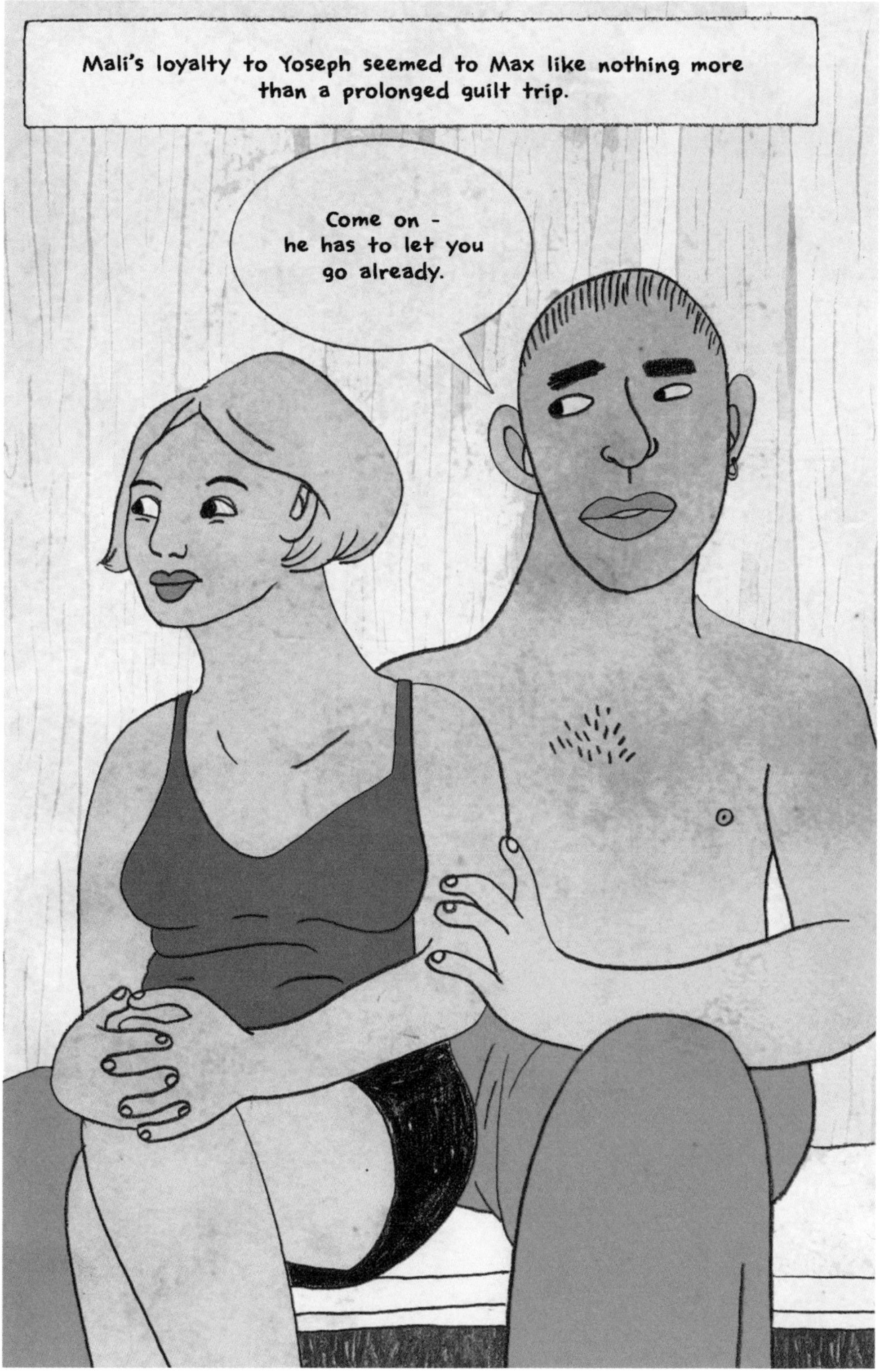
Mali's loyalty to Yoseph seemed to Max like nothing more than a prolonged guilt trip.
Come on - he has to let you go already.

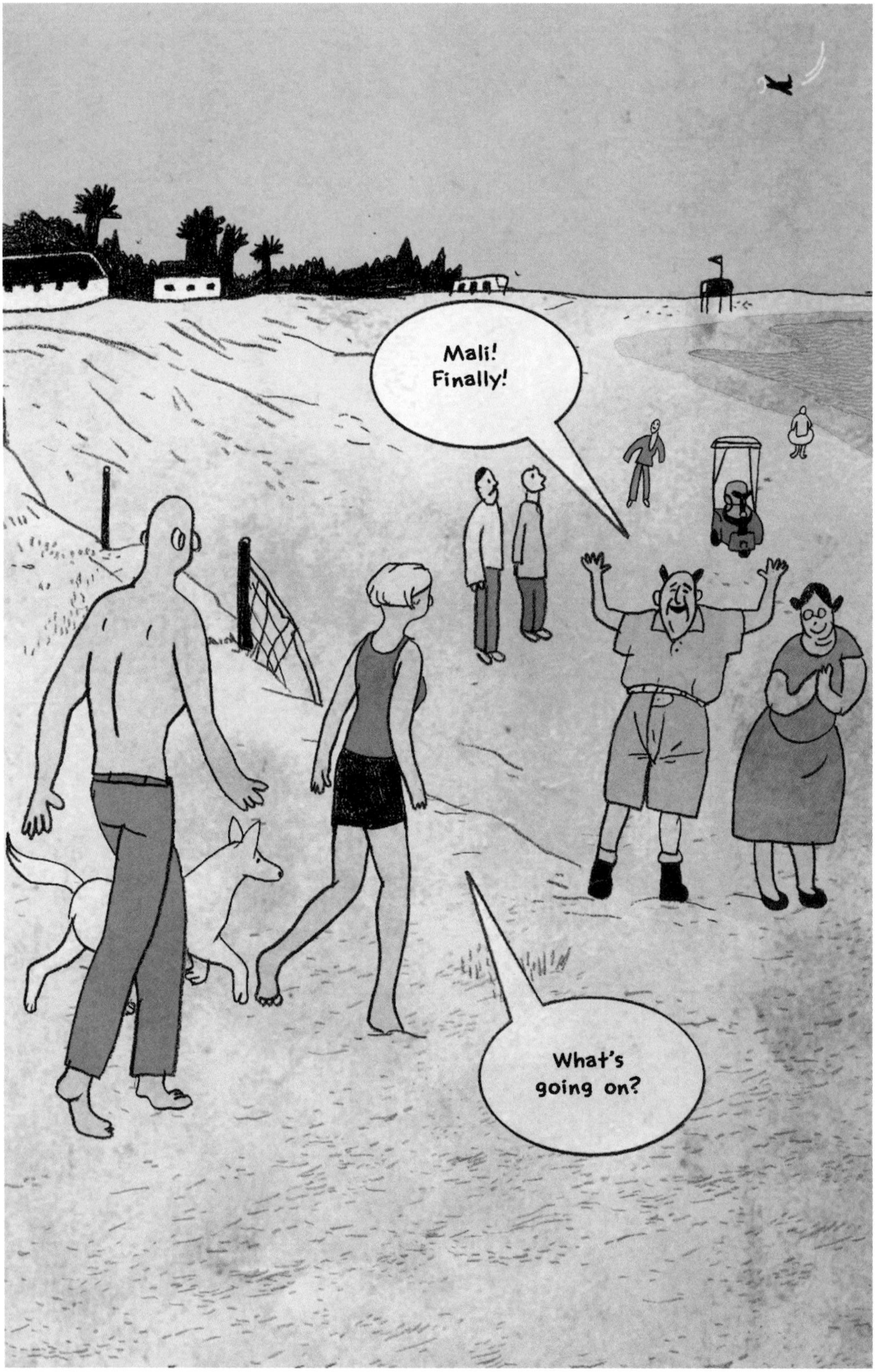
Mali! Finally!
What's going on?

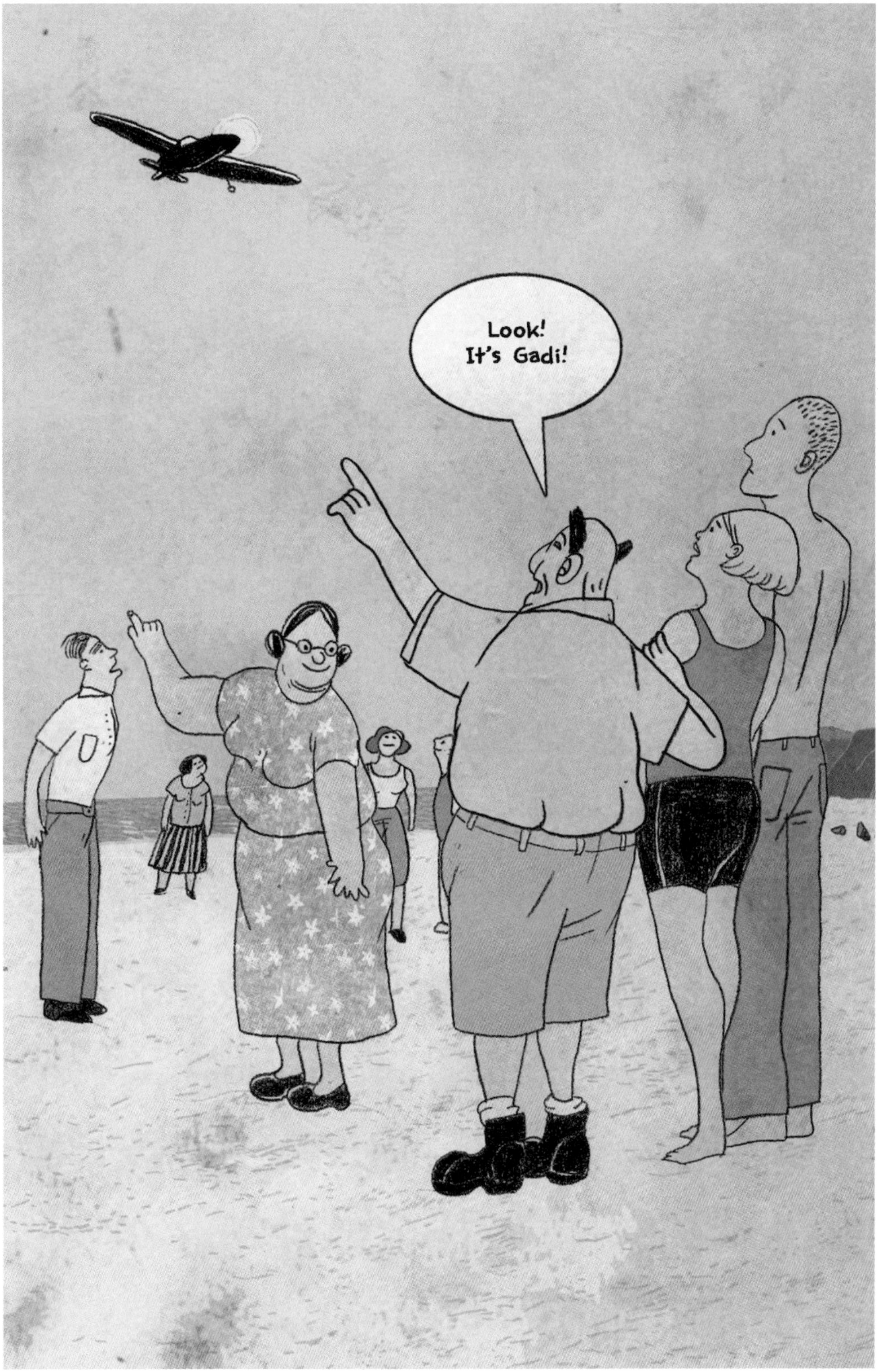
Look!
It's Gadi!

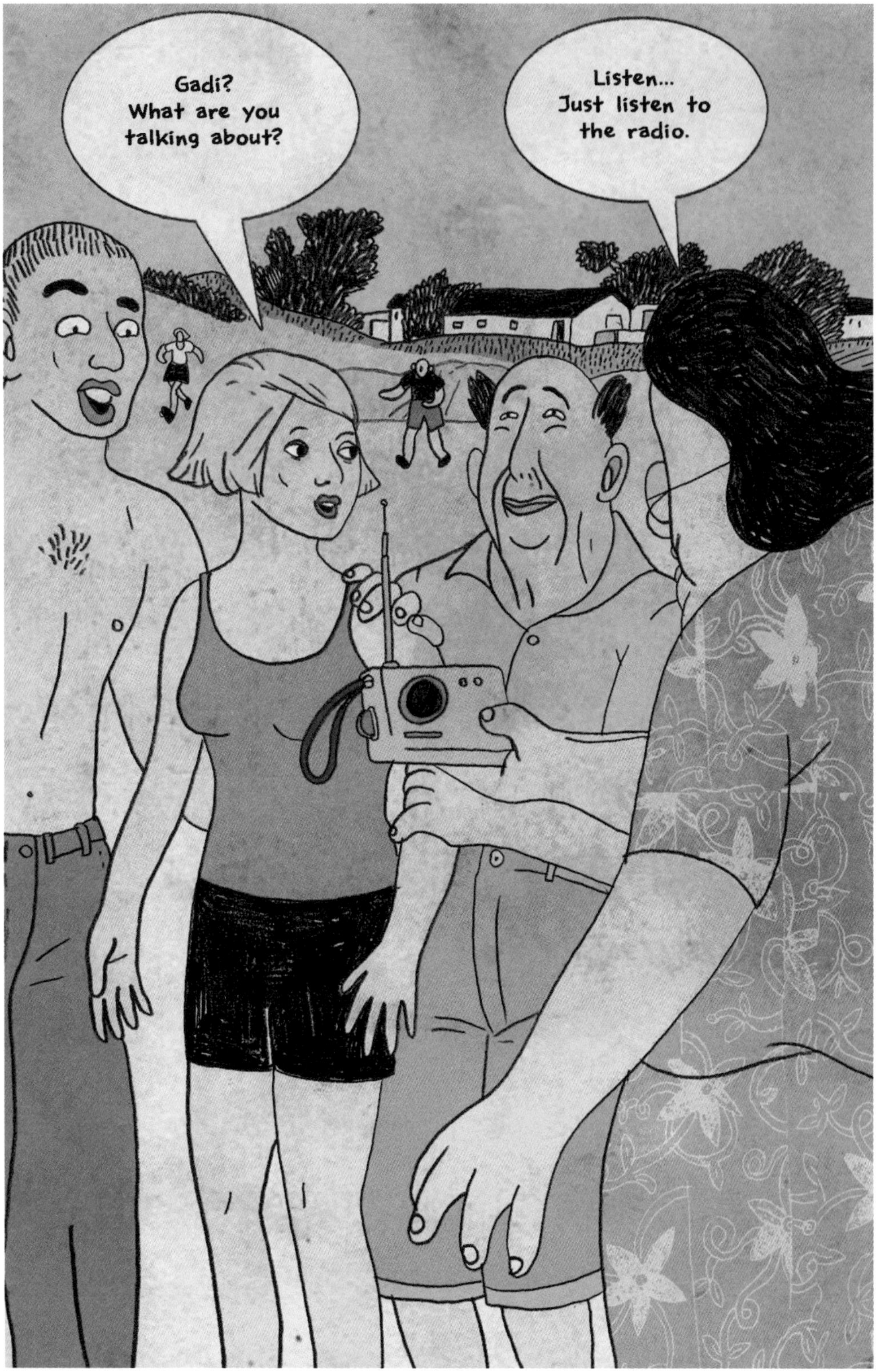
Gadi? What are you talking about?
Listen... Just listen to the radio.

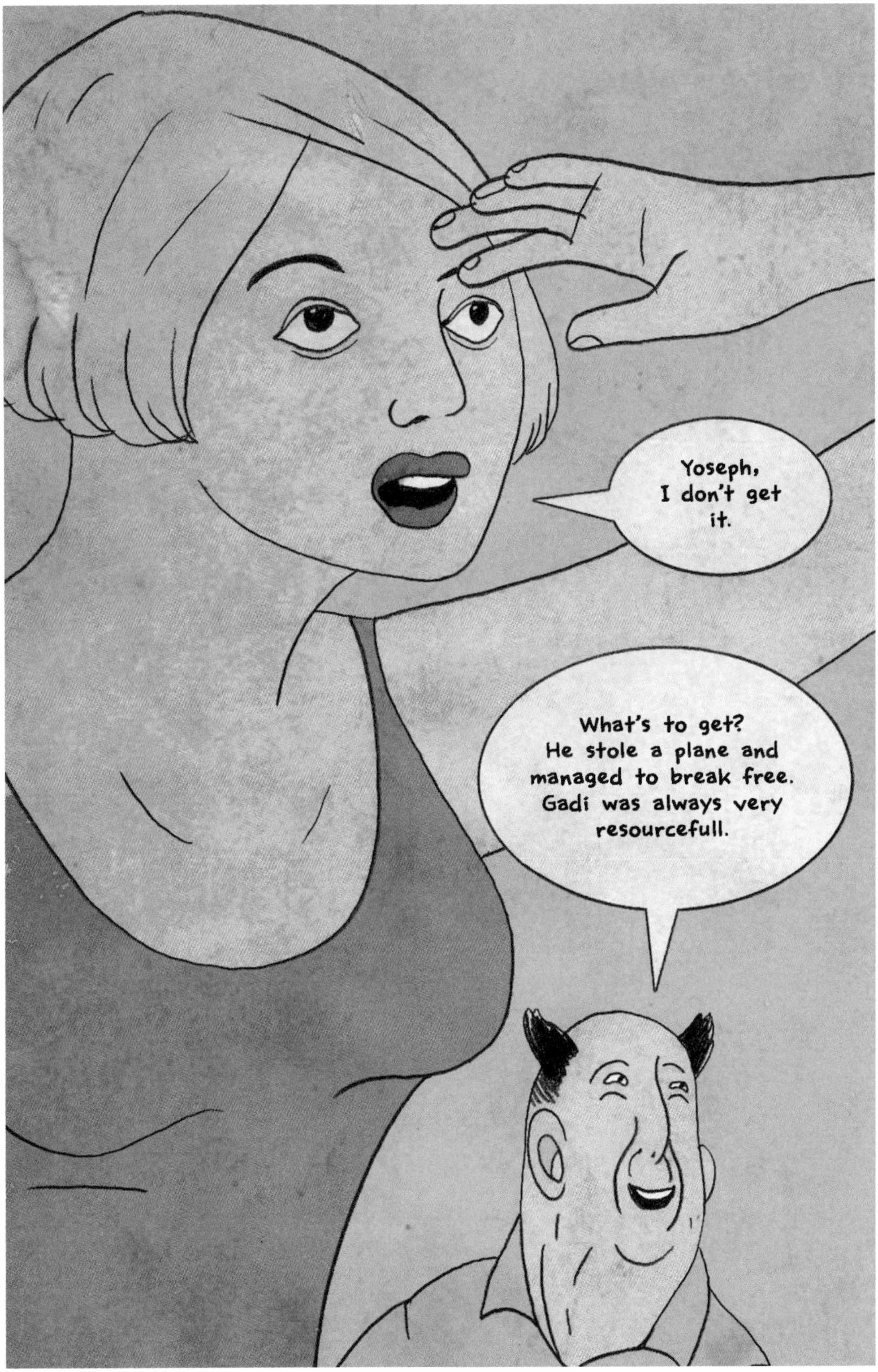
Yoseph, I don't get it.
What's to get? He stole a plane and managed to break free. Gadi was always very resourcefull.

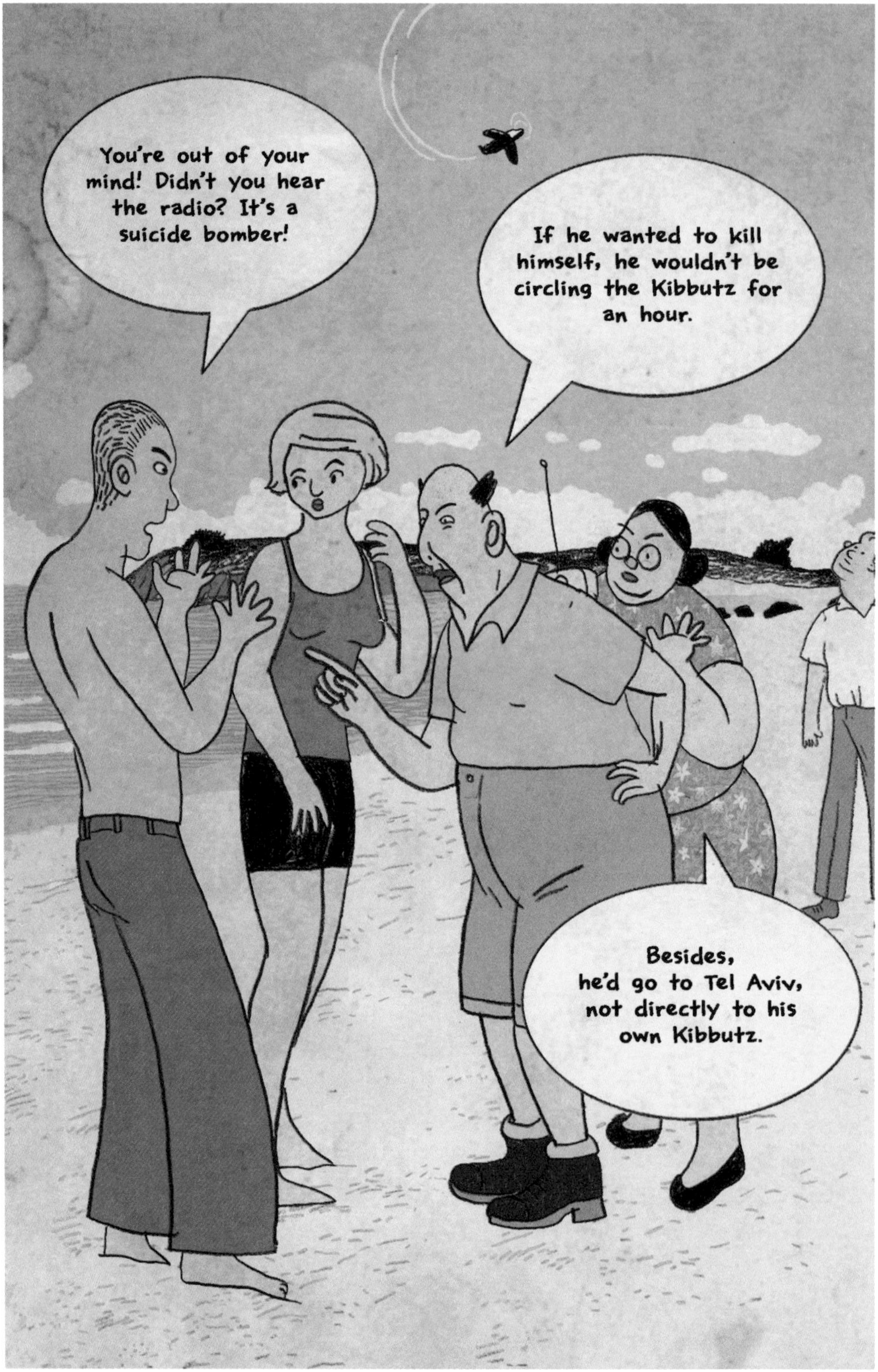
You're out of your mind! Didn't you hear the radio? It's a suicide bomber!
If he wanted to kill himself, he wouldn't be circling the Kibbutz for an hour.
Besides, he'd go to Tel Aviv, not directly to his own Kibbutz.

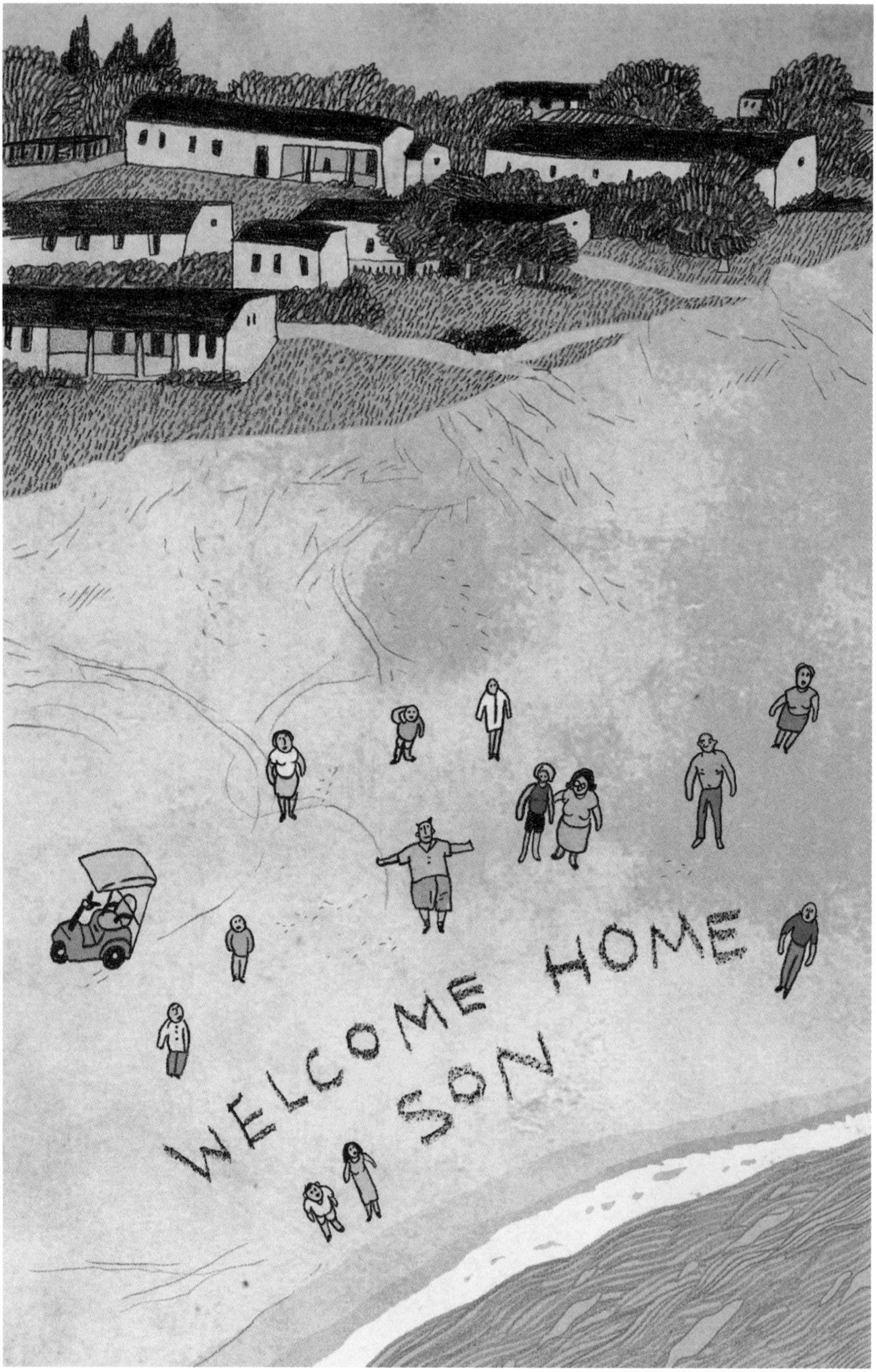
WELCOME HOME
SON

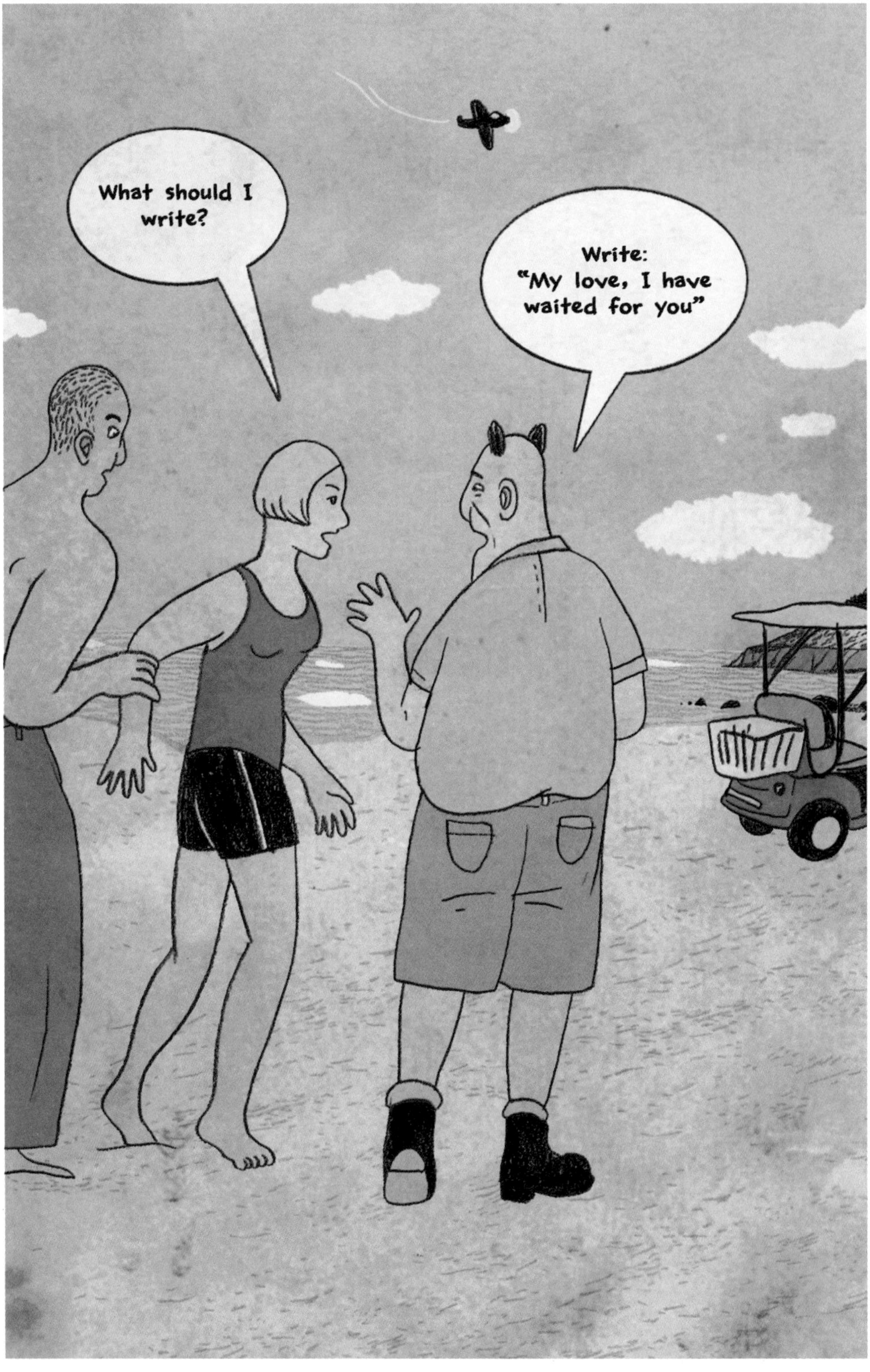
What should I write?
Write: "My love, I have waited for you"

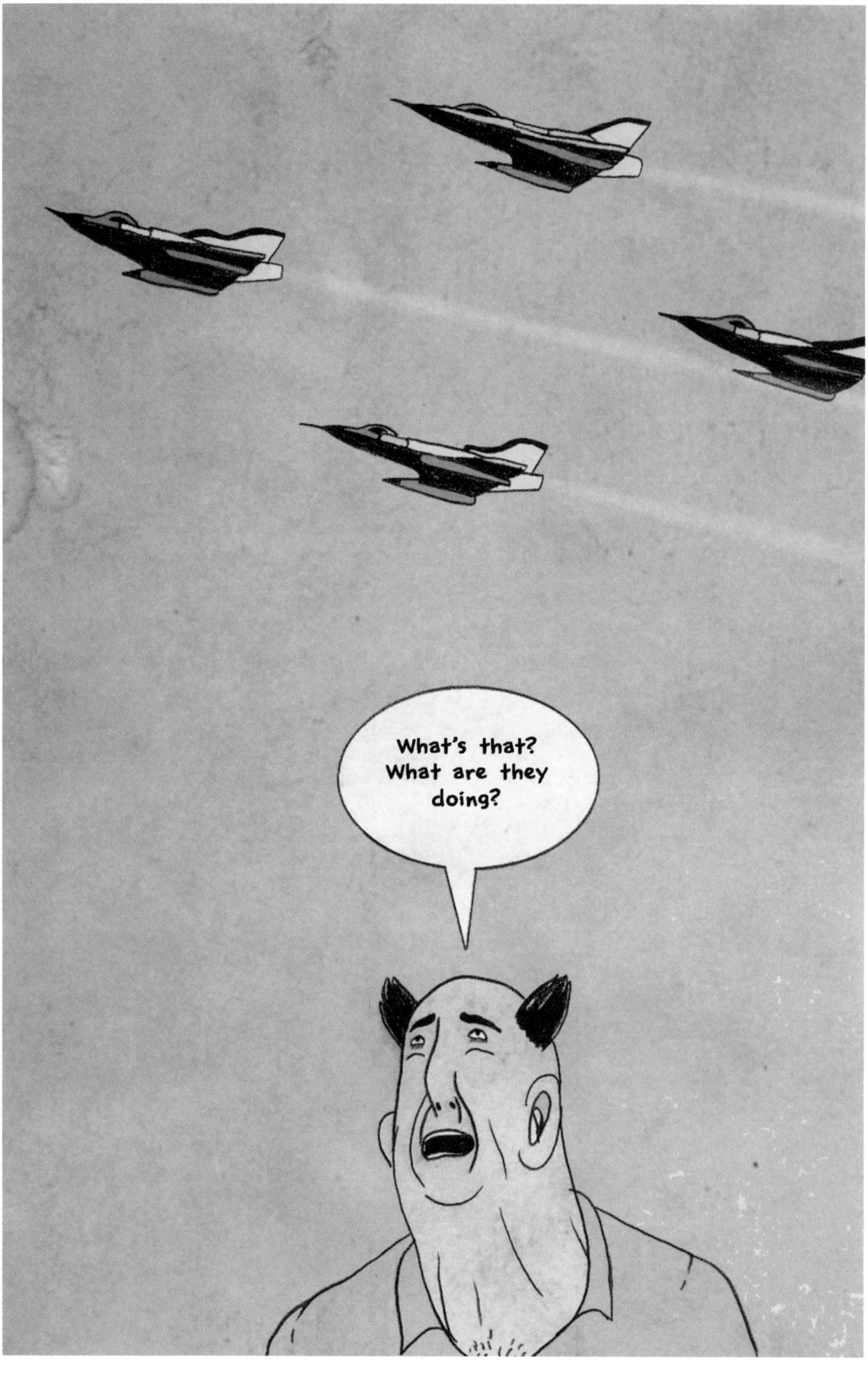
What's that? What are they doing?

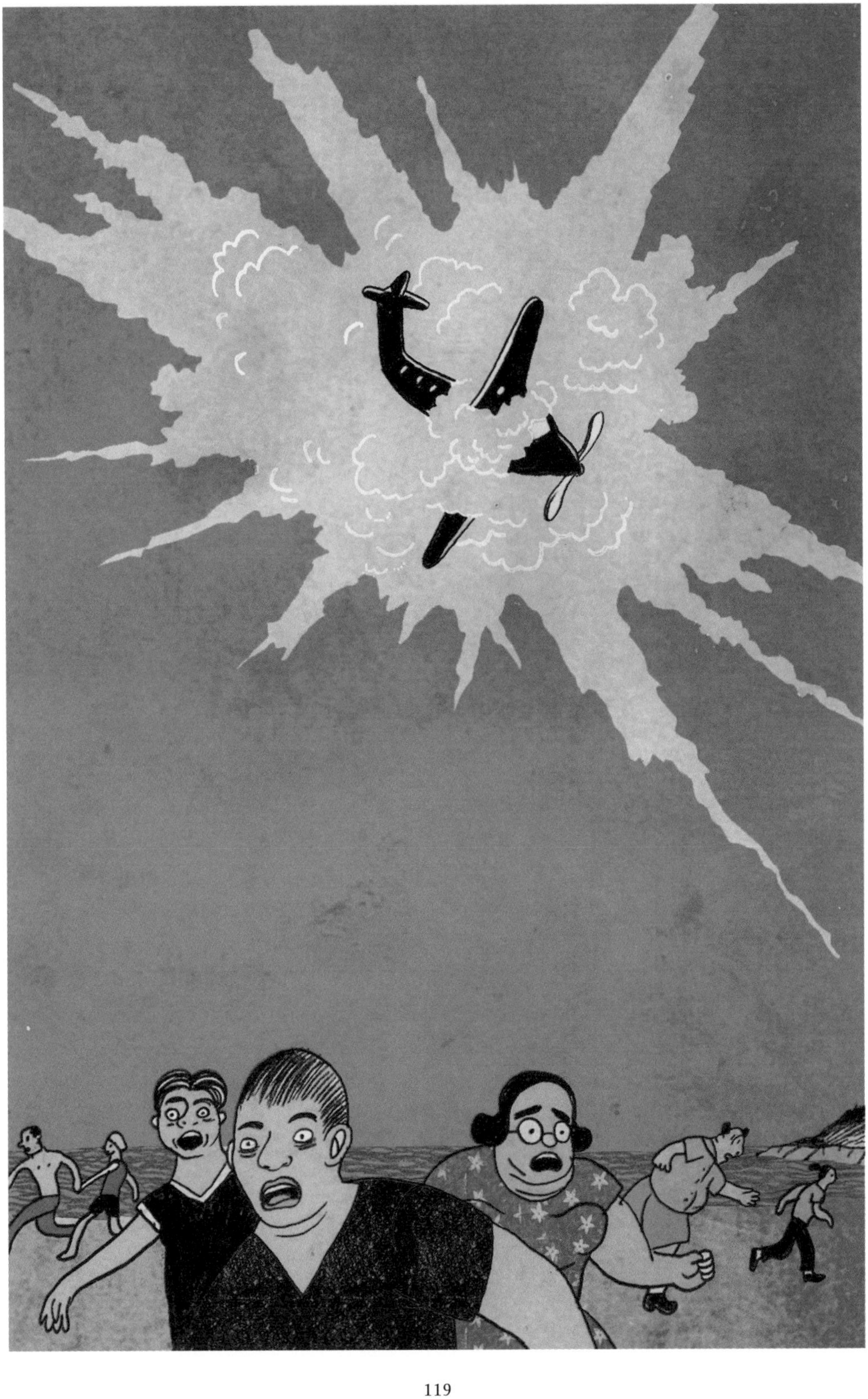

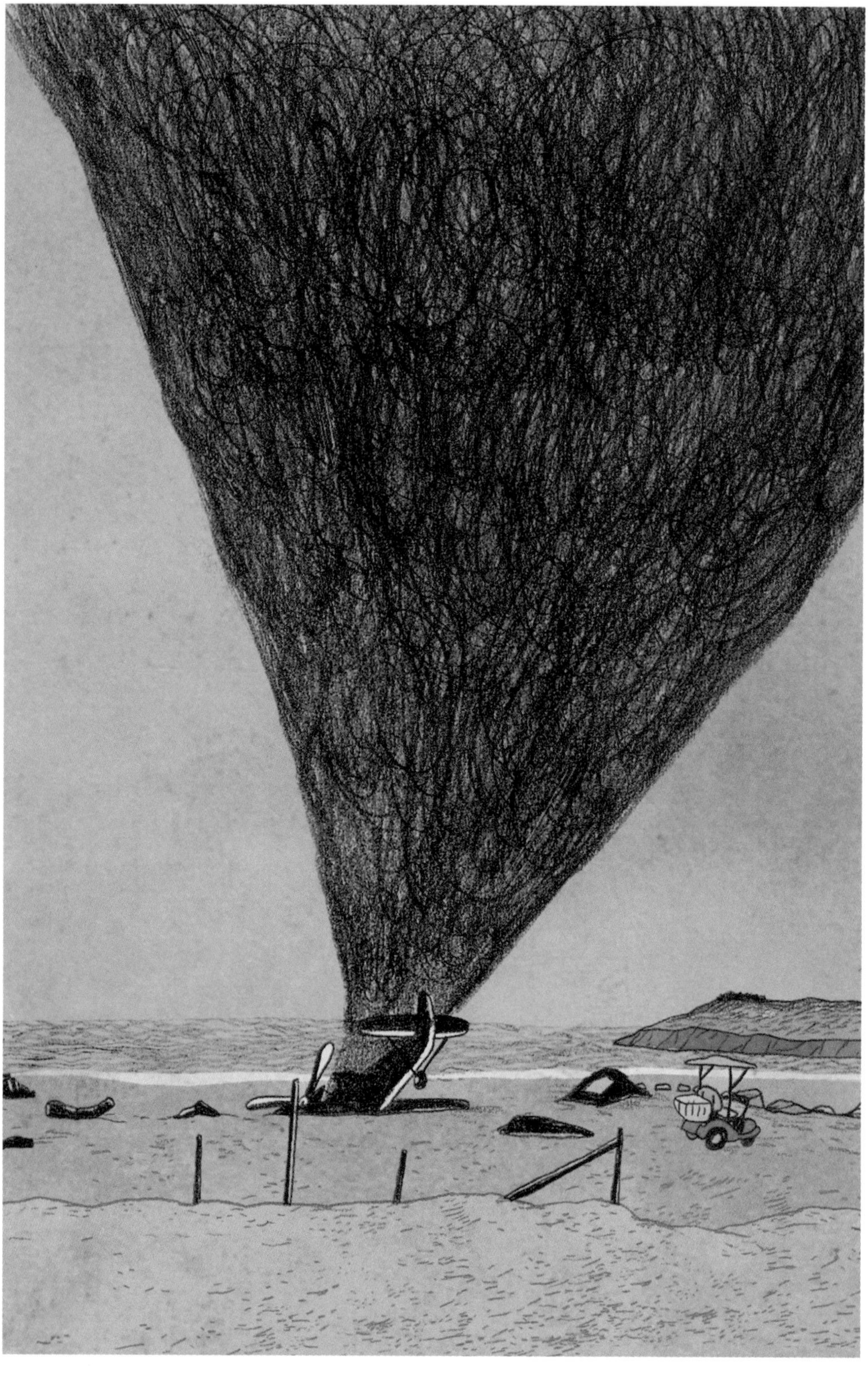

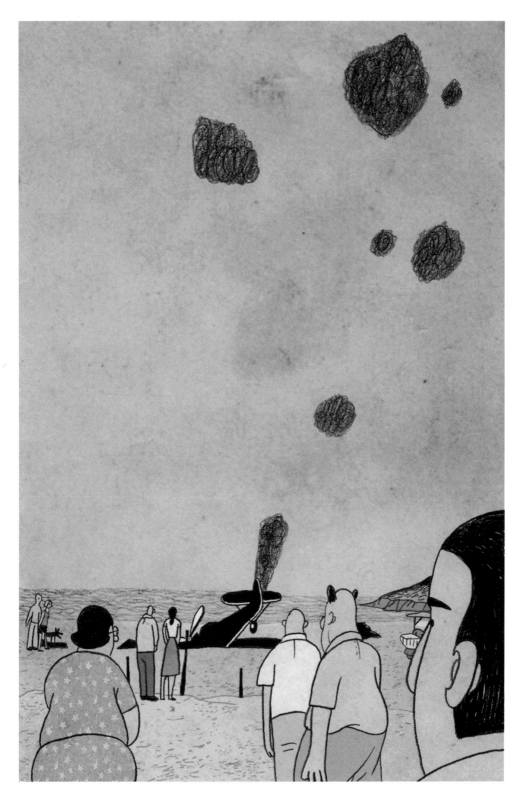

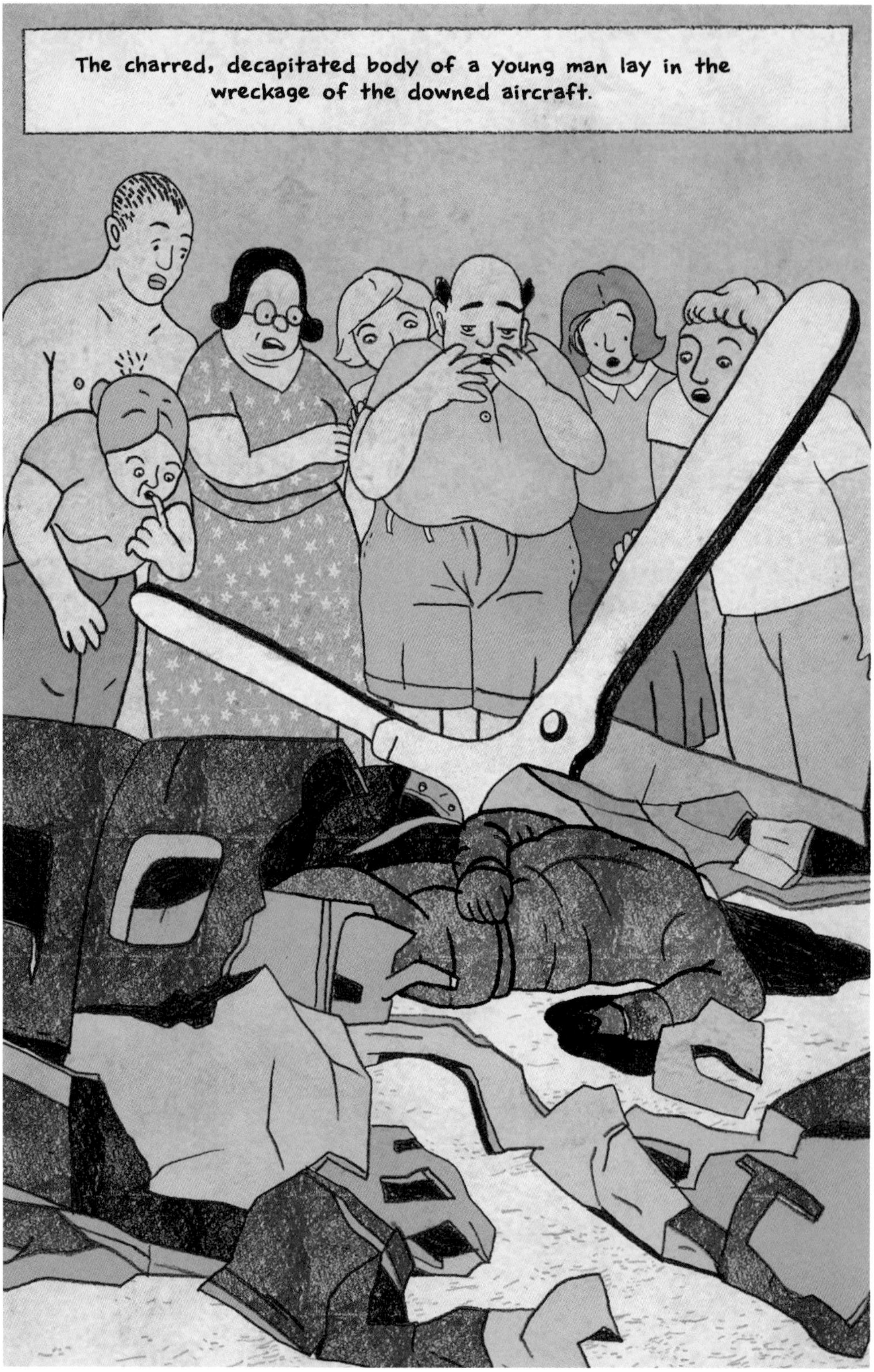
The charred, decapitated body of a young man lay in the wreckage of the downed aircraft.

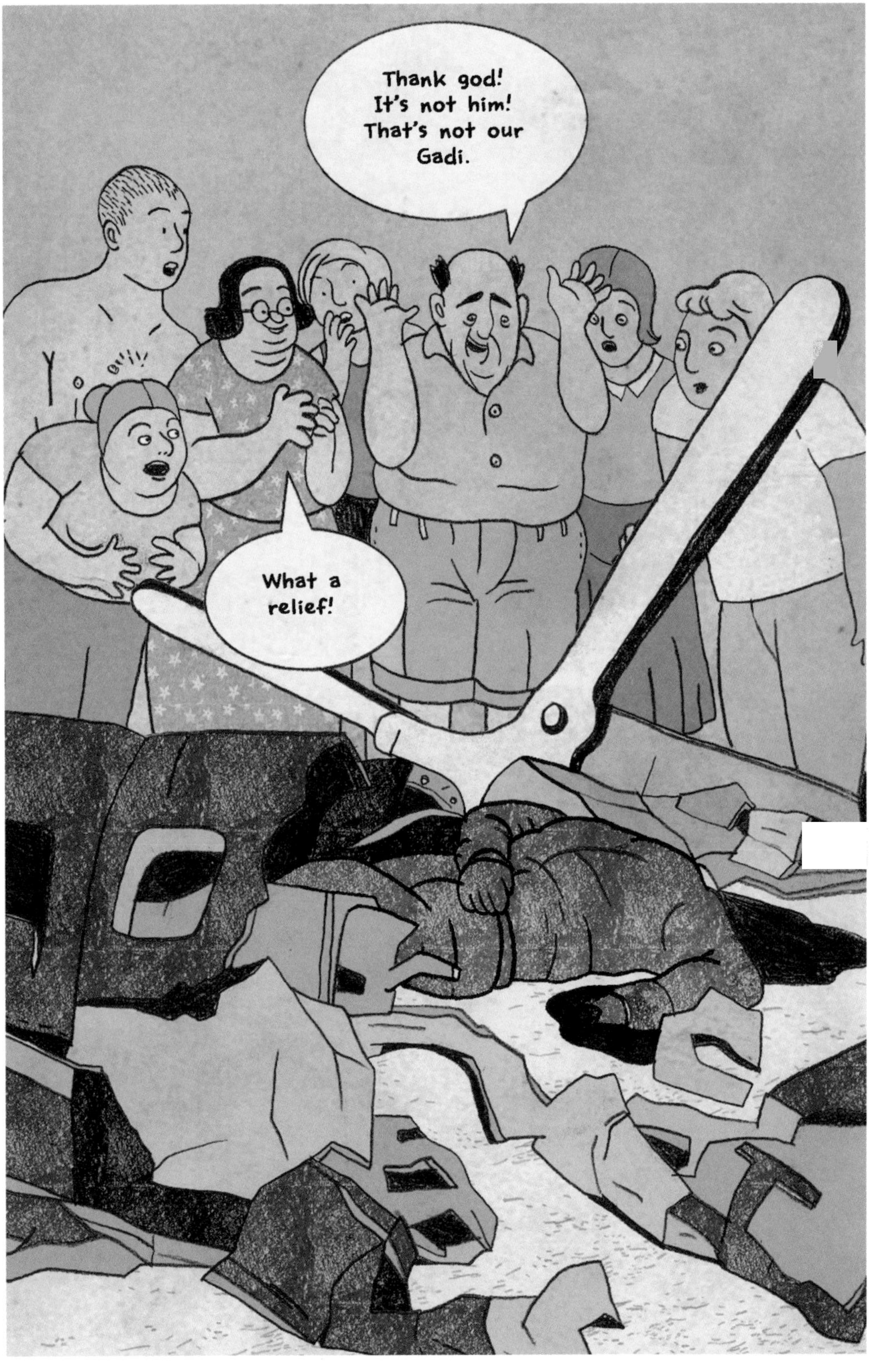
Thank god! It's not him! That's not our Gadi.
What a relief!

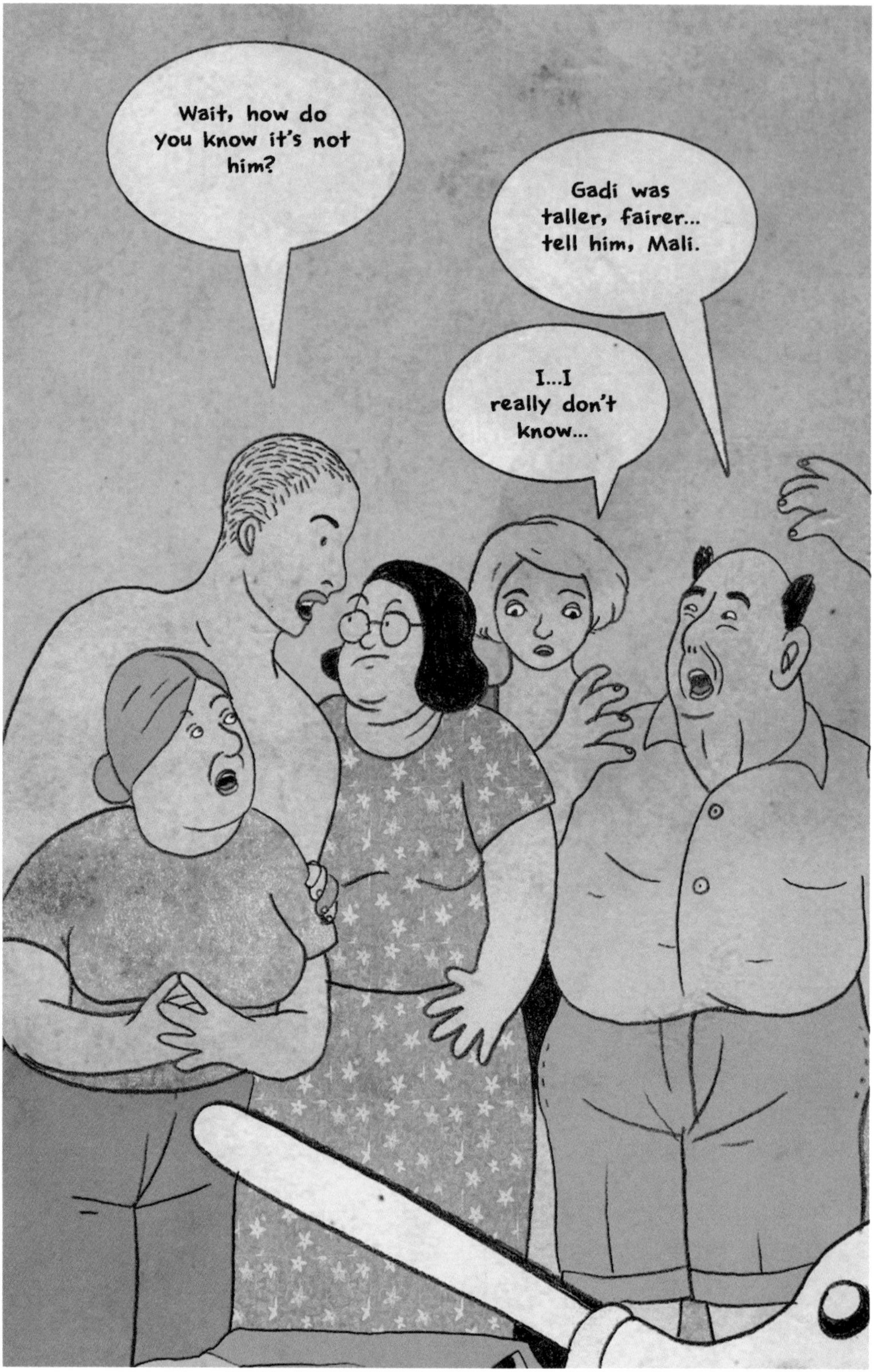
Wait, how do you know it's not him?
Gadi was taller, fairer... tell him, Mali.
I...I really don't know...

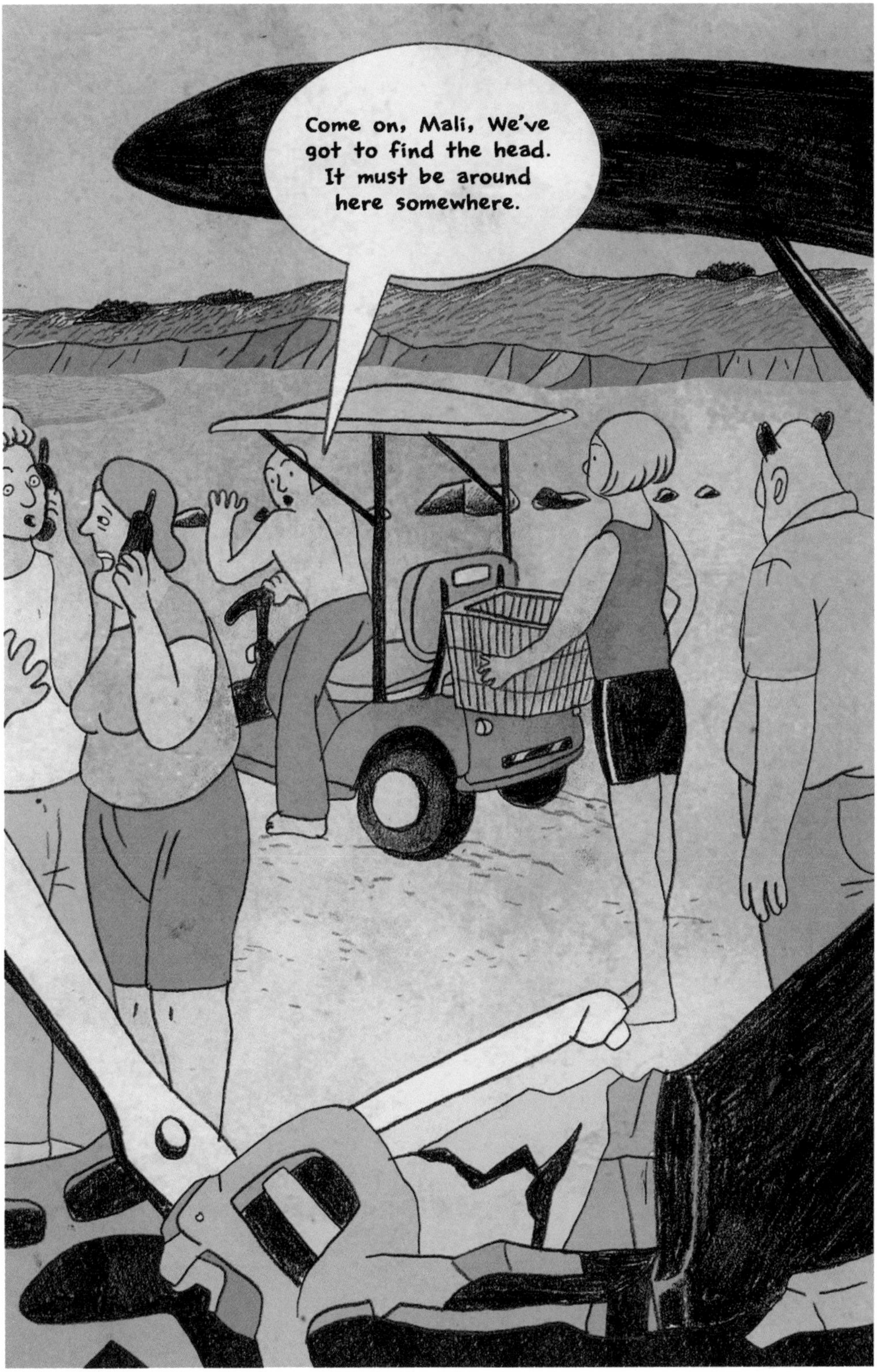
Come on, Mali, We've got to find the head. It must be around here somewhere.

THE KING OF THE LILLIES

Louise Wagschul was in a quandary; Her daughter Lilly had
already turned 12, and was showing no signs of acrobatic
aptitude. They had been getting by so far, but the applause was
growing weaker with every show, and the other day
two men had walked off right before the double-back somersault. No
man had ever left her little show in the middle before.
"I'm getting older," Louise said to herself.
"Sooner or later my audience will abandon me. I think it's time for a
career transition."

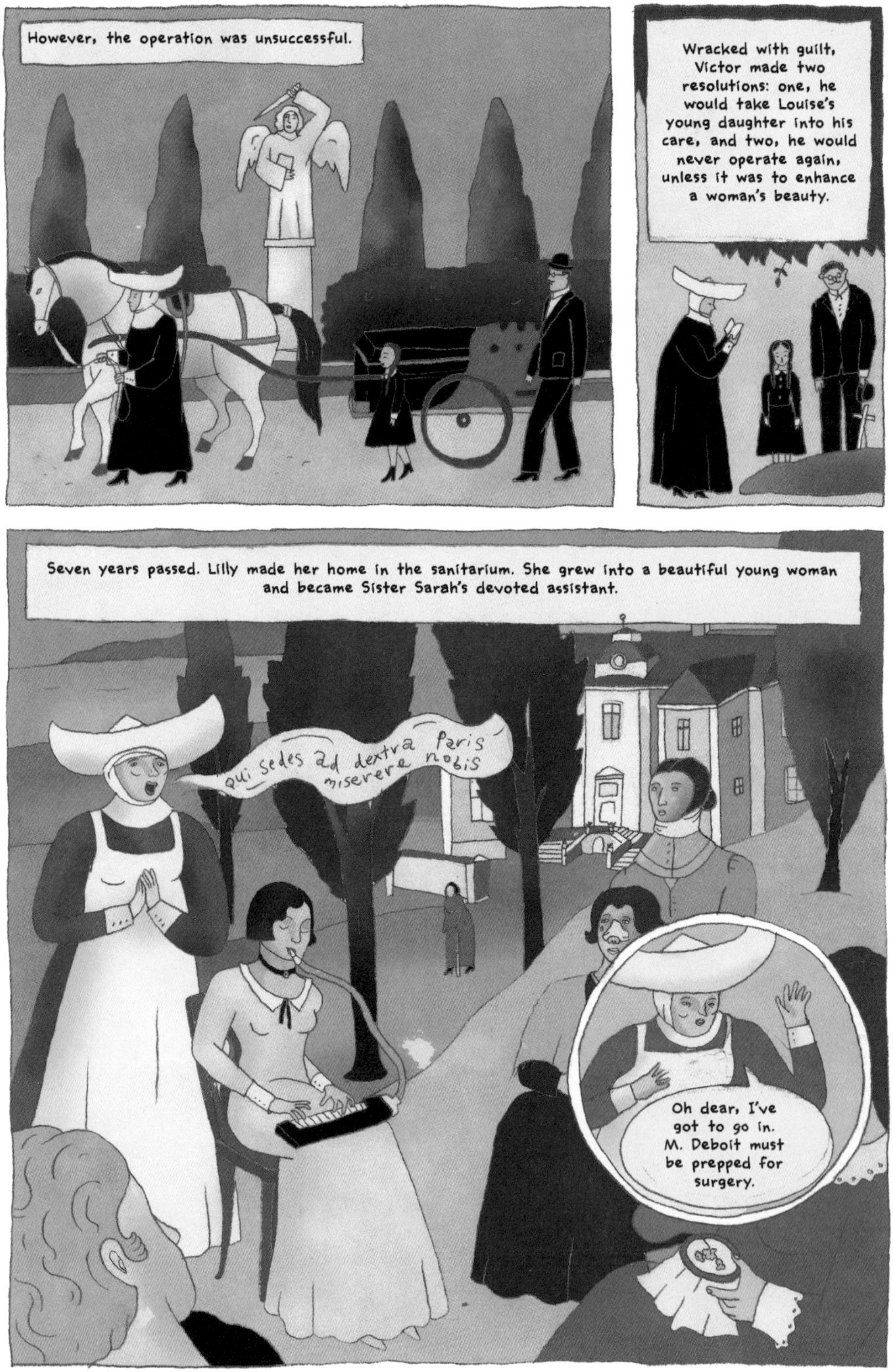
However, the operation was unsuccessful.
Wracked with guilt, Victor made two resolutions: one, he would take Louise's young daughter into his care, and two, he would never operate again, unless it was to enhance a woman's beauty.
Seven years passed. Lilly made her home in the sanitarium. She grew into a beautiful young woman and became Sister Sarah's devoted assistant.
qui sedes ad dextra Paris miserere nobis
Oh dear, I've got to go in. M. Deboit must be prepped for surgery.

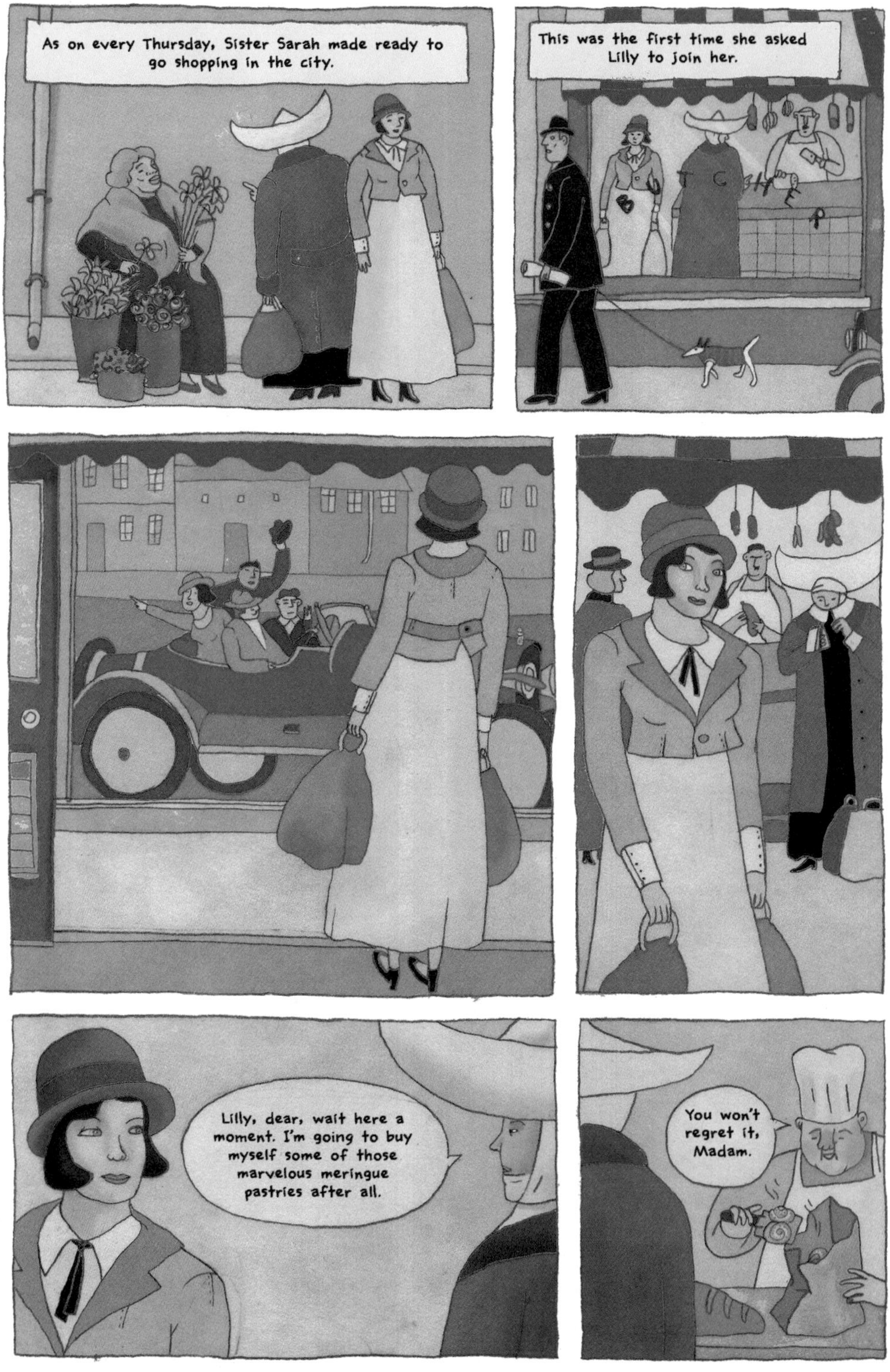
As on every Thursday, Sister Sarah made ready to go shopping in the city.
This was the first time she asked Lilly to join her.
Lilly, dear, wait here a moment. I'm going to buy myself some of those marvelous meringue pastries after all.
You won't regret it, Madam.

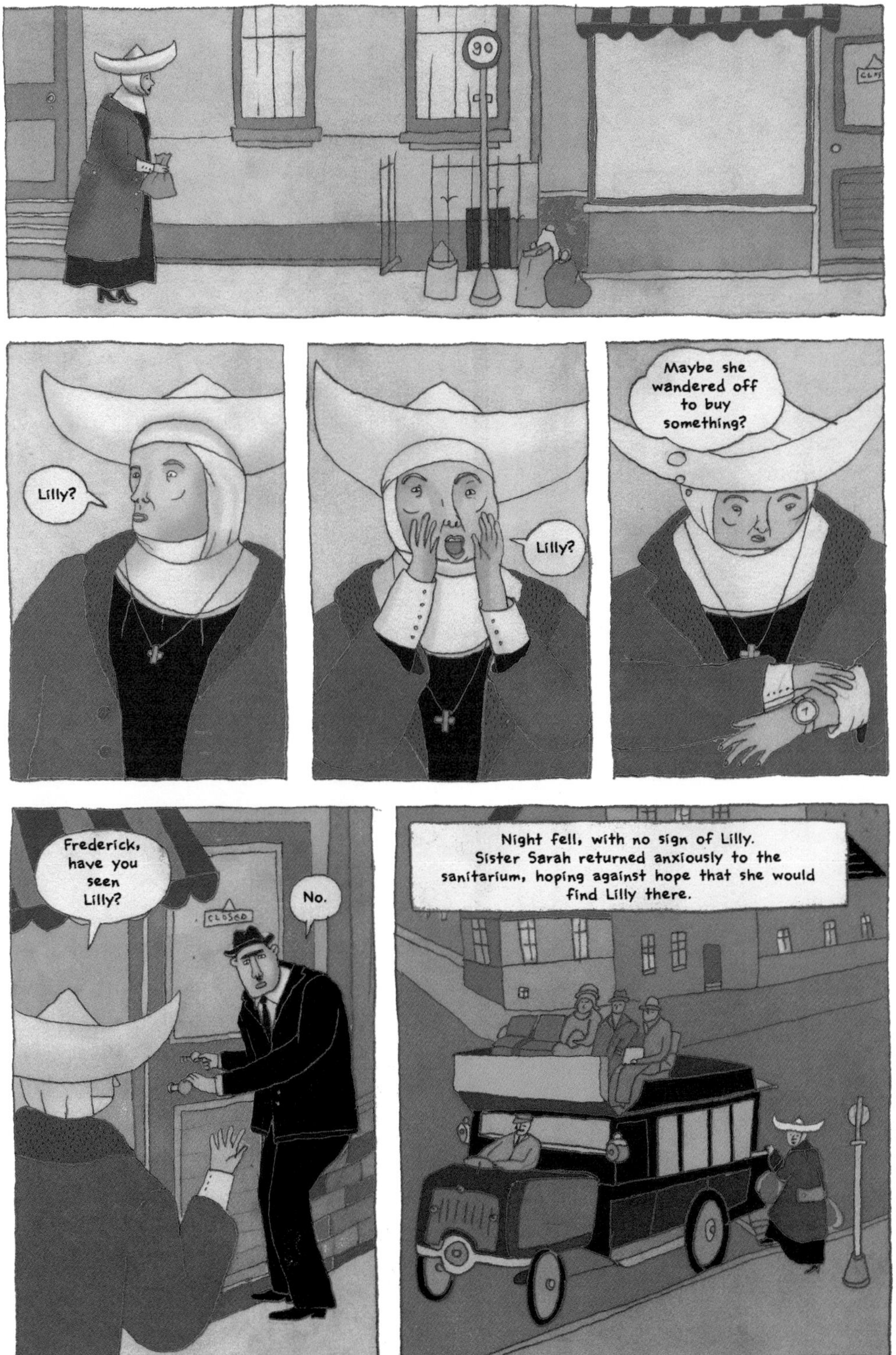
Lilly?
Lilly?
Maybe she wandered off to buy something?
Frederick, have you seen Lilly?
No.
CLOSED
Night fell, with no sign of Lilly. Sister Sarah returned anxiously to the sanitarium, hoping against hope that she would find Lilly there.

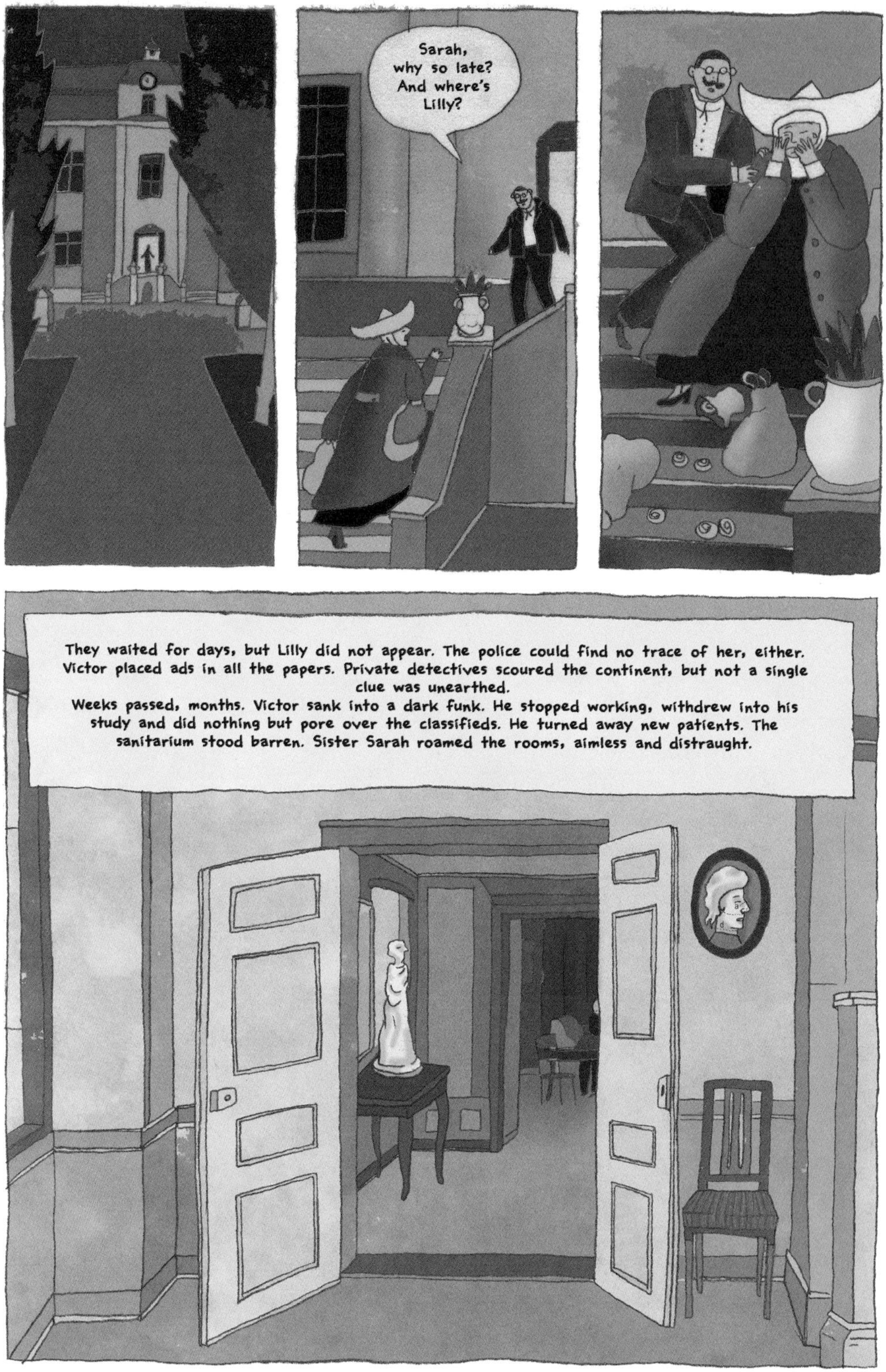
Sarah, why so late? And where's Lilly?
They waited for days, but Lilly did not appear. The police could find no trace of her, either. Victor placed ads in all the papers. Private detectives scoured the continent, but not a single clue was unearthed.
Weeks passed, months. Victor sank into a dark funk. He stopped working, withdrew into his study and did nothing but pore over the classifieds. He turned away new patients. The sanitarium stood barren. Sister Sarah roamed the rooms, aimless and distraught.

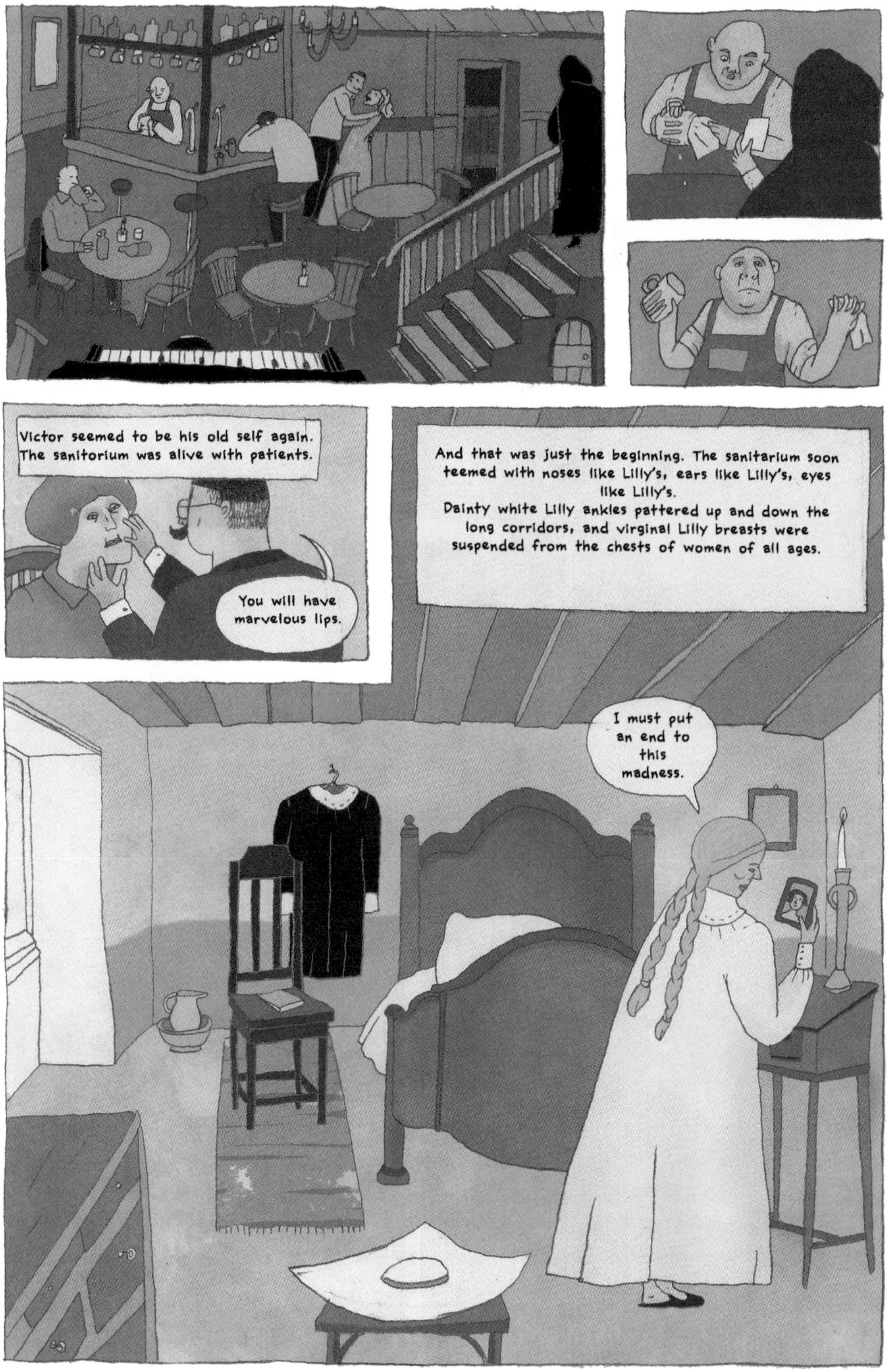
Victor seemed to be his old self again. The sanitorium was alive with patients.
You will have marvelous lips.
And that was just the beginning. The sanitarium soon teemed with noses like Lilly's, ears like Lilly's, eyes like Lilly's.
Dainty white Lilly ankles pattered up and down the long corridors, and virginal Lilly breasts were suspended from the chests of women of all ages.
I must put an end to this madness.

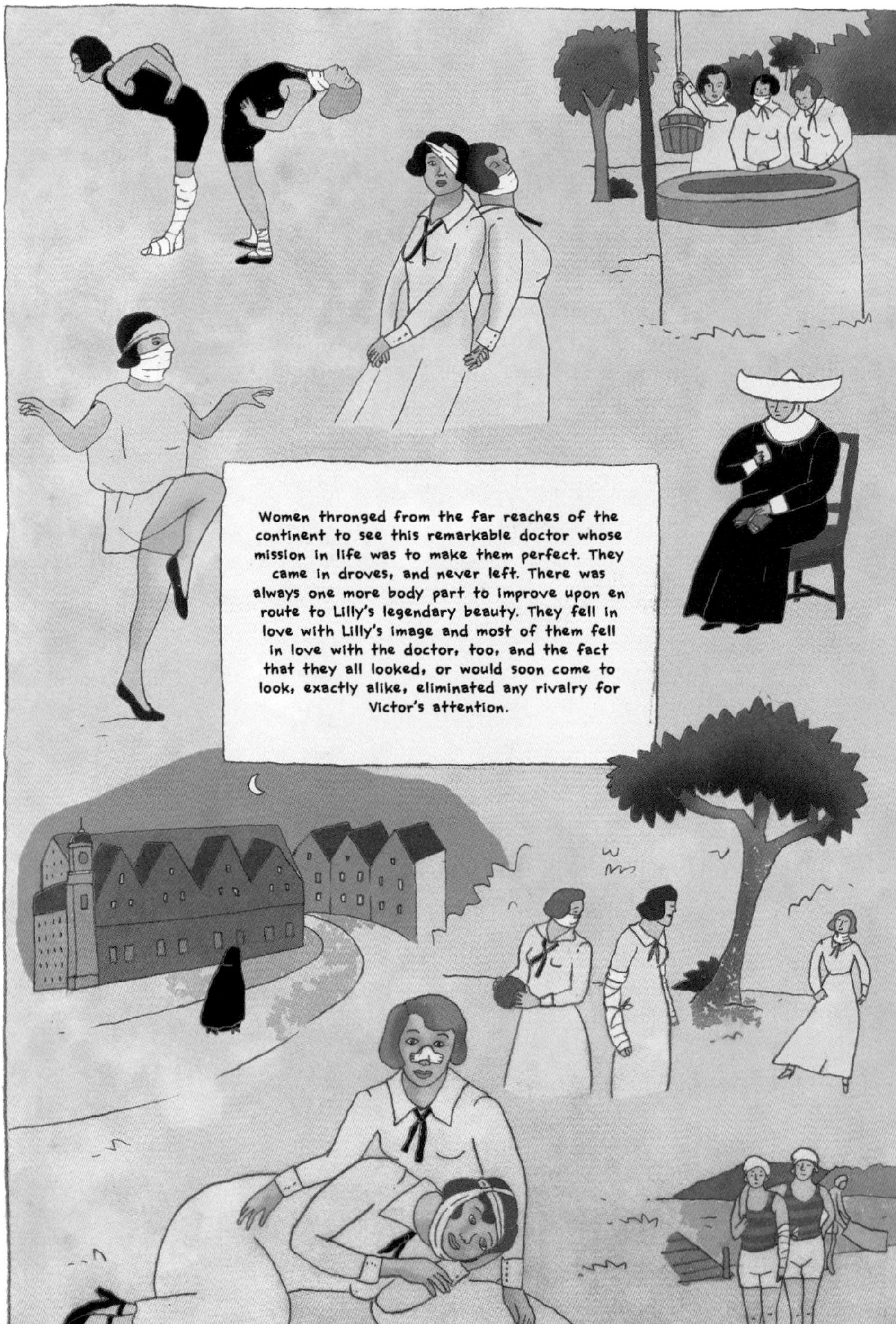
Women thronged from the far reaches of the continent to see this remarkable doctor whose mission in life was to make them perfect. They came in droves, and never left. There was always one more body part to improve upon en route to Lilly's legendary beauty. They fell in love with Lilly's image and most of them fell in love with the doctor, too, and the fact that they all looked, or would soon come to look, exactly alike, eliminated any rivalry for Victor's attention.

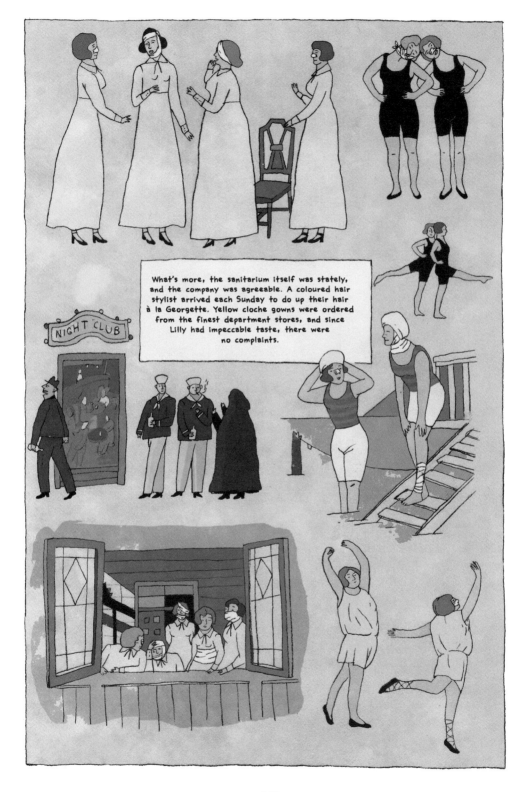

What's more, the sanitarium itself was stately, and the company was agreeable. A coloured hair stylist arrived each Sunday to do up their hair à la Georgette. Yellow cloche gowns were ordered from the finest department stores, and since Lilly had impeccable taste, there were no complaints.

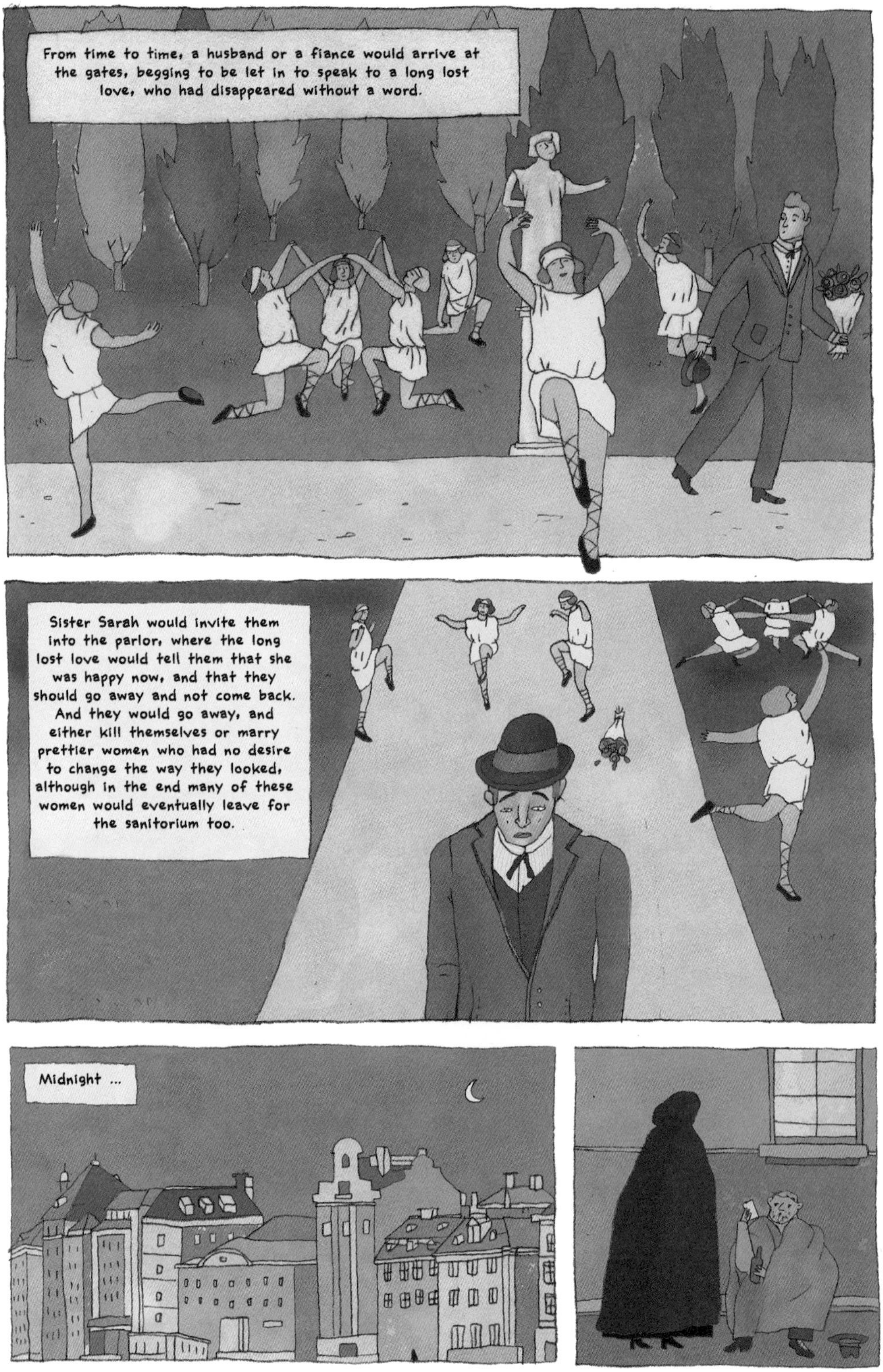
From time to time, a husband or a fiance would arrive at the gates, begging to be let in to speak to a long lost love, who had disappeared without a word.
Sister Sarah would invite them into the parlor, where the long lost love would tell them that she was happy now, and that they should go away and not come back. And they would go away, and either kill themselves or marry prettier women who had no desire to change the way they looked, although in the end many of these women would eventually leave for the sanitorium too.
Midnight ...

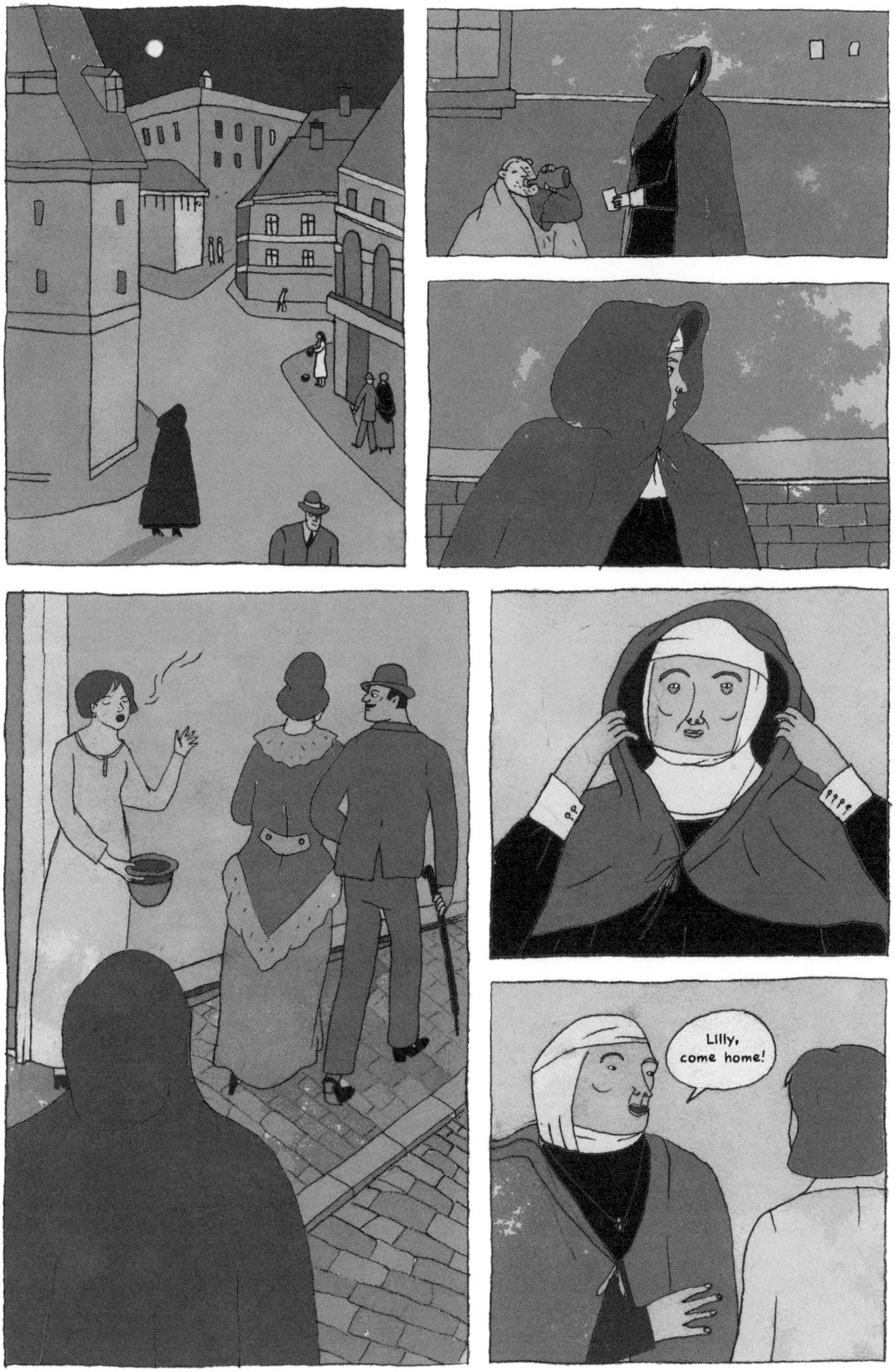
Lilly, come home!

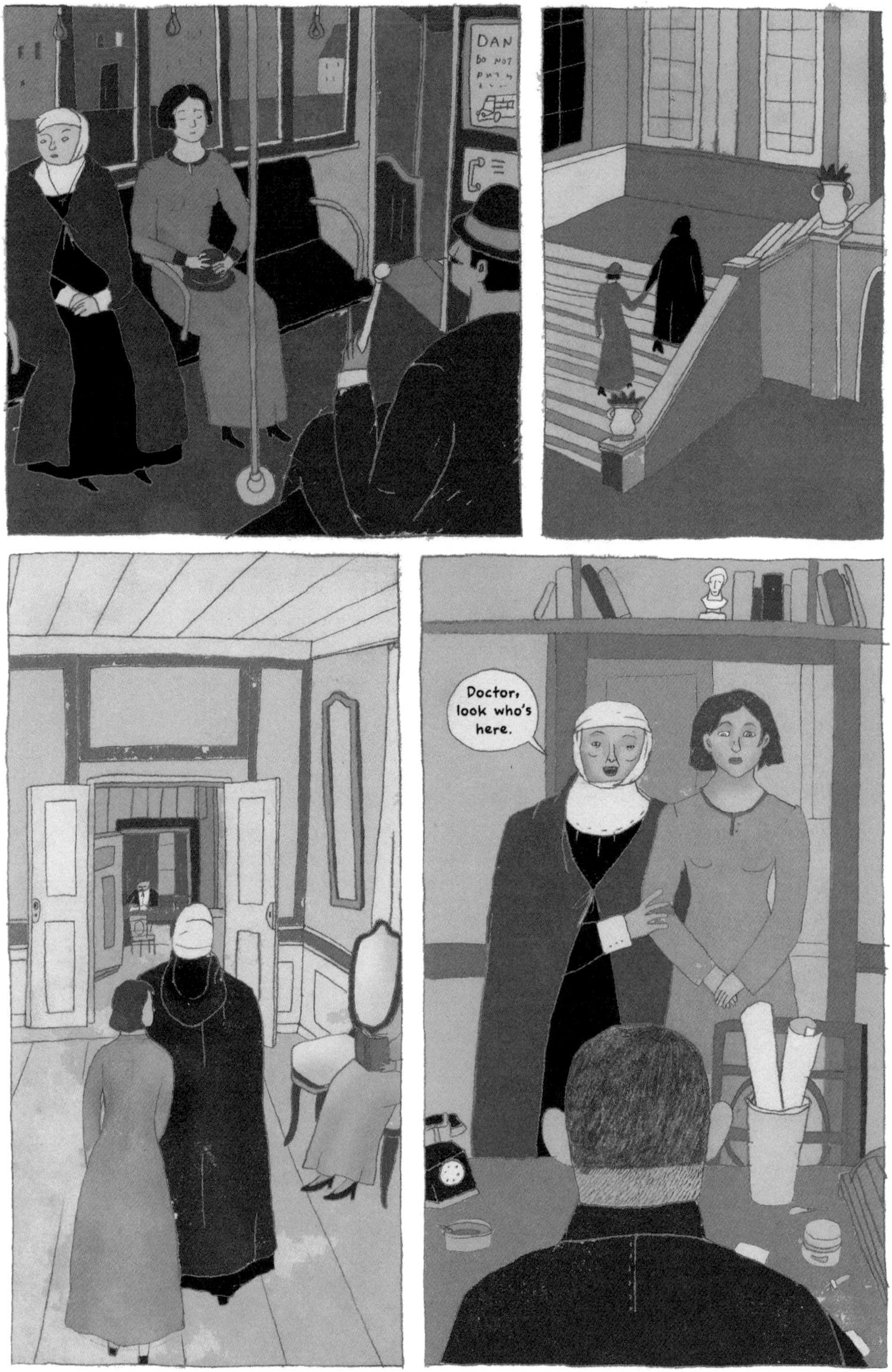
DAN
DO NOT
Doctor, look who's here.

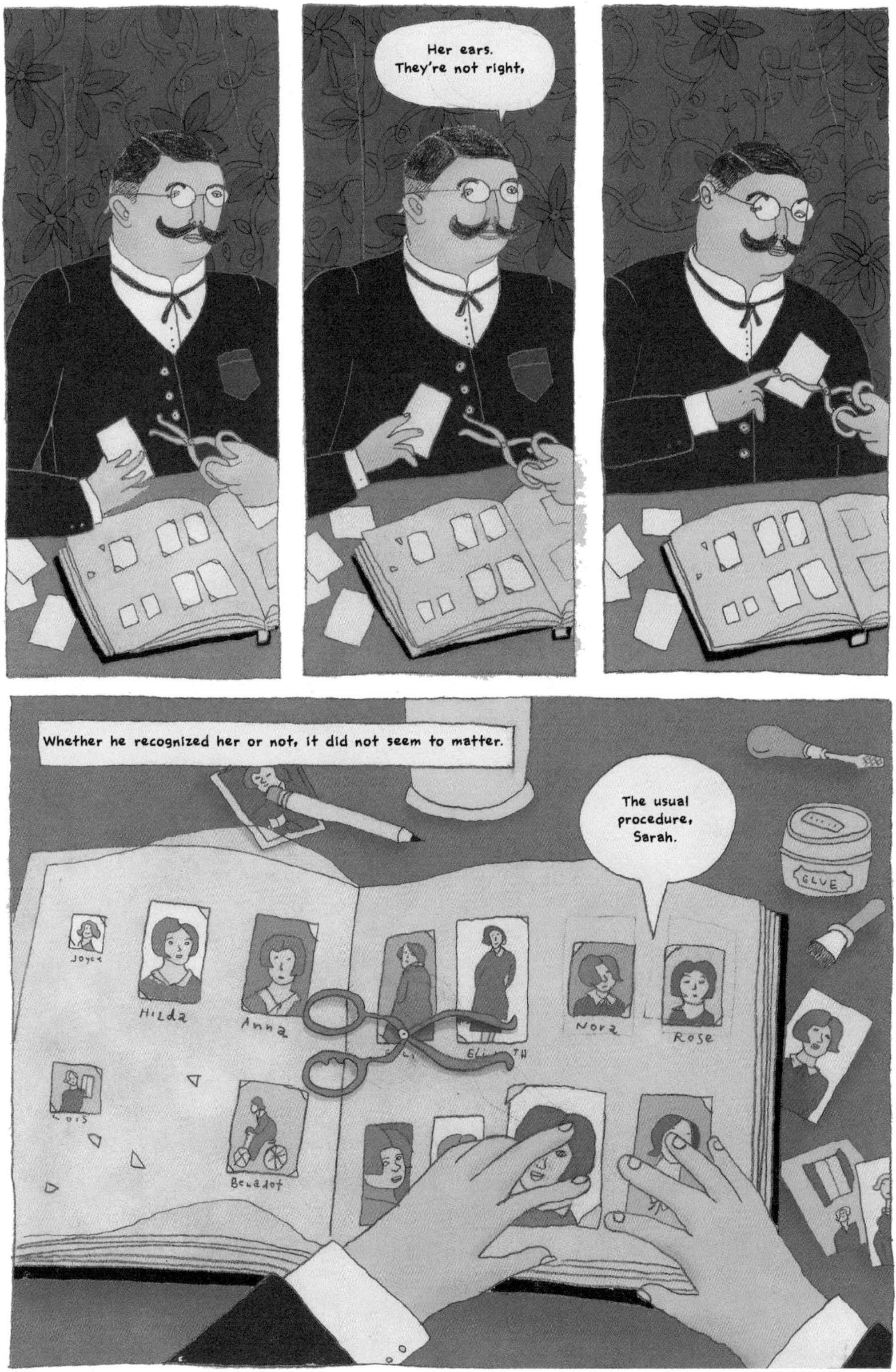
Her ears.
They're not right.
Whether he recognized her or not, it did not seem to matter.
The usual procedure, Sarah.
Joyce
Hilda
Anna
Nora
Rose
GLUE

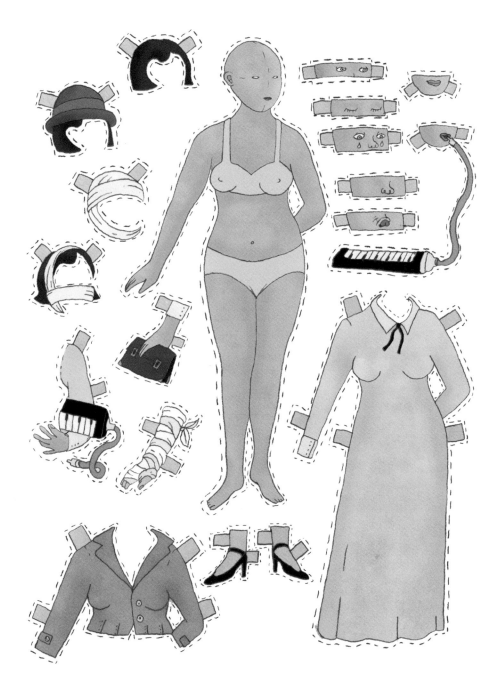

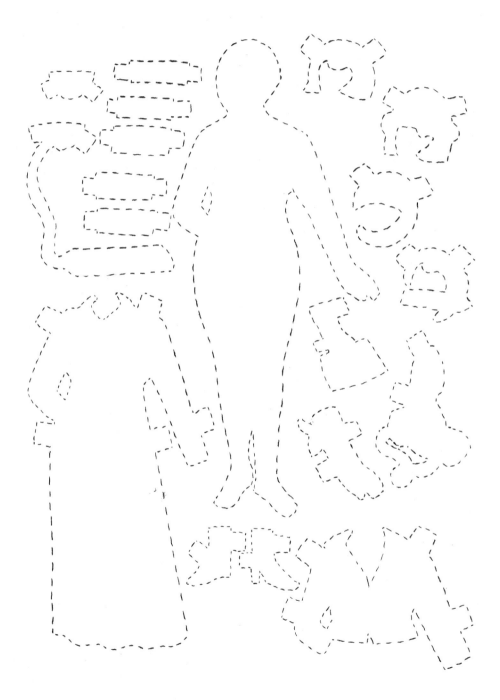

YOUR NUMBER ONE FAN

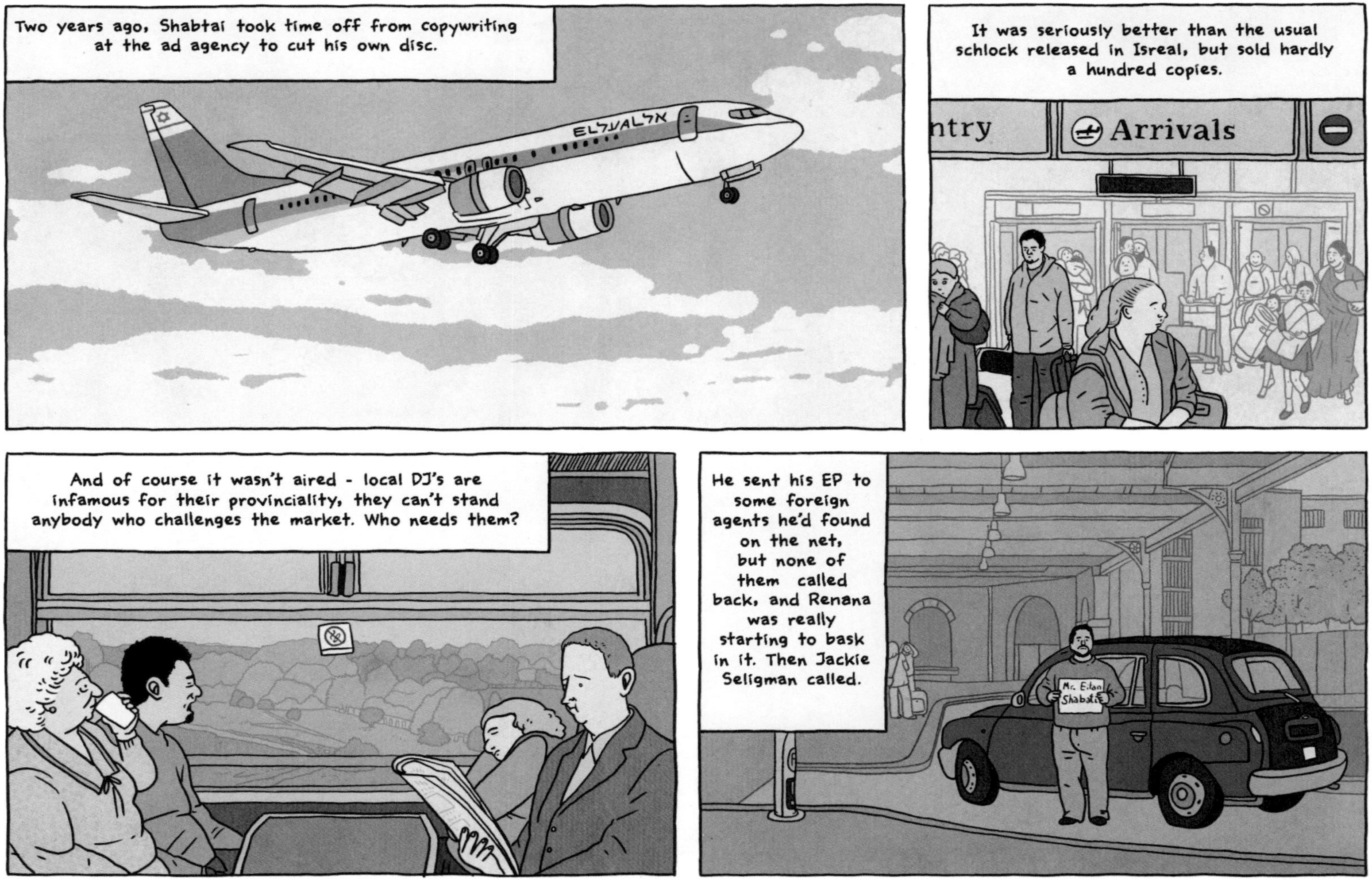
Two years ago, Shabtai took time off from copywriting at the ad agency to cut his own disc.
ELAL
It was seriously better than the usual schlock released in Isreal, but sold hardly a hundred copies.
ntry
Arrivals
And of course it wasn't aired - local DJ's are infamous for their provinciality, they can't stand anybody who challenges the market. Who needs them?
He sent his EP to some foreign agents he'd found on the net, but none of them called back, and Renana was really starting to bask in it. Then Jackie Seligman called.
Mr. Eilan Shabatie

156

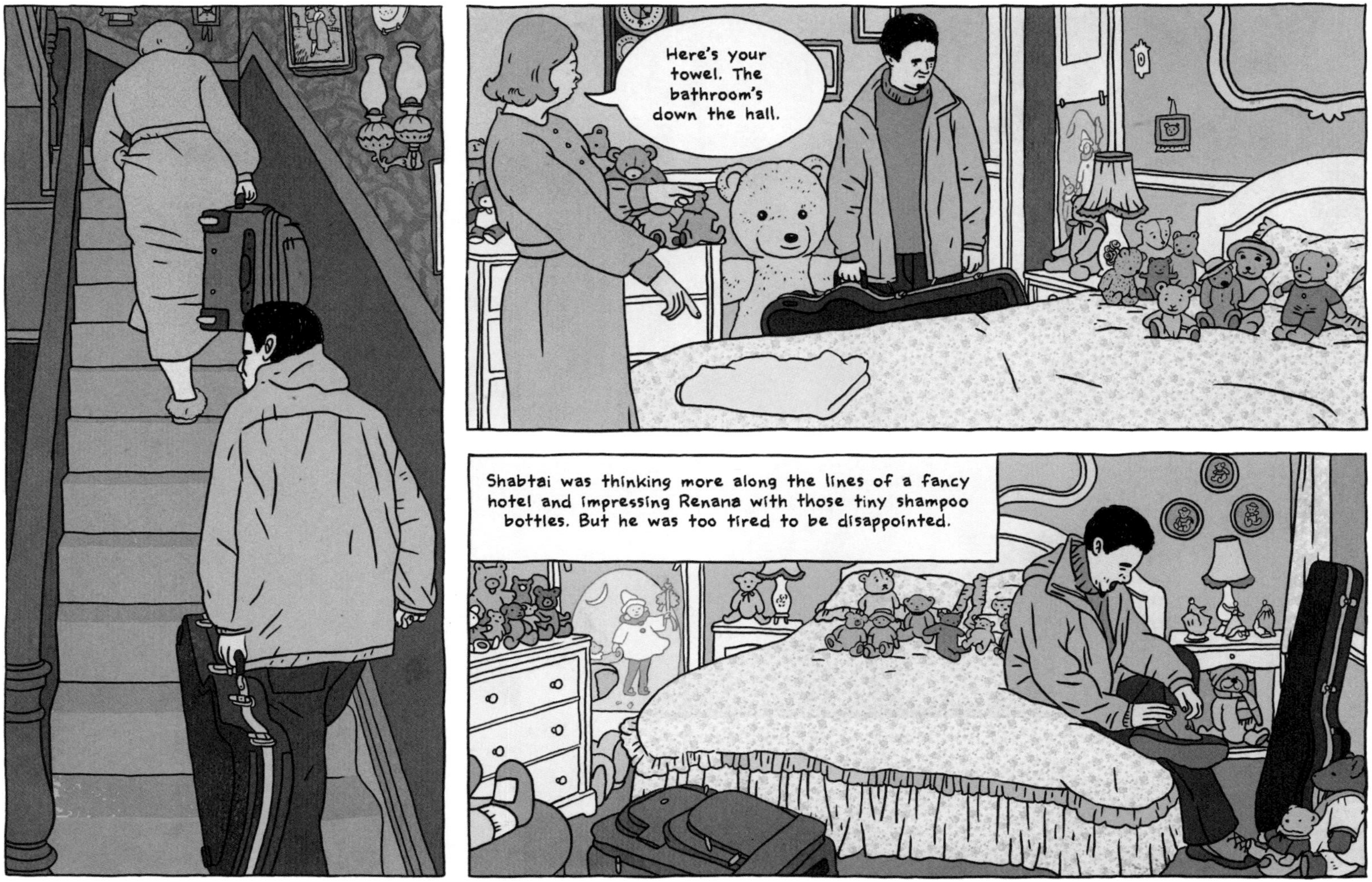
Here's your towel. The bathroom's down the hall.
Shabtai was thinking more along the lines of a fancy hotel and impressing Renana with those tiny shampoo bottles. But he was too tired to be disappointed.

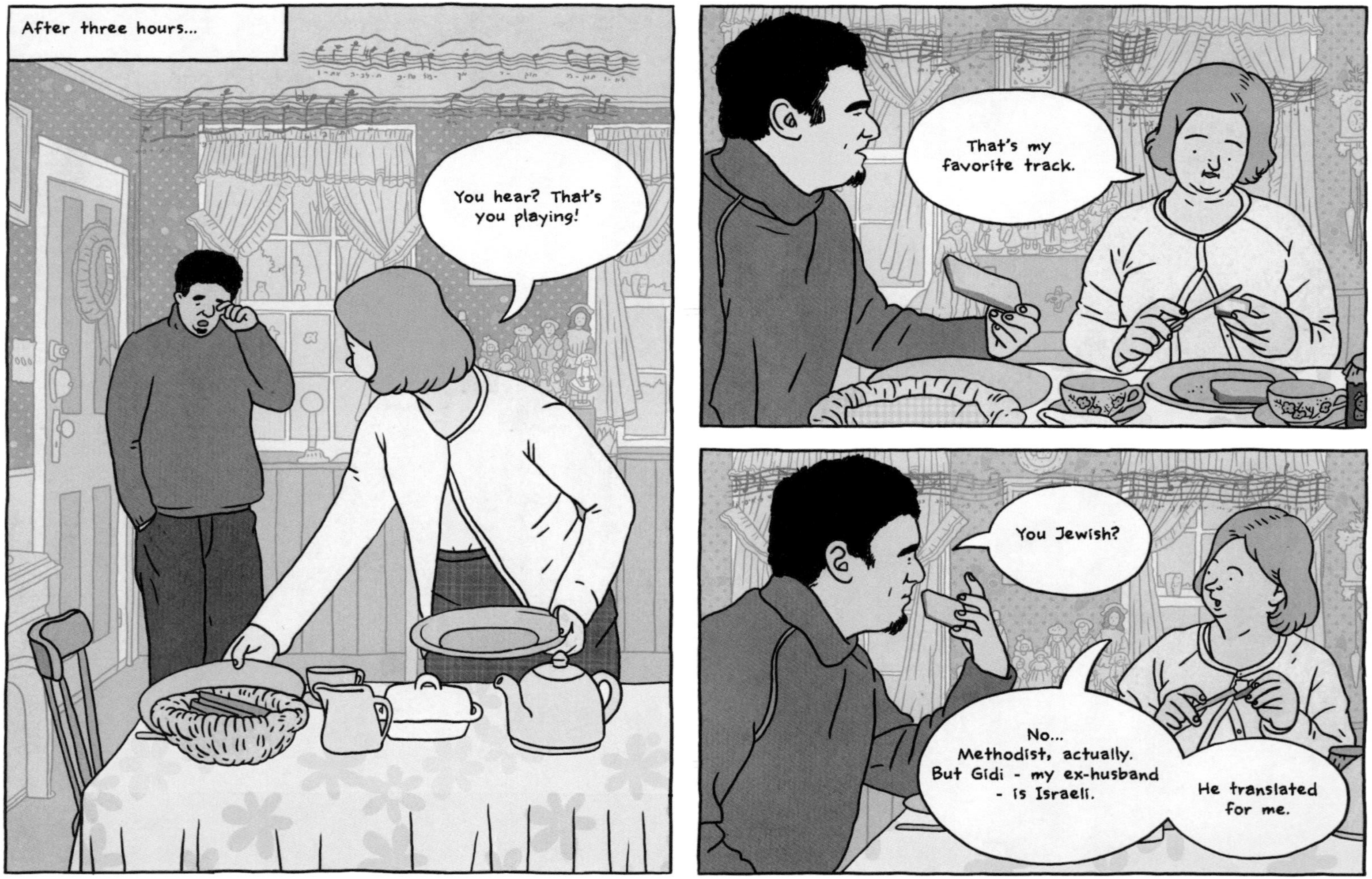
After three hours...
You hear? That's you playing!
That's my favorite track.
You Jewish?
No... Methodist, actually. But Gidi - my ex-husband - is Israeli.
He translated for me.

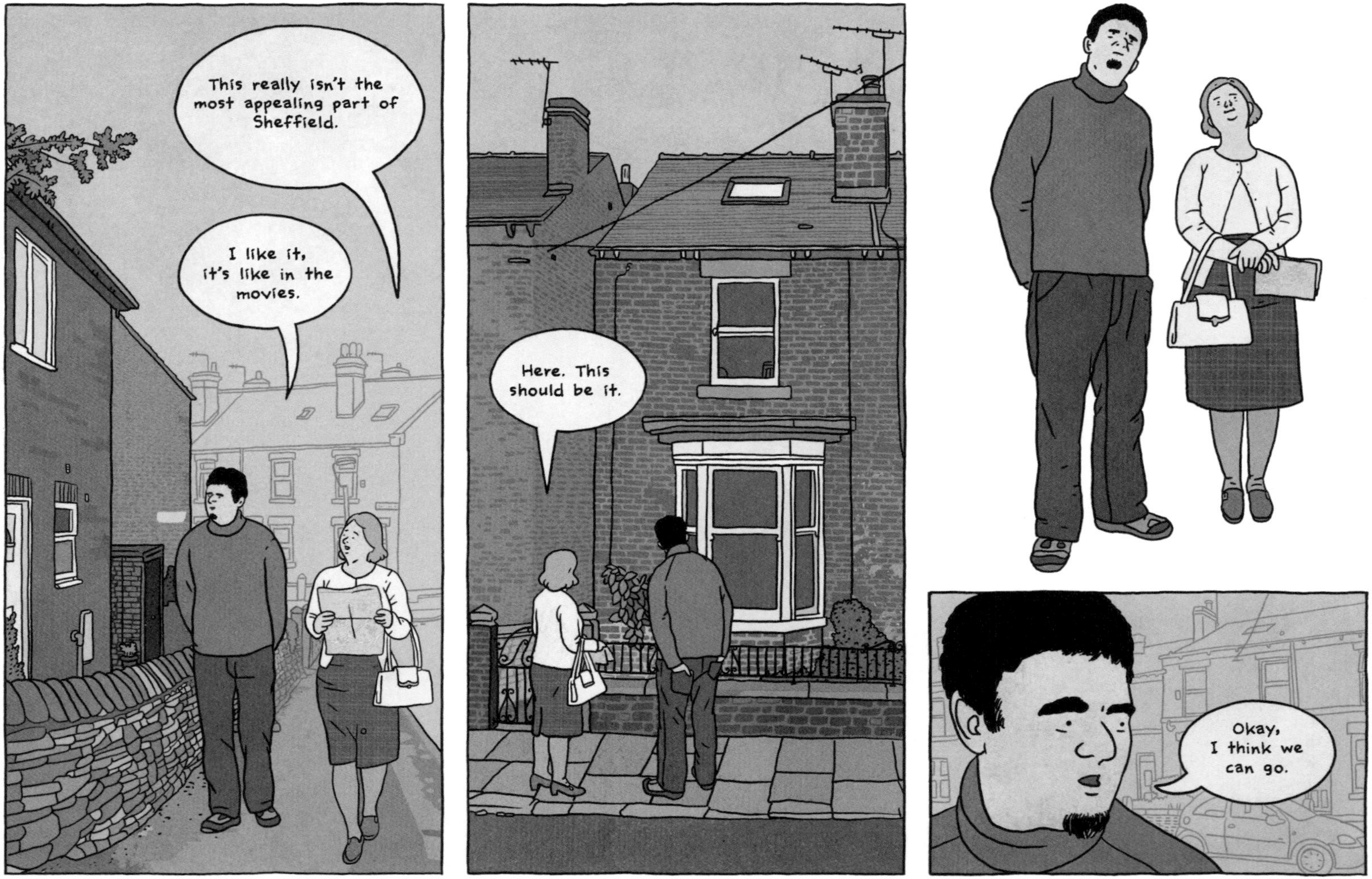
This really isn't the most appealing part of Sheffield.
I like it, it's like in the movies.
Here. This should be it.
Okay, I think we can go.

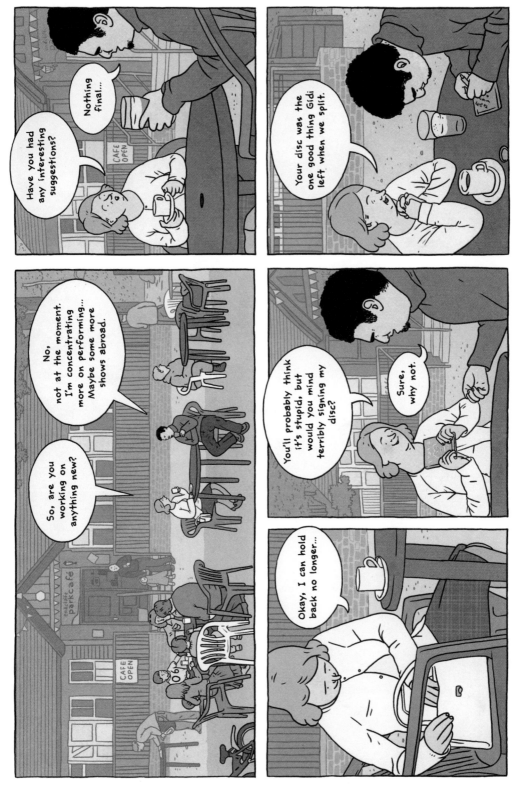

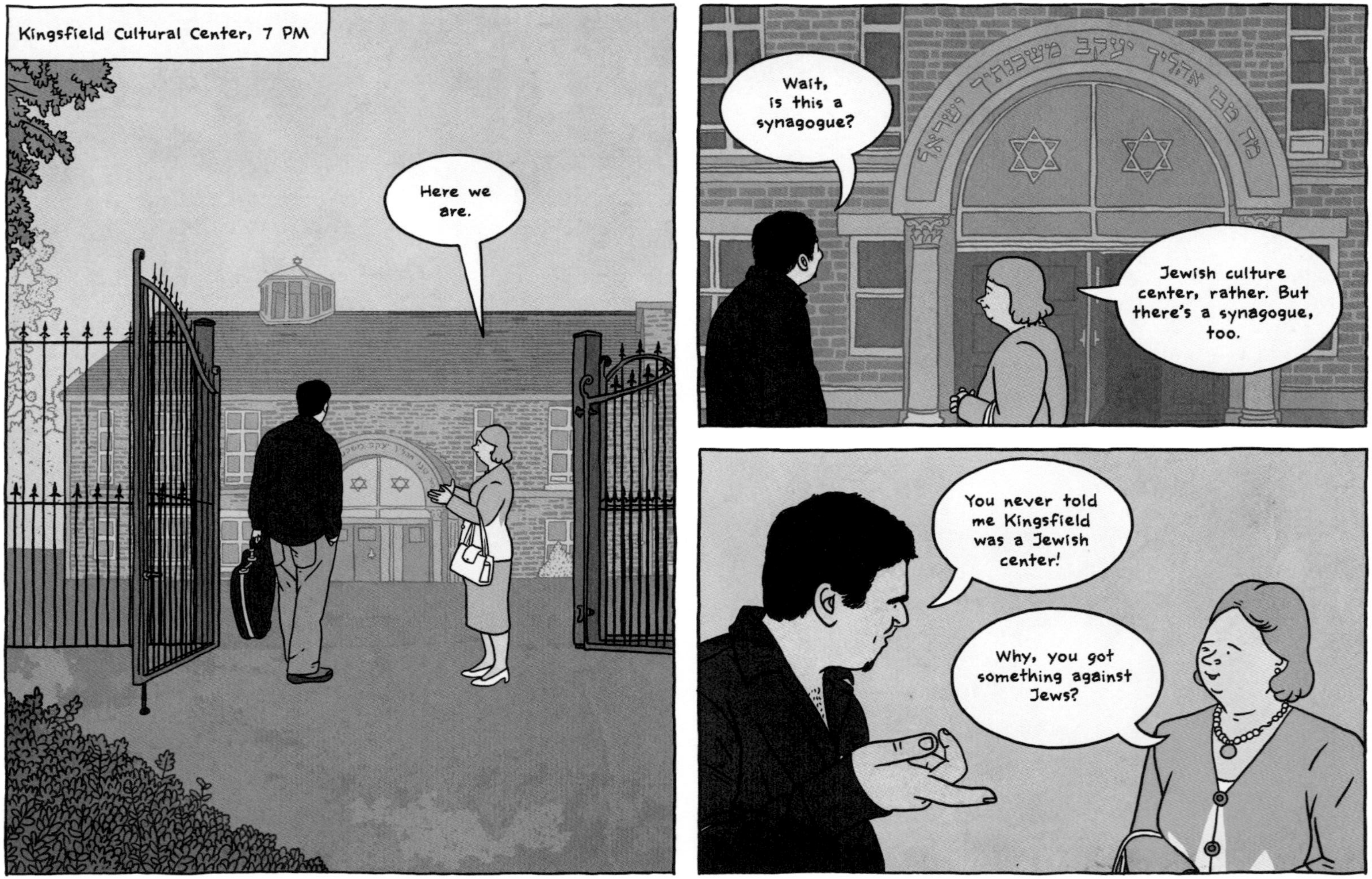
Kingsfield Cultural Center, 7 PM
Here we are.
Wait, is this a synagogue?
Jewish culture center, rather. But there's a synagogue, too.
You never told me Kingsfield was a Jewish center!
Why, you got something against Jews?

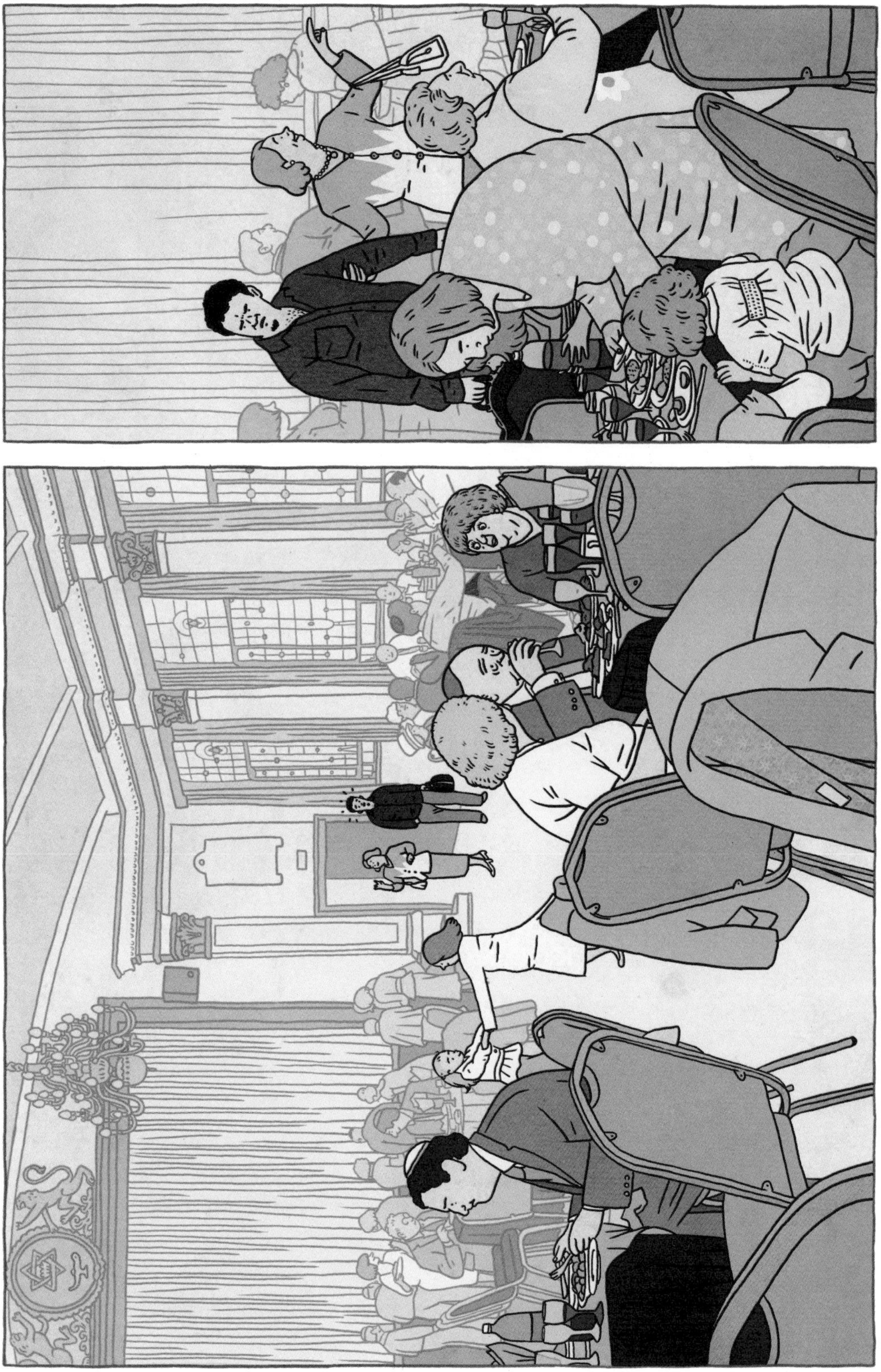

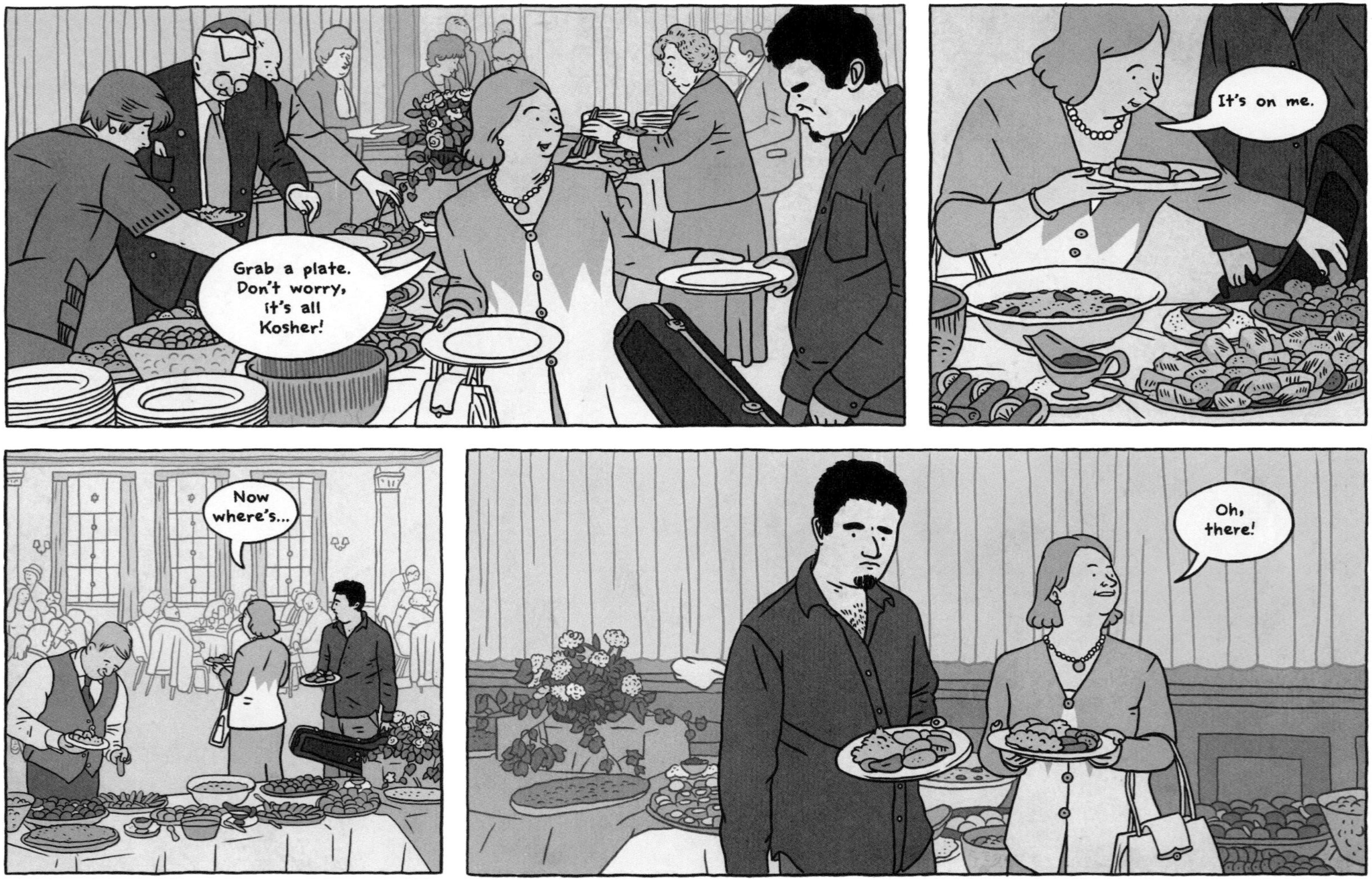
Grab a plate. Don't worry, it's all Kosher!
It's on me.
Now where's...
Oh, there!

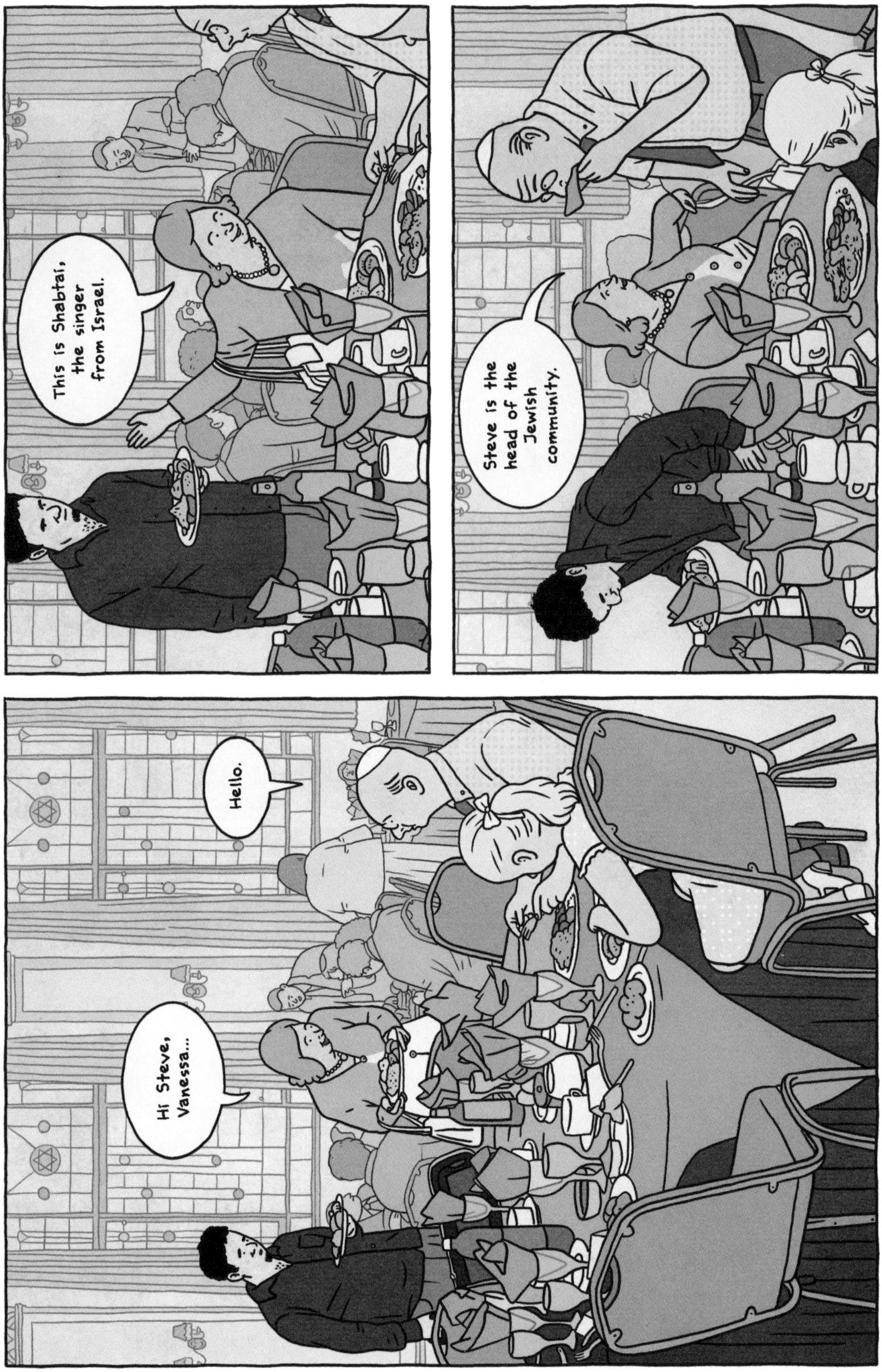
Steve is the head of the Jewish community.
This is Shabtai, the singer from Israel.
Hi Steve, Vanessa...
Hello.

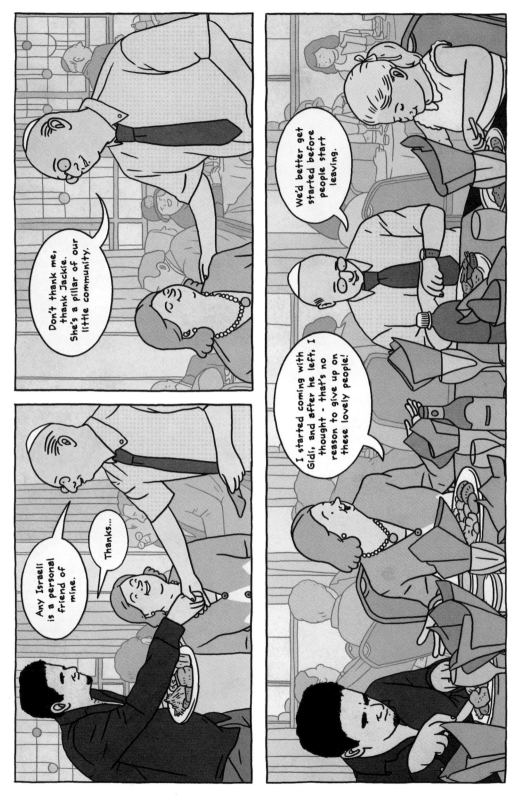

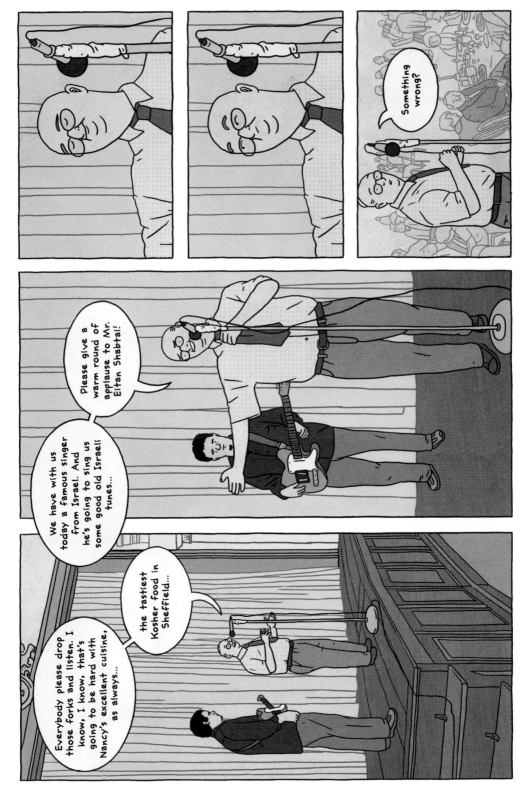

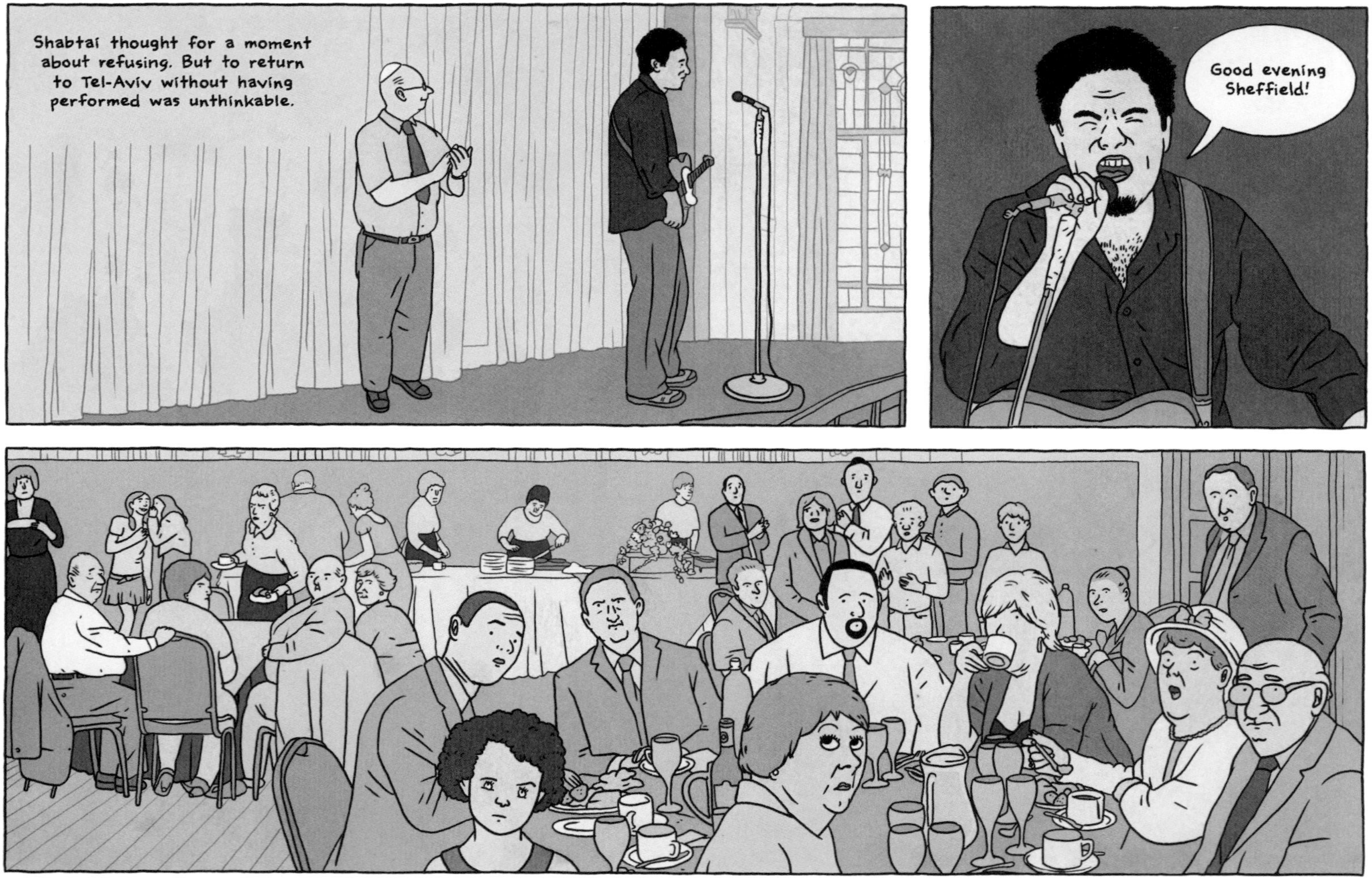
Shabtai thought for a moment about refusing. But to return to Tel-Aviv without having performed was unthinkable.
Good evening Sheffield!

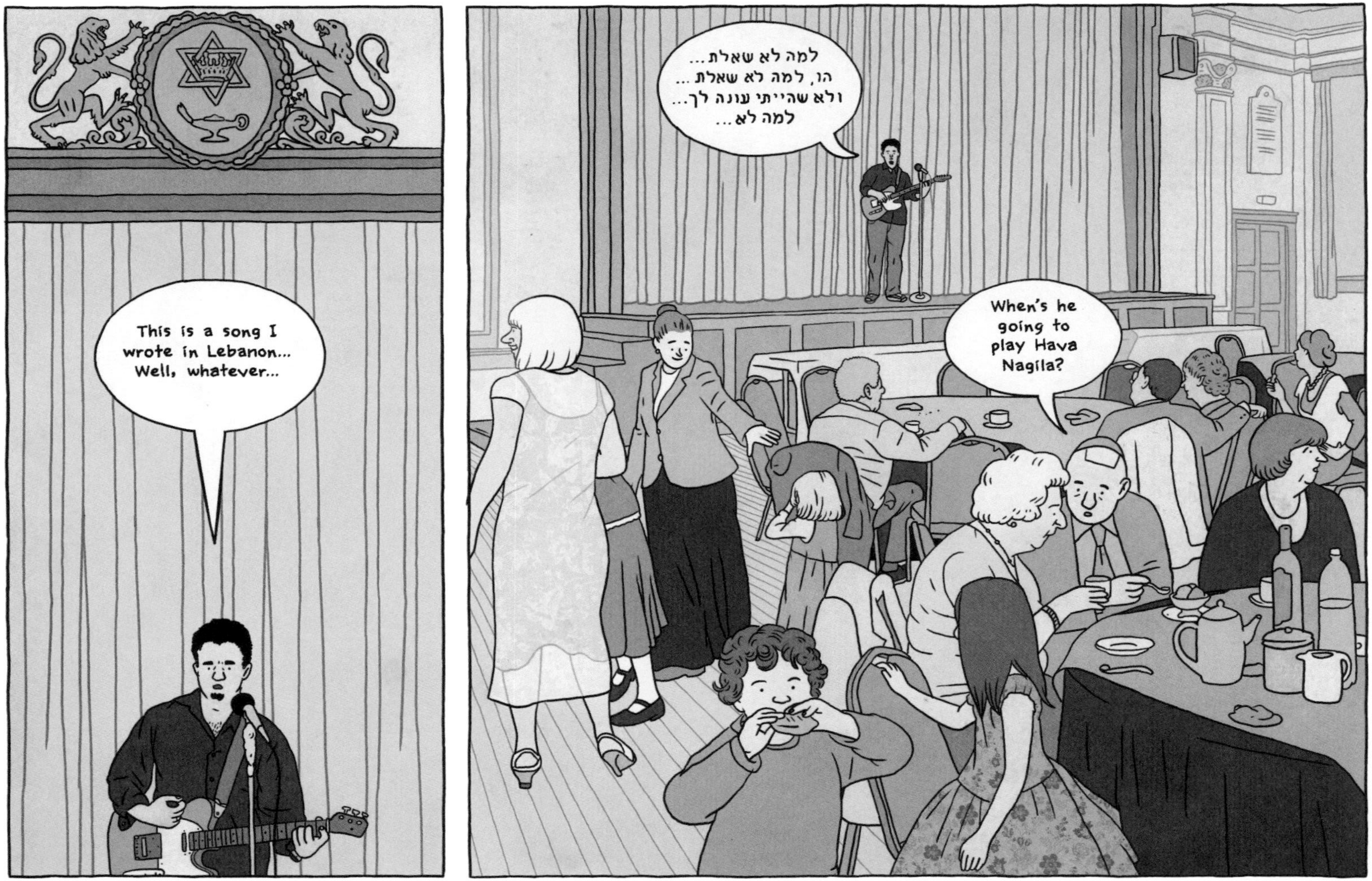
This is a song I wrote in Lebanon... Well, whatever...
למה לא שאלת...
הו, למה לא שאלת...
ולא שהייתי עונה לך...
למה לא...
When's he going to play Hava Nagila?

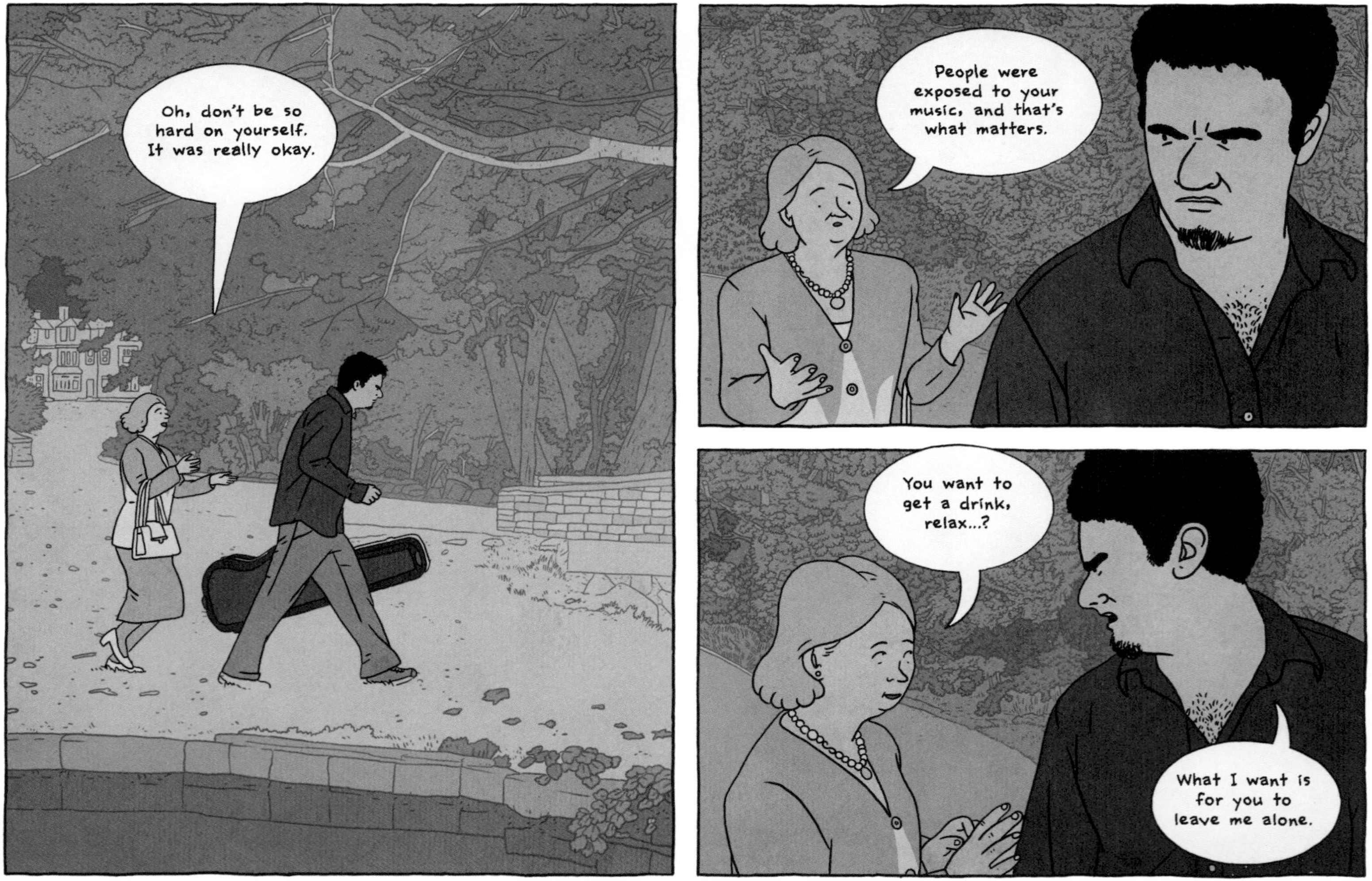
Oh, don't be so
hard on yourself.
It was really okay.
People were
exposed to your
music, and that's
what matters.
You want to
get a drink,
relax...?
What I want is
for you to
leave me alone.

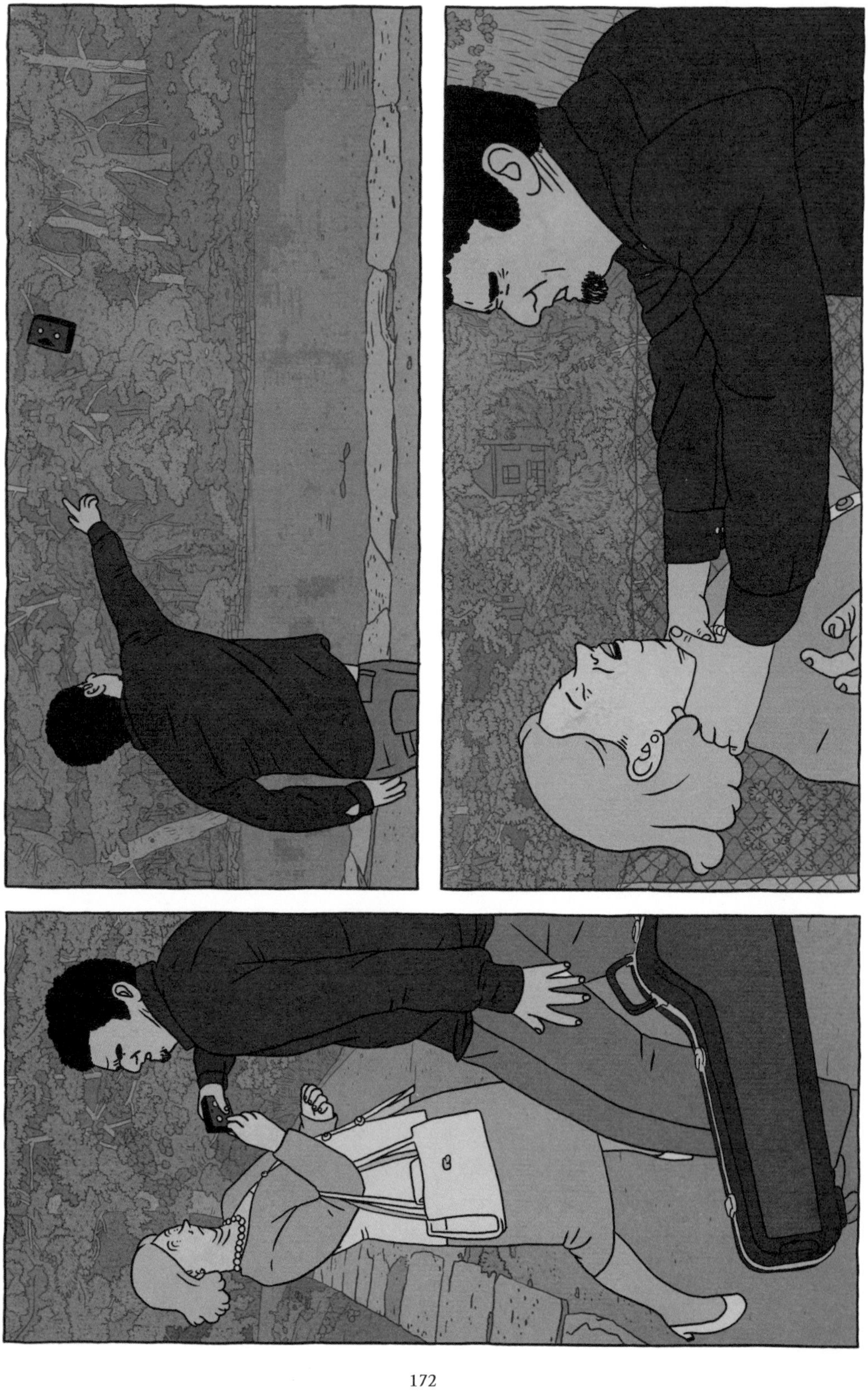

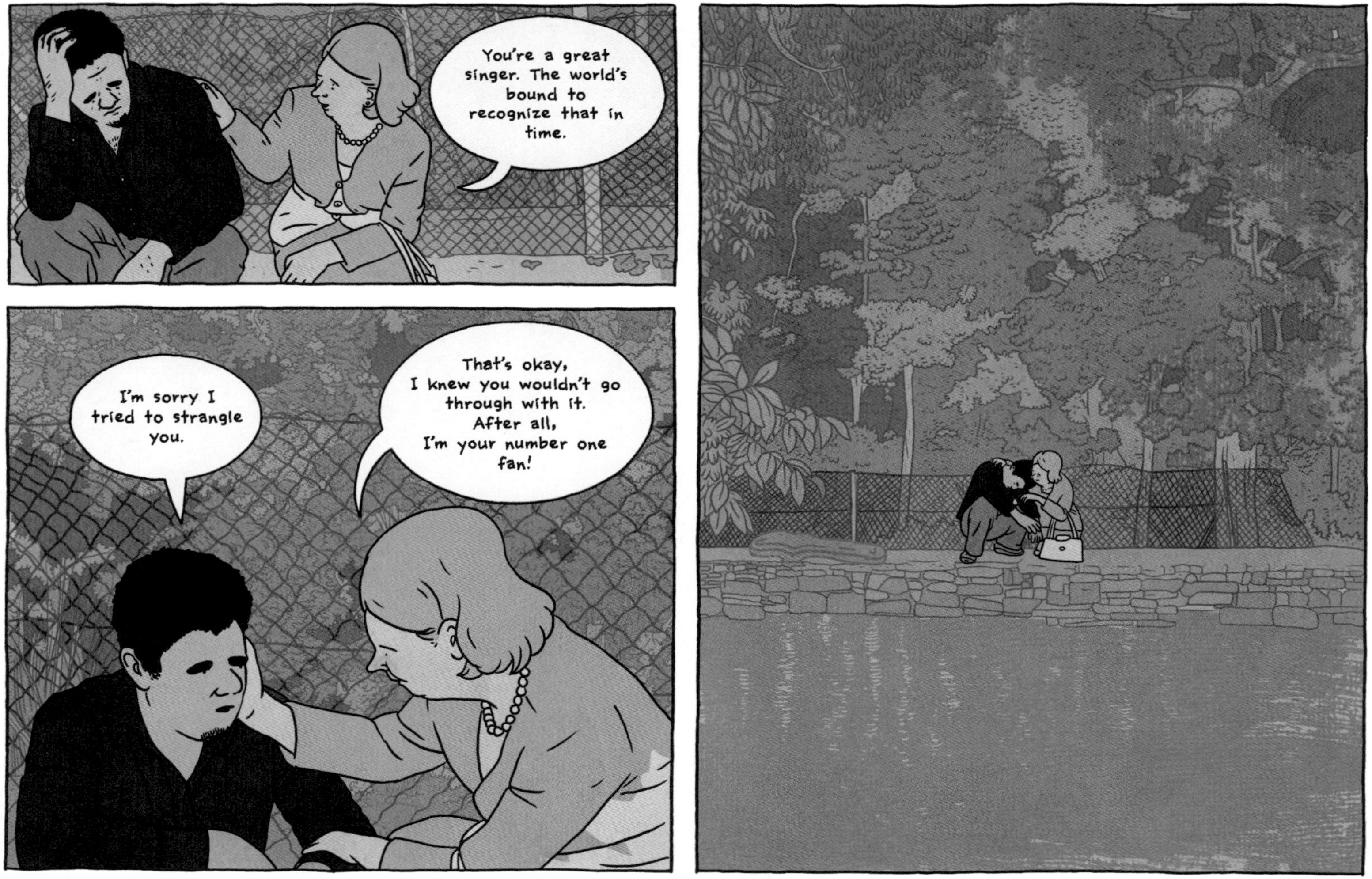
You're a great singer. The world's bound to recognize that in time.
I'm sorry I tried to strangle you.
That's okay, I knew you wouldn't go through with it. After all, I'm your number one fan!

Author's Note

The stories in the collection were written between 1998–2007. The oldest one is "King of the Lillies." At the time, I still believed that only in far away places and times—like Sweden of the early 20th century—could crazy stories happen.

"Bygone" was written a year afterwards—my first story set in Israel, but it was only in "Homecoming" (2002) that I was able to use what is unique to the Israeli reality, which led to "Jamilti" (2003) and later on to *Exit Wounds*.

It was a process of development, both artistic and personal, to realize that real life is bizarre and grotesque enough to base a story upon, and this insight/understanding affected the style of the drawings as well.

Most of the stories have some issue around old family photos. I have an obsession for family photos as objects as much as I have for families as a subject. The photograph focuses on a moment in life but hides a bigger issue, which is much the same as making a comic. Besides, it is really fun to draw from old photos.

All the stories (except "Jamilti," which first appeared in *Drawn & Quarterly* volume 5) were published originally by Actus independent Comics. I want to thank my colleagues and friends in the Actus collective—Yirmi Pinkus, Batia Kolton, Mira Friedmann and Itzik Rennert—for their support and help in creating these stories.